D Kane

FIFTH DRAGON

Tempest
Book III

Fifth Dragon: Tempest

tellwell

Tellwell Talent
www.tellwell.ca

ISBN
978-1-77370-286-5 (Hardcover)
978-1-77370-285-8 (Paperback)
978-1-77370-287-2 (eBook)

The Fifth Dragon series is dedicated to Renée and Brandy.

BY D KANE

FIFTH DRAGON

Book One: *Cumulos Capers*

Book Two: *Rider Magic*

Book Three: *Tempest*

FIFTH DRAGON

Tempest

Chapter 1

"I don't want to hear about it Cyril! You're not even supposed to be here! What if someone sees you? Who'd believe a rat the size of a house dog would be dumb enough to remove his fur and get tattoos? In this country, animals can't talk, and some idiot would blame me!"

Although muffled, his nasally voice emanated all too clearly from the satchel. He yelped as I jostled him against a lamp post and hurried across an intersection. Halfway over, I bestowed a fake smile on a curious pedestrian and quickened my steps, wishing I hadn't chosen to wear heels.

"Cyril, if you don't shut-the-hell up, I swear I'll drop you in a dumpster!"

The satchel went silent.

If I'd had my broom, I'd have stepped into the nearest alley, cast an invisibility spell, and taken a shortcut to my apartment. But the average American doesn't want to consider magical people could live amongst them, and I'd found it safer to keep that fact out of their faces. It was an unspoken agreement. They didn't want to know, and I didn't want to tell them.

At the next light, I tapped a foot as I waited for traffic to pass and hoped Cyril would remain quiet for the remaining two blocks. A young man with a four-day beard sauntered up, and my gaze canted to the terrier that trailed behind him. The dog sat as we waited for the lights to change.

Cyril must've been uncomfortable as he fussed about, for the soft sides of the satchel bulged and flexed. With mounting anxiety, I noticed the dog's attention was caught by the motion. Its ears perked, and it gave the bag a sniff. A low growl commenced.

The young man glanced at the dog. "What's the matter, Thor?"

Before I could step away, the terrier sprang, fastened its teeth into the satchel, and jerked it from my hand. As it whipped the bag from side to side, its horrified owner grabbed the frenzied creature by its collar.

"Drop it, Thor! Drop it!"

Thor appeared to be deaf.

I made a hand motion behind my purse. The satchel jerked from Thor's mouth to launch against a concrete wall where it dropped to the sidewalk with a dull thud. As the owner wrestled the dog to some sort of control, the snarling canine remained focused on the bag, aquiver with murderous zeal.

"I . . . don't understand," choked the man as he knelt over the dog, a forearm across its throat. "The only thing that'll get this kind of reaction is a rat! He's a rat terrier, you see. He's never, *ever* done anything like this. I'm so sorry!"

"Umm . . ." Nearby pedestrians decided the event didn't require further attention so moved off in a clump as the light changed. I glanced at the bag. "I'm carrying an area rug from an old house. Maybe it smells like rats."

At his raised brows, I added, "I do needlework and wanted the pattern. I'm sorry if it upset your dog. There's no harm done. It's an old leather satchel. Lots of scratches already."

He glanced across the street, wanting the experience to be over.

"You should go. I'll get my bag and be on my way."

"You sure you're alright?"

"I'm fine. I'll clean the rug before handling it though."

Thor still growled but was on a short leash when the man let him up. With a self-righteous sniff and final glance at the satchel, the terrier stalked across the street with his owner.

I scurried to the satchel. "Cyril! Cyril! Can you hear me?"

A low moan came from the bag. People were staring. I picked it up and trotted after the clot of people crossing the street. I'd have to wait to check on Cyril's welfare. Ten more minutes.

The elevator doors opened on my floor to reveal a rubber ball on legs. It had horizontal stripes on its tee shirt, thick glasses, and buck teeth. Pale reddish hair stuck out in a variety of directions.

"What are you looking for, Reg?" I asked, brushing past him. The kid was a ten-year-old blot on my existence and always underfoot. Although he lived with his mother in the apartment below, he liked to skulk outside my door. His reason for existing had morphed into his personal challenge of exposing me to the world as a witch.

"What's in the bag?" he asked.

I prayed Cyril was too stunned to move.

"Nothing that concerns you, Reg. Just some of my stuff."

"How come your hair's so long? Only witches have black hair like yours. You can sit on it!" The kid had both the instincts and persistence of a blood hound.

"You watch too many movies. Do you see a pointy black hat?" I fumbled in a pocket. *Where the hell were my keys?*

"It's in your apartment." His eyes were solemn, mud-grey, and tinged with olive-green. "Does that bag have stuff for your magic brews?"

The key slid into the lock, and I heard a muffled groan as the satchel slammed against the door jam.

"What was that noise?"

Apparently, the kid also had the ears of a bat.

"Nothing. My stomach growled. I'm hungry. Go away so I can eat."

I set the satchel on the floor, dropped my keys into a brass bowl in the shape of a coiled snake, and turned back to the kid. "Reg, I've got stuff to do."

Reg stared at the satchel. "It moved! There's something alive in there!"

"No, there isn't. It's my lunch. Now, go home so I can eat."

Quick as lightning, Reg darted in and unzipped the bag. Before I could grab him, he'd turned the satchel upside down. Cyril tumbled onto the rug, the crystal on his collar refracting light from the kitchen window. All four legs were stiff, and he looked dead. Even Reg seemed horror-stricken at the sight.

He recovered with lightning speed and poked Cyril in the ribs. When there was no response, he asked, "Is it dead? Where's its fur? What are those marks? How come it's so wrinkly?"

I grabbed Reg by an arm and propelled him towards the door. "No, it isn't dead! It's a statue. I'm taking an art class, and I have to draw it. Now, go home."

He turned to glare at me. "You're a liar! It's not your lunch or a statue! That's a rat! I'm going to tell my mom you've got a giant rat up here!" And he scrambled down the hall to the stairs.

I closed and double-locked the door. My day was only half-over and already in the toilet. I jammed a rug against the bottom of the door so Reg couldn't sneak back and stick a periscopic device under it. No, I wasn't being paranoid. He'd done it before.

"Cyril! Are you alright?"

Unlike Reg, I recoiled from touching Cyril. Bald rats resemble bald cats. They want you to touch them, but you'd rather eat glass than pet one.

"Is he gone?" Cyril's voice was shaky.

"Yes, Cyril, he's gone. Let me help you . . . how about you roll onto this towel, and I'll carry you to the couch?"

Cyril rolled to his stomach, a glazed look in his eyes. When he could focus, he shot me a steely glare. "What, in the name of magic, did you do that for?!"

I searched my memory. "What are you talking about?"

"You could've killed me with all that shaking!"

It dawned on me he hadn't seen the dog, and it took some convincing to get him to believe it hadn't been me.

He felt his head with careful paws. "I probably have a concussion!"

"I told you not to come to Denver, Cyril. There are dangers here magical people can't imagine."

"How can I be your familiar if I don't know your origins? After all, it's hard to believe a world like this even exists."

"It exists. And it's not safe. Return to Cumulos before something eats you or Reg stuffs you in a cage. Magic isn't reliable in the mortal world."

His little nose tilted. "My magic is always reliable."

"Don't count on it, Cyril. Trust me on this. I grew up here."

"You just need more training."

I resisted the impulse to throttle him. I'd have loved to let him learn through hard experience, but that would most likely involve me somehow, and not in a good way.

"Look, Cyril. It's late. How about you sleep on the couch tonight? I tossed a thick towel at him. "Here's a blanket."

I marched into the bedroom and locked the door. Cyril is supposed to be my familiar, that is, my magical companion but, not only does he have a snotty upper-class attitude, I can't get past the fact that he's bald. Did you know rats have wrinkles under their fur? I hadn't known that, and I'd been happy in that ignorance. Wish I could go back to it. Anyway, one way or another, Cyril was returning to Cumulos in the morning if I had to use a spell to send him there myself.

I revelled in a long, hot shower, snuggled into fuzzy warm pajamas, and crawled into bed. After a few weeks of floating in the clouds in Cumulos Castle, I had a new appreciation for showers, electric lights, and environmental controls.

I switched off the lamp and closed my eyes. A few errands in the morning and I'd be back in the magical realm before sundown.

Chapter 2

I was comfortably ensconced in a drawing room of Cumulos Castle with the trio who managed the local magical realm. Cyril was in his favourite position on the mantle, ropy tail hung over the edge, soaking up heat from the fire.

The cloud castle was my absolute favourite place to be. Although it had been nearly a year since I'd started to visit the magical realm, I still hadn't created a place for myself. Probably because my magic wasn't reliable. Everyone knew why King Dorian had been invited, but I seemed to be a tag-along that people were mostly nice to. Side-long glances confirmed nobody seemed to know whether I belonged in the non-magical world of the Americas or in the realm of magic. I'd liked to have given them an explanation, but I was more in the dark than anyone. So, I shuttled between the two worlds in hopes of figuring it out.

In Cumulos Castle, I had the opportunity to be with witches, mages, and others who could teach me what I needed to know. Although I had significant abilities, I was badly in need of instruction. A childhood spent in North America did not prepare one for the realities of magic.

Angus was the trio leader, a powerful mage with curly red hair and bright blue eyes. He was leaned back in a comfy chair with a foot propped on the corner of a low table. This would be fine except for the fact that he wore a kilt. I don't know why he does this. No self-respecting woman would sit like that in a skirt sans underwear.

He sipped meadowfair nectar from a crystal glass. "Since Mydryth is still a bug in a stream, we can be sure he's nae helping Myrador."

Frost, a beautiful Transylvanian witch in a flowing gown, reclined in an upholstered chair next to Angus. "I haven't had any luck tracking down the dark mage, Myrador yet, but I'll keep looking."

"Thank ye, Frost. I appreciate your efforts."

A purple creature that looked like a cross between a plush carnival toy and an alien was perched on the back of a Pegasus statue. Talon wasn't my favourite individual, but we'd developed a live-and-let-live relationship because he believed I saved his life. It's a little more complicated than that, but I'll leave it there.

I was drooped in a comfortable position with my head on one arm of a chair, my legs over the other. I heard a "prrrrt?"

Green cat eyes peered up. Sin had spotted a vacant lap. He had black fur, white paws, and was significantly overweight. As he prepared to leap, I dropped my hand in preparation. As I'd learned from harsh experience, twenty pounds of cat hanging by his front claws is less than pleasant. He danced from one front paw to the other, head bobbing like he was an Olympic competitor. Then he scrunched down, gave a terrific lunge, and managed to get to my lap – the front half of him anyway. I gave him a shove to avoid being left punctured and bleeding.

As he extricated his face from the back of the chair, he shot me a scathing look and whipped his tail . . . but the lap was warm and soft. He made some turns while casting sharp looks my way and formed himself into a furry ball. With a sigh of satisfaction, he plunked down, closed his eyes, and began to purr. It seemed he didn't hold a grudge – so long as he got what he wanted.

I groaned at the flutter of tiny wings. I'd hoped Scarlet would stay on Altaria. Dorian, now King of Altaria, had inherited three magical gifts from his mother: an amulet, a jewel-encrusted short-sword, and Scarlet. Although the fiery-haired, ten-inch pixie had fierce loyalty to the Altarian Royal Family which included Dorian, she had less respect for yours truly. Cute in a Barbie-doll kind of way, she was brash and opinionated (in my opinion), and we had a tendency to rub each other the wrong way. She thought I should be her personal slave, and I tended to disagree – quite loudly on occasion. Angus has been known to send us to different corners of the room.

But I was safe with Sin on my lap. He thought Scarlet was an exotic bird that could be delicious. An ear flicked, and his eyes opened to slits as he tracked her movements, hoping the bird would get close enough to bat out of the air. Scarlet spotted him, fluttered out of reach, and settled on the table in front of Angus where she eyed his goblet.

"Is that meadowfair nectar?"

"Aye, Scarlet. Would ye like a wee drop?"

"I was thinking more like a thimble-full. You've got lots."

Angus used an eye dropper to fill a tiny glass with nectar, set it before the pixie, and added a short straw. "There ye be."

Scarlet knelt beside the (to her) large glass and began to drink. After several gulps, she gave a satisfied burp. "This was a great year. When was it made?"

"Tis from the spring, lass; fresh as can be."

"Good thing it isn't wine, then."

"We've wine if ye'd prefer?"

She blinked enormous emerald eyes. "Probably not a good idea. I have trouble flying when I drink wine. Don't know why that happens."

"It's called getting drunk," I growled, shoving in an uninvited oar.

She narrowed her eyes at me. "Pixies don't get drunk! We're immune to the effects of alcohol!"

"Keep telling yourself that." I took another swallow of meadowfair nectar.

Scarlet fluttered to hover nearby, little fists on tiny hips. "Not all of us have such weaknesses!"

"No. Some of us have other weaknesses." I slid my gaze to Sin whose ears had flicked and narrowed eyes watched her movements. As Scarlet shot away, I retorted, "At least I can't get eaten by a common barn cat!"

Sin's gaze transferred to me. Oops! Better go easy on the "barn cat" comments.

"Ladies," sighed Angus, "can ye nae get along?"

We shot hard glances at one another then lapsed into silence. It was true. I needed to get a handle on my temper where Scarlet was concerned. She was a pixie, after all. Better to ask water to run uphill than expect her to be human.

As I stroked Sin's marshmallow sides, he resumed purring. I was forgiven.

Talon's pale eyes swung like a pendulum between Scarlet and me. As usual, he showed no inclination to humour. His voice was dry, carrying as always, the flavour of condescension. Maybe when you're mauve and, let's face it, not very attractive, it could affect your disposition.

"I assume the pixie has a reason for coming to Cumulos. Perhaps she'd be good enough to share," he said.

Long toes that twitched in a spidery fashion forced me to look away. I'd been wrapped in a spyder's web in the not-too-distant past so was sensitive to such movements. But he had a point. Why was she here? The last I'd seen of Scarlet, she'd been catching up with old friends on Altaria. Maybe it'd been a short list. No surprise.

After a second belch, Scarlet wiped her mouth and fluttered to the top of a two-foot hourglass that sat on a side-table beside Angus.

"King Dorian asked me to invite Talon and (she swung towards me with her pretty eyes looking pretty vindictive) White Raven to his castle on Altaria. There've been strange happenings, and he wants people he trusts to look into events." She threw her arms in the air in a theatrical gesture. "Of course, he never asked me who *I* trusted! It's not like I was born yesterday like some people!" Her green orbs fastened on mine.

It was true I was still a couple of years short of thirty, and heaven knew how old she was, but I was bigger the day I was born than Scarlet will ever be. As I took a breath preparatory to pointing that out, Angus made a hasty interjection.

"Perhaps we should discuss King Dorian's request."

Talon's long fingers played with long toes; floppy ears drooped onto his chest. He reminded me of a bunny crossed with a purple alien on stork legs – some kind of bizarre mutation that'd gone to mold. Whenever he sat or leaned against something, his fur flattened and stayed that way until he brushed it. At least, I hope he brushed it. The idea of him licking himself like a cat was too gross to contemplate.

"King Dorian sent a Cathesach bird yesterday asking if I had cannabis amongst my herbs," said Talon.

My ears perked. "Are you serious? Are you talking about pot?"

He stopped stroking his toes and turned my way, something that always makes me wary. He's a particularly nasty little . . . bunny. "As usual, you make no sense. What possible connection can there be between cannabis and a pot, besides something in which to store it?"

"Amongst humans, pot is what they call marijuana, which is a strain of cannabis."

"Why confuse the name?"

Good question. "Uh . . . I don't know. But possession of it has been illegal in most of North America for years."

"That's ludicrous!"

"Most people would agree with you. Making a plant illegal wasn't my idea."

"I can understand why you weren't consulted." As my back teeth began to grind, he returned his attention to Angus. "I will depart this evening."

Cyril stood on hind legs and cleared his throat. "I'm teaching a course on magical applications of mushrooms and other fungi. I leave in the morning for a month so will be unable to assist."

I'd noticed that Cyril avoided any kind of personal exertion or danger for which I was profoundly grateful. It meant I could leave the castle without him. With a sense of relief, I shot to my feet. The sudden movement was followed by a heavy thump and yowl of umbrage. Sin cast a narrow-eyed glance over his shoulder and stalked to a mat by the fire.

I turned my attention to Talon. "He asked for me too!"

Talon gave me a condescending stare. "Do you require assistance to find Altaria?"

"No. I just . . . I thought . . ." I sighed. "Never mind."

Scarlet cast calculating looks between Talon and me, no doubt trying to determine who'd be the least offensive travelling companion then, little wings aflutter, popped into the air. "I'm off. See you there." And she was gone like a shot.

As I climbed to my room, I wondered what Dorian could want with marijuana. He wasn't into drugs as far as I knew, and I'd never have pegged Talon as a pot-smoker. Odd indeed.

Chapter 3

I descended to the cobblestones of Odenai, capital city of Altaria, and dismounted from my broom. Dorian leaned against the castle gates looking Royal in embroidered tunic and black trousers. Dark-haired and dark-eyed, King Dorian was a gorgeous example of manhood. We'd spent a couple of great years just hanging out as friends in Denver, Colorado before he'd acquired his royal inheritance. Having my own brand of magical abilities, I'd followed him to the fairy-tale realm to assist in the recovery of his father's throne.

He enveloped me in a warm hug during which I realized I'd missed him – a lot. Probably more than I should. This could get confusing since a while back, I'd become involved with a Rider of Gaia named Valgren. As the hug lengthened, I kissed his cheek and pushed away.

"Welcome back," he said. "I've missed our time together." He gestured to the castle. "You wouldn't believe how much work it takes to run a country!"

"I imagine it never ends. Any regrets?"

His lips quirked. "No – except for the absence of my best friend."

Friend? Ouch! Dorian had kissed me once – a real one – but, before I'd had time to think about it, Valgren had returned and . . . well, the subject had been dropped.

"Talon's setting up in the cellars."

I sent my broom to park itself as we climbed the wide staircase to the carved castle doors.

"Setting up for what?"

"Cellar slugs."

My brows rose. "Cellar slugs?"

"Tenacious little things that can destroy anything. We're lucky one of the grooms noticed them in time to nip the infestation in the bud."

"What do they do?"

"They multiply faster than rabbits, crawl everywhere, and grow dark magic. Everything in their vicinity eventually disintegrates."

"What's the cannabis for?"

"Slugs don't like cannabis. Talon will scry where they're getting in and sprinkle it there.

"Have you ever . . .?"

His glance held a twinkle of humour. "A king could never admit to smoking pot. It would be unprofessional."

I chuckled. "Not very dignified."

"What about you?"

"Once or twice. Didn't catch my interest though. Hated the stomach cramps."

He gave me a mute questioning glance.

"From chronic laughter and overindulgence in junk food."

Dorian looked wistful. "True. I believe they were called 'munchies' at one time." At my sharp look, he opened the massive front door and grinned. "Not that I'm admitting to anything."

I laughed. "I grew up North America too."

As we entered the light-filled marble foyer, I craned my neck like a tourist. "This is incredible, Dorian! I'm so happy for you. The castle is stunning!"

He glanced around the massive hall. "I'm already getting used to it," he said. "Shame, really. Something like this ought to be appreciated every day."

"By the way," I said, returning to the subject, "if Talon can get rid of the slugs, what do you need me for?"

He slid a look my way – a look I knew contained a secret. "Thought we could both use a break."

"And . . .?"

"And what?"

"Don't look innocent, Dorian! You're hiding something!"

He laughed. "You know me too well! I found a toy in the attic."

"Ah . . . boys and their toys."

"This one's great! It's a magic carpet!"

I stopped to check for signs of a practical joke. "Seriously?" The thing about being in a magical world is you never know if something is true or not, and it's easy to be suckered into somebody's bad idea of fun. Dorian however, well aware of my abhorrence of practical jokes, was unlikely to think playing a trick on me would be worth enduring my wrath. I felt my brows draw together. "This better not be some kind of . . ."

He held his hands up, palms out. "It's not, Raven. It's real! I've taken it out for short hops, but I want to share it with you . . . right after we check on Talon."

"Must we?"

He tugged my hand. "It'll only take a minute."

I trotted along, hoping he was right, but my relationship with Talon had always been chilly and, if he could screw up my fun, he would. He was ingenious that way; one might even call it magic.

We wound down many stairs until we came to a broad area ringed with halls and cells. Most of the cells stood open though the area showed signs of previous heavy use. Dorian's Uncle Gargeran, no doubt. Dorian had given his greedy uncle a choice to stay imprisoned on Altaria or accept banishment. Thankfully, he'd chosen to leave – minus his magic. He'd been an unhappy man as he'd stomped onto the ship that would take him away. Of course, he'd made a melodramatic threat against Dorian's life and promised to return. Blah . . . blah . . . blah . . . If he'd been in Dorian's position, he'd have already been dead. But I'm sure it never occurred to him to be grateful.

We negotiated dark corners until the hallway brightened. I sniffed then sniffed again. "Recognize that smell?"

Dorian inhaled. "Hmm. Been some time since I've come across that particular aroma. What in the name of magic is Talon doing?"

We picked up the pace until we came to an open cell where a couple of glow-globes made a weak attempt to illuminate a thick wall of haze. Talon, barely visible against the back wall, was leaned over a small fire wafting smoke into a jagged opening with a rag.

We coughed upon stepping into the cell. "Talon, what's going on?"

"Oh! Hi, Dorian! I decided smoke would be better to drive the little devils out! It'll get into all the nooks and crannies of the tunnels!" He returned to his task.

Dorian and I exchanged a look. Maybe cannabis smoke didn't affect . . . whatever the hell Talon was, but he sounded suspiciously cheerful. Taking shallow breaths, I inched closer and noticed his purple fur was singed in places. It wasn't like him to be careless.

"Talon, do you know what humans use cannabis for?"

"Slugs in the garden?" he quipped as he wafted more smoke into the hole. He did a double-take, stopped waving the rag, and turned to me. "Raven!" he burst as if I was his oldest friend. "Didn't see you there! Give me a hand! We'll have the little sods choking in no time!"

I leaped behind Dorian in terror. Talon had a *lot* of sharp little teeth – and they all showed in a frightening grin. At least, I think it was a grin. I'd never seen him do that. Dorian winced as my nails sank into his arm.

A ground elf arrived and handed a folded note to Dorian who gave it a quick scan. The creature wrinkled its nose and scurried away to cleaner air. I shot Dorian a look filled with daggers and whispered, "Don't you dare leave me alone with this sky-high idiot! He's even scarier loaded!"

As Dorian tucked the note into a pocket, we watched Talon manoeuvre smoke into the opening, getting worse at it by the minute. A strange sound began which, to my shock, was Talon humming.

I figured the answer to my previous question was, no, he didn't know what cannabis smoke did to people – and apparently to him as well. We stared in stupefaction until it came to me that somebody should do something. I made a move to latch onto Talon's skinny arm but thought better of it in time. He could act like a rabid badger with little provocation, and I wasn't willing to bet he was that cheerful.

I looked at Dorian then gestured towards Talon. Dorian leaned close to whisper, "I'm not touching him! He's crazy on a good day!"

"We've got to do something. He looks so . . . goofy!" An unladylike guffaw burst from me. As I leaned towards Talon, he slipped into the smoldering cannabis where he yelped, rolled to the side, and swatted at singed belly-fur. Without thinking, I squatted and rubbed at the glowing spot to put it out. This had the strange effect of causing him to burst into giggles – high-pitched and uncontrollable. Who knew the little guy was ticklish? In fact, who knew he could laugh? He sounded so hysterical, I couldn't help but join in.

I looked up at Dorian's expression of disbelief. "Come on, Dorian! You've got to admit this is funny!" Tears streamed down my face. I don't know if they were from laughter or the clouds of smoke.

Dorian stamped on the smoldering leaves which didn't do much good as the air was already thick. Talon staggered to his feet, purple eyes decorated with bright red veins. He pointed at Dorian's efforts and, through gales of laughter, tried to tell him to stop, but somehow it wouldn't come out right.

I crawled over to an area covered in clean straw and laughed until my stomach ached. As Dorian stamped out the last of the glowing cannabis, he could no longer resist a grin as Talon staggered to a wall and slid down, skinny arms and legs at awkward angles, giggling helplessly.

Dorian sank to the straw beside me. "We have to . . ." He choked back laughter. ". . . get out of here." After another bout of mirth, he managed, ". . . It's affecting us too!"

"I know!" I could barely form the words through my hysteria.

Talon rubbed his singed belly. "I'm starving! Is there anything to eat?"

This sent us into further peals of hilarity as Talon rolled to hands and knees and crawled to the door. “I’ll die if I don’t eat,” he whined amidst giggles. “I could eat a dragon! I know there’s one around here somewhere!” He crawled from the cell and disappeared down the hallway where his cackles were interspersed by “Ouch! Ouch!” I’m pretty sure he was stepping on his ears.

I leaned into Dorian’s shoulder and blurted between giggles. “Think he’ll be back?”

Dorian slipped an arm around me. “Not a chance. Probably lost already. He sure is a strange little dude.”

“That’s an understatement!” I put a hand to my spinning head. “That’s some powerful stuff! I don’t think I’ve ever been quite so . . . loaded,” I said on an upsurge of renewed laughter. “Whoever was stupid enough to make this stuff illegal?”

Dorian lay back onto the straw, dragging me with him. “Ah . . . this feels good,” he said. “I haven’t had a good laugh in, I don’t know how long.”

“Uneasy is the head that wears the crown?”

“Sounds like you’re quoting somebody.”

“I think so, but I’ve no idea who.”

Nor did I care at that point. It felt good to have Dorian’s arm around me, his voice sending shivers and warm spots throughout my body, and to feel the deep, regular rhythm of his heart. He clasped my hand where it rested on his chest, and his warm breath stirred my hair as we lay in a silent, dim cocoon.

It would feel so good to . . .

We turned towards each other at the same instant, our normal reticence drifting away with the smoke. Dorian brushed my hair back, a different look in his eyes – warm, questing, open.

"Raven, I . . ."

I've tried to rationalize my next action with every fibre of my being, but there's just no excuse – other than being high, I guess, but I should admit for the record that it merely relaxed me enough to do what I'd always wanted.

I kissed him.

A light kiss at first. He returned it gently then gave a sigh and pulled me to him, transformed it into something deep and sensuous. My head swam from more than the drug. Dorian's lips were magic, his touch inviting. *I may burn in hell for this*. I ran my fingers through his white streaks, inhaled his light, spicy fragrance. Somehow my legs were entangled with his as he tugged at the ties of my tunic.

As I felt warm, exploring hands and lips move down my throat, I had a feeble thought that this might be a bad idea. As his mouth settled on sensitive body parts and delicious sensations shot through me, I decided to ignore that first thought. I'd had enough of controlling myself, of always doing the right thing.

Dorian raised his head and unclipped the snap of his tunic. "Don't move," he whispered. He kissed me and shrugged out of the cloak. "Don't talk."

Guess he knew me pretty well. I'd probably say something stupid.

He spread the cloak over the straw and lifted me onto it. Shivers of pleasure shot through me at his light touch. As I stroked his shoulders, I realized I'd never noticed how his darker skin contrasted with mine. Black hair, blue eyes, and alabaster skin were the result of my mother's Irish ancestry. His background was obviously different.

"You are so beautiful," he whispered.

I stroked his face. "You think so?"

He gazed into my eyes. "Why do you think I've kept my distance? You're the one woman I couldn't risk. Beautiful, brave, funny – not to mention, magic. I didn't dare change our relationship while we were in Denver – or even hint that you were special."

"You fooled me," I said. My head spun, but I was pretty sure it was no longer the drug.

"I'm sorry. There was no other way." He kissed me again then sat up, there was a rustle of clothing, and he was warm against me, dusky skin reflecting the dim light.

I had the presence of mind to glance around. "What if somebody comes?"

He smiled. "One: Nobody voluntarily tours the dungeons. Two: Nobody would interrupt the king for any reason. Capital offence."

"You wouldn't . . ."

"No, but they don't know that."

My trousers landed in a corner, and Dorian stretched over me. *My god, his body was as perfect as I'd imagined!* Smothering a weak bleat of conscience, I opened myself to the experience – and slid into a new heaven.

Much later, Dorian shoved our clothes into a pile and performed a translocation spell which put us into a warm bed. I snuggled beneath the blankets and pressed against him for warmth. The dungeon had been cool.

As Dorian gathered me close, I heard him murmur he'd never again think of dungeons in the same way.

Chapter 4

I opened my eyes to a luxurious room flooded with morning light. Odd. I'd had the most incredible dream of Dorian on a bed of straw, the two of us laughing together. I remembered his body in dim light, warm kisses . . . Wow! An erotic dream about Dorian!

I shot upright. No! Surely, I hadn't . . ! I lifted the blankets. Naked! My hair reeked of pot smoke, and I felt energized.

Oh . . . my . . . god!

I flopped back onto the bed. There it was – proof I couldn't be trusted. Had I even had one thought of Valgren? How could I have done something so colossally stupid? I wasn't sure being loaded out of my head was any kind of excuse. What could

I have been thinking, for crissake? How the hell was I going to explain this to Valgren?

Of course, thinking had been kicked far out of the driver's seat the previous night. A whole other part of me had taken control – what some would call baser urges. At least, I hoped that's what they'd been. I could live with that, even if it did make me somewhat promiscuous. That I may have strong feelings for Dorian was the real issue I didn't want to face. I tried to remember what I might've said during the event (multiple events).

Surely, I hadn't used the "L" word . . . had I? Memories were jumbled. A faint hope glittered. If I couldn't remember what we'd said, maybe he couldn't either.

Hold on. Had *he* used the "L" word? There'd been a lot of stuff happening, most of it pleasing beyond belief, so I'd been distracted from any bits of conversation that may've transpired. I had clear memories of a lot of feeling fantastic. Finally, I huffed out a breath. It wasn't worth worrying about. Anything either of us had said could be discredited by the drug. What a relief!

I scanned the room. I couldn't imagine Dorian leaving me in his bed and going off to trade-talks, so he'd be back soon. I'd escape before he returned.

I was halfway to a jumble of familiar clothing on the floor when the door opened and, of course, it was Dorian, fully clothed, carrying two cups of coffee, his face wreathed in a knowing smile. "Trying to sneak away?"

I dove for the bed and yanked the sheet over me. He sat on the edge and handed me a steaming cup. "Cream, no sugar, extra-large. Thought you might need a stimulant this morning." He surveyed me from under his brows as he took a sip. ". . . and a reason to delay your escape."

I tried to look relaxed while scanning for the nearest exit. As I pulled the sheet higher, Dorian chuckled. "It's too late, Raven – way too late." He surveyed me with a smug smile and twinkling eyes.

"Dorian," I said, chewing my bottom lip, "do you think we could forget this ever happened?"

"Why would I want to do that?" He held my gaze and sipped more coffee.

"Well . . . after all, we were both drugged to the gills last night!"

"We can't blame marijuana for everything, and the experience is pretty well burned into my brain."

"I thought pot was an amnesiac," I growled.

"Within limits. And we were far outside those limits last night." He straightened and blew out a burst of air. "Come on, Raven! Don't expect me to believe you didn't want this every bit as much as I did!"

More was coming back to me. Wow! He was right. He'd never buy that. In fact, I had a vague recollection of me being the one to initiate the activities. I congratulated myself. I could now add *stupid* to promiscuous. Have I mentioned how much I hate introspection? This is why. It usually makes me look bad.

Dorian watched me over the rim of his cup. "Okay, Raven; I see the wheels turning." He sighed. "I don't suppose there's any chance of keeping this simple?"

"A few months ago, it would've been simple."

"Valgren," he said through tight lips.

I nodded. "I feel like I've betrayed him. Christ! I have betrayed him!"

Dorian angled a knee onto the bed. "Raven, last night might not have been the choice either of us would've made under normal circumstances, but it did happen."

Contrariness stabbed me at that statement. Neither of us? It had taken being drugged for him to touch me but, now it'd happened, he'd live with it?

Dorian must've seen it in my eyes. "Maybe I should rephrase that." He put a hand on my arm. "I explained last night why I'd kept my distance in Denver. I couldn't show any interest in you. It was too dangerous, but now . . ."

"Now there's Valgren," I said, my lips firm.

"I know. I just wanted you to know in case . . . I just want you to know. And last night when you kissed me, I couldn't walk away."

I chewed my lip. "Look, Dorian; let's just say I started it and forget it ever happened."

"You *did* start it."

"You know what I mean! I can't just hop from Valgren's bed to yours! What kind of person would that make me?" I ground my teeth. "And I'm not ready to give him up!"

Now I was on familiar ground – a reason to be mad. I leaped at it like a starving chicken and bounded out of bed, forgetful of my nakedness. Coffee slopped as I slammed the cup on a table, shoved on my clothes and called for my broom which sailed in the open window.

"Raven, wait! We need to talk!"

"Dorian, no matter how I feel about you – and believe me, I'm damn confused right now – I'm still a commoner and you're a king. Had you forgotten? Commoners need not apply. And I wouldn't make a good concubine!"

I spotted a knife on the side-table, picked it up, and made a nick on the perfect bed post. "There!" I dropped the knife with a clatter. "When you're finished with this post, use the others. You'll probably need them. Lots of women will wait in line to sleep with the king!"

I grabbed my broom and, not trusting myself to look back, shot out the window into crisp morning air. I had a stray thought for Talon which I ignored. I expected he'd be found in a drugged stupor beneath a kitchen table like an overstuffed python. I wasn't dumb enough to be the one to wake him.

***

Angus and I shared a bottle of meadowfair nectar before a roaring fire in his study. Cyril was perched on the back of my chair, his snake-like tail giving me goosebumps as it drooped too close. I shifted away. Perhaps just to ruin my day, Talon floated into the room in his usual twisted-legs meditative position looking like he'd been blow-dried – except for a shaved portion on his belly. I'd never seen him so clean. It must've taken a lot of scrubbing to make him look like a fuzzy, purple balloon.

Talon shot a narrow-eyed look in my direction then turned his back. I supposed that was his embarrassed face though it was hard to tell since his expression doesn't change much. I imagined he hoped the drug had erased my memory. Not bloody likely. It was ammunition for the next time he was a pompous ass, besides which, maybe my subconscious blamed him for my predicament with Dorian. And, yes, of course I realize it wasn't his fault, but I was trying to spread the blame. I hated that most of it pointed at me.

"Good morning, Talon," I said with a bright, fake smile. "How are you today?"

He narrowed bloodshot eyes. "Why do you want to know?"

I maintained the smile. "Just being friendly."

He sniffed, ignored me, and addressed Angus. "It will take longer than anticipated to eliminate the cellar slugs. Also, I checked the tunnels beneath Cumulos this morning." Talon's expression became grave. "The cloud island is infected too."

Angus straightened. "How did they get here?"

"Good question. It's an odd coincidence they showed up in both Altaria and Cumulos at the same time."

Angus tossed his tam onto the floor and scrubbed fingers through curly red locks. "I dinnae care for the sounds o' that!" He turned to me. "By the way, Dorian also sent for ye, lass. What did he have o' ye?"

A gallon of nectar sloshed into my lungs. The violent choking that followed explained away a flaming red face as my brain scrambled for a response.

"Are ye alright, lass? Sounds like ye swallowed the ocean."

"I'll be fine. It just . . . went down the wrong pipe." When the coughing spasms lessened, I added, "Dorian wanted to show me a magic carpet he'd found in the castle."

"A magic carpet? I have nae seen one o' those for centuries! Did he take ye for a ride?"

I cleared my throat several times and found something interesting in the fabric of my chair. "Umm . . . we didn't try it out. Um . . . something came up."

"Must've been important. Flying carpets are rare. Ye've got te let Dorian take ye on the carpet, Raven. Ye'll have a grand time!"

I swallowed at the image that leapt to mind. "Maybe the next time I go to Altaria." Which could be never considering the way I'd left things with Dorian.

"Talon," I burst in desperation, "tell us more about the castle slugs!"

Angus seemed confused as to why I'd find castle slugs more interesting than riding a magic carpet but refrained from comment.

It was one of the few times I appreciated Talon's preference for being the centre of attention. It took it away from me. He explained in excruciating detail how the slugs started small vortices that formed dark magic and attracted anything in the vicinity. If left undetected, the area beneath Cumulos castle would begin a slow rot that would progress throughout the cloud realm. Dark creatures would start arriving and, the more that gathered, the harder they'd be to expel. Although the slugs lived in the realm of dark magic, they were opportunistic and could survive in the light. Constant vigilance was the price of keeping the realm pristine.

"Talon, could ye take a couple o' the mages and make a tour o' Cumulos? We need te know the extent o' the infestation."

"A survey has already been started. We'll have a good idea of what we're dealing with by tomorrow afternoon."

I turned to Angus. "What can I do?"

"Do ye think ye could feel the presence o' the slugs?"

"I haven't been close enough to find out, but I'll give it a try."

"Don't go into the tunnels alone, lass. Take Cyril or Cash."

The idea of bringing my own rat into dingy tunnels was less than appealing. "Cyril is leaving later today, so I'll ask Cash."

Cash was an eight-foot giant in charge of the Cumulos military. His bald head was the size of my exercise ball in Denver, and muscles bulged whenever he moved.

"By the way," said Angus, "tell me more o' this magic carpet ride."

I shot to my feet. "Umm . . . I should be going. Don't want those slugs taking over. We can talk about the magic carpet later."

I created a draft as I shot out the door.

Chapter 5

"There's another one!" Cash pointed with a finger the size of a sausage, his bulk making me feel like a child as we picked our way through the gloom of yet another tunnel. As usual, he clanked whenever he moved due to the multiplicity of weapons that hung from his person.

It happened that I made a reliable detector as the presence of cellar slugs gave me a crawly sensation. As I inched closer to one of the slimy creatures, my wand light caused it to cringe. It might be able to live in the light but definitely didn't like it. Five times the size of a garden slug, it was dull grey. Traces of visible darkness drifted from a slime trail – a darkness with a reality of its own. I was beginning to comprehend why the others were concerned that Cumulos could be swallowed by the equivalent of tiny black holes.

I pondered the odd position of being a citizen of two different worlds – one magic and the other its polar opposite. Black holes were scientific; black magic was not. When I tried to merge the two realities in my mind, I got a headache.

After pointing out two new invaders, I erected a protection spell in the shape of an umbrella and edged away from Cash's simple remedy which was to stomp them into the ground. His enthusiasm caused rocks to fall from the ceiling.

A couple of hours later, I perched on a rock and guzzled from a canteen as I wondered if stone-walking would help. With this rare magical ability, I could move through solid ground. Although useful, stone-walking was the scariest of my magical abilities – so far. A loss of focus could transform the stone around me into a coffin.

The darkness the slugs exuded hadn't affected my magic so far, but I'd only encountered a few at a time. I chewed my lip. I'd have felt better if Valgren had been there. Call me chicken if you will, but the idea of being embalmed in stone if something went wrong gave me the heebie-jeebies.

Valgren. Since my night with Dorian, I'd been dreading Valgren's return. Even though we'd made no commitments, and he'd tried to explain what being part of Gaia meant, I felt guilty. Valgren had told me love wasn't lessened by being shared, only by an expectation of entitlement. Nobody owed anyone love. Love was given as a gift, and every day was a new gift. You couldn't purchase love, and you couldn't demand it.

Love was always experienced in the present and *as* a present. It was possible for two people to share love only with each other, but that was rare.

That was the problem. I could handle the situation with Dorian if it wasn't love.

I gave myself a mental head slap. Like a hamster on a wheel, I'd gone over it a hundred times. What was done was done. *For god's sake, get over it!* I jerked my attention to Cash who stared at me.

"What?"

"I asked if you wanted to go for lunch – twice."

"Sorry. I was wondering if stone-walking could help find where these creepy little things are entering."

"Don't know much about stone-walking."

"Unfortunately, neither do I, and I'm concerned the dark energy from the slugs might affect my magic as they increase in numbers."

"Valgren could help with that."

I chewed my lip. He could indeed. I sighed. I had to see him sometime. Might as well get it over with. "He should be finished his task for Gaia. Angus expects him this afternoon."

"The Riders of Gaia are a strange bunch, Raven. Kind of keep to themselves. Not that they aren't great people; they're just so tied to Gaia, they don't think like the rest of us. Guess they don't have to; they've got so much magic."

That was true. Along with an inherent sensuality, a river of magic flowed through Valgren, and it was impossible to be near him without being affected by both. Shoulder-length honey-blond hair and moss-green eyes made it difficult for a red-blooded woman to ignore him. I made an effort to relax my shoulders and, for a selfish moment, considered not telling him at all. Stupid, I know. He probably already knew.

I glanced at Cash's craggy face. "Hungry?"

He looked at me as if I had a screw loose. "Yes," he said. "Would you like to go for lunch?"

"Thought you'd never ask. Great idea! Let's go!" I started off without a backward glance. Sometimes it's better to baffle them with bullshit.

***

I was at the top of one of the castle towers, elbows on the stone balustrade. A cool breeze felt good as it lifted my hair . . . *when I felt him*.

Without conscious volition, my heart raced and palms dampened. On the one hand, I hated he could do this simply by being near but, on the other, I loved it. He moved into my vision and leaned against the wall.

Moss-green eyes found mine. "I've missed you." As the scent of flowers and shaded groves enveloped me, I couldn't answer. A hand stroked my hair. "You need to breathe, Raven." His breath was soft. Strong hands grasped my upper arms as he turned me to face him. A gentle, intimate smile made my legs turn to rubber.

"How do you do that?" I whispered.

He stroked my cheek. "We are of Gaia, you and I. There are no barriers between us."

I lowered my eyes. "Yes, there are. I've . . . I've . . ." I stuttered to a stop.

His voice remained gentle. "You've what?"

"I . . . Dorian . . ."

"Ah," he said. "You feel you've betrayed me." He lifted my face to his. "You *cannot* betray me, Raven. We're part of each other and will remain so whether we're together or not. Riders create bonds that supersede all other relationships."

"You have relationships with female Riders?" I didn't want to hear about that.

"No, Raven. I have a relationship with *one* Rider." Gentle humour swirled in moss-green, waiting for me to put it together.

I stared. "Rider?"

He brushed my lips with his. "Have you not yet realized you are Rider-born?"

I couldn't figure out if my head swam because of what he'd said or what he was doing. I decided I didn't care. My arms slipped around his neck.

After a time, he touched his forehead to mine and whispered, "I've prepared a lovely swinging nest for the night if you're interested."

I was so lightheaded from his scent and touch, I don't remember what my response was but, since I ended up high in the trees on a flower-scented evening, I'm guessing "no" wasn't part of it.

***

Knock! Knock! Knock!

Please let that be a woodpecker! I groaned and turned over to snuggle against the gentle strength that was Valgren. He made a soft sound and slipped an arm beneath me so I rested on his shoulder.

Knock! Knock! Knock!

"I know you're in there!" Talon's scratchy voice carried through the woven cover that Valgren had made to cover the hatch. "I'm not leaving until you open the door! Angus wants Valgren!"

"So do I," I mumbled, stroking the muscular chest beneath my cheek.

"Angus overrules you by about five thousand years!"

I sighed. "Curse his Vulcan hearing!"

Valgren chuckled and stroked my hair. "We'll be at the castle shortly," he said through the closed entrance. He chuckled at my groan. "Don't worry," he whispered, "you won't be tired today."

"What makes you say that?"

"A lot of energy moved last night." He kissed the top of my head. "Much of it will fill you today."

I pushed masses of hair from my face and sat up.

Valgren watched me with a soft smile as the woven cover fell away. "You are so perfect," he whispered.

How does one resist that? I snarled vile threats at Talon and snuggled against Valgren who chuckled as the knocking stopped. "You seem to have frightened him off. Considering what a powerful mage he is, should I be nervous of you?"

"Not at the moment," I murmured.

As he smiled and moved towards me, I forgot all about Talon.

***

Much later, Valgren and I entered the study to find Talon perched on the back of the Pegasus statue, the only sign of recognition a slight tightening of fuzzy lips. Angus was at his desk in his favourite pose, feet crossed at the ankles over one corner, knees peeking from beneath his kilt. I averted my gaze and moved to a loveseat.

Frost lounged in a chair, a colour-coordinated vision of beauty. She glanced at Valgren and me, likely wondering why the Rider would be interested in a half-trained waif from the human realm. As we sank into the loveseat, Valgren draped an arm behind me in a casual gesture of possession.

"It's good te see ye, Valgren. Thank ye for responding te my request."

"It worked out well, Angus, as I'd finished my errand for Gaia. It's good to be back."

"I dispersed Cathesach birds this morning hoping te get some idea o' where the cellar slugs are getting into Cumulos." He turned to me. "It might be good te have Bluescale back for a wee bit. He seems te have a knack for finding the dark mages. One o' these days, I might nae be tempted te stop him when he's pulled one o' those rats from their holes."

I recalled the dragon's fury at being prevented from making a vengeful snack of Mydryth, the image of Angus' magical binding cords clear in my memory. I shuddered and glanced around the room at scorch marks on the books. Bluescale had been so enraged, the library would've been incinerated if Angus hadn't stopped him. Unfortunately, the distraction had given Mydryth a chance to escape – which he'd snatched like the vermin he was.

As Talon cleared his throat, Angus glanced at him. "O' course it might be better te wait til we get Talon back home."

"How are ye . . . *you* going to get either of the dark mages to help Talon?" I asked.

"Tis an unsolved challenge, lass, but if anyone knows how te transit the dimensions, it'll be one o' those two." He rubbed his chin. "Myrador seems te have a bit o' respect for Bluescale. Might even call it fear. Could work te our advantage. If Bluescale can help us find Myrador, we might be able te stop the infestation o' the cellar slugs before they cause more damage. I've nae doubt the dark mage is involved somehow."

"Bluescale's in Denver." An unnecessary comment since everyone in the room knew that. Master of the obvious. "Umm . . . I can get him."

"I'll nae have ye travelling alone, lass. I'd feel better if Valgren or Dorian were with ye, maybe both. Cyril might be o' help too. Perhaps he could delay his teaching appointment."

Before I could object, Cyril chimed in. I hadn't noticed him perched behind my shoulder. He wore a tiny red backpack. "If it's all the same to you, Mage Angus, I've decided to stay here. My students are pleased to make the trek to see me in my, ahem," he preened, "natural habitat. Besides, humans in Denver seem to have an aversion to rats. Can't understand it."

It wasn't a surprise to me that Cyril's insistence on coming to Denver had resulted in his being targeted by Reg. After spending several hours in hiding, my tattooed companion had decided that, if human children were that dangerous, he had no desire to interact with adults. He'd returned to Cumulos while I visited my dragon friend, Bluescale, who lived in a stream near Denver.

As I heaved a sigh of relief, Valgren slanted me a secret smile. "The three of us together should be interesting," he said.

I shuddered at the thought. "Uh . . . I think Dorian's busy."

Valgren beamed a delighted smile. "I seldom get to human cities. This will be fun!"

"Could ye release the great beastie today? I'd not like te wait until tis too late."

I sent a questioning glance at Valgren who nodded. "We'll leave this afternoon," he said. "I understand the dragon's motivated when it comes to Mydryth and Myrador." He looked at me. "Besides, I'd love to see Raven's home."

My worldview jarred at the image of Valgren in my apartment. It'd always been Dorian and me in Denver. I pasted a smile on my face. "That'll be great."

Chapter 6

We materialized in a grove of spreading elms next to my apartment building, Valgren looking almost normal in jeans and a tee shirt that molded a muscular torso. My hair was piled in a messy knot on top of my head, and it felt strange to wear jeans. When a super-fit runner in short-shorts slowed to get a better look at Valgren, she caught my scowl, gave him a disappointed finger wave, and trotted on. He wore a broad smile as he watched the tight derriere disappear around a shrub.

When I snapped my fingers in front of his face, he gave me an unrepentant grin. "Gaia does some fine work!"

I tried to remember his values were different from the rest of us. After all, he hadn't blinked an eye at my . . . indiscretion with Dorian. I didn't have a leg to stand on – and knowing that made me cranky. I have te admit te being a wee bit illogical from time te time, as Angus would say. I hate introspection. I believe I've mentioned that before. It never ends well.

I expelled a deep breath, spun on my heel, and strode towards my apartment with Valgren craning his neck at the sights. As I pointed out my building, his only comment was to ask how I could live in a box so far above Gaia's plant energies. I'd never thought of it that way. I remembered my great view. It had been enough. Was it still?

In the elevator, Valgren watched the floor indicators light up. "Humans have a lot of unnecessary stuff," was all he said.

The air in my apartment was stale, so I dropped my keys onto the kitchen table and swung the patio doors wide. As Valgren took in the view from the balcony, I went to my room to gather some things.

With a sigh, I left an electronic e-reader on the dresser since its dozens of books couldn't be read on Cumulos. I tossed paperbacks into a sack and pulled the drawstring tight. The Cumulos library was wonderful, but it had a serious lack of rainy-day fiction. A framed picture of my mother and me taken just before I'd left Canada joined the books.

I glanced around. Why did I have so much stuff? Material things were losing their gloss. Even my attachment to childhood trinkets was fading. The room felt deserted, emptied of the human life for which it'd been designed.

I gave myself a shake. Were my new skills making me crazy? I loved the bumpy ceramic plate I'd made in fourth grade!

I wrapped it in a towel and stuffed it with the photo. And I reminded myself that rooms didn't feel anything. They were empty spaces for heaven's sake!

The air pressure altered, and I knew he stood behind me. As I turned, he glanced at the bed then down at me. "Looks comfortable."

I flushed. "Probably not as comfortable as a nest, but I believe it would do." His green eyes held mine, the aroma of a forest enveloped the space – and I swear the room smiled. I know I did.

***

City lights were sprinkled along the horizon as the sun dipped behind the mountains. Valgren was behind me on my broom, an arm around my waist enjoying the unusual method of travel, unusual because he never required technology to move anywhere. As our feet touched the stream bank, I sent a telepathic call to Bluescale.

Valgren strode to the edge of the stream, spread his arms, and intoned a spell. The calm surface of the water began to burble. In seconds, it looked like it was boiling, and there was a deep rumble. As the rumble increased in volume, I grew concerned the neighbours might hear. Then a gigantic scaly monster burst from the water. It shook its enormous head and exposed eight-inch teeth in a vicious snarl.

Of course, it only looked like a snarl. It was, in fact, a happy grin.

"Raven! Valgren! Great to see you!" The dragon turned his head to the side and spewed a column of flame followed by a great roaring laugh. "I love doing that!"

"Great to see you too, Bluescale," I said, "but we don't have an invisibility spell cast yet. Might want to avoid torching the countryside and alerting your neighbours."

He maintained his grin even though he sighed. "You always were a party pooper, Raven." After showering us with water by shaking like a dog, he said, "Well, hop on. Let's see why you need a dragon to save the kingdom this time!"

We floated to his broad back to settle between thick, vertical scales where I leaned into Valgren's chest. I cast an invisibility spell and, with powerful strokes of membranous dragon wings, we lifted into the evening sky.

Using time compression, we were at the enormous cloud that was Cumulos within a half-hour, Bluescale chatting the whole way. I missed Bluescale when he was away; yet, within minutes, I remembered what I always found so irritating about him. He believed everyone should be as happy as he was and seldom shut up. Unfortunately, some of the things he called fun such as terrorizing people, I found less than entertaining.

Many years ago, mages had changed the dragons into water bugs and placed them into streams around the world so they wouldn't keep killing people. Through a magical error a few months back, I'd met Bluescale, and we'd become . . . well . . . friends, I suppose. Hard to stay mad at someone who's so filled with such joie de vivre. Of course, you could get frustrated and impatient on a regular basis – which I did.

Bluescale turned his head so we could see one eye. "Somebody want to open the gate?"

Of course, there was no gate, just a spell that hid Cumulos from the non-magical and uninvited guests. As we approached the edge of the cloud, the air shimmered. There emerged a sight that never ceased to delight me – my own fairy realm where anything could happen. A crystal castle of children's dreams twinkled in the darkness, its towers lit by torchlight.

"Whoo . . . weee . . !" chortled Bluescale as he went into a spinning dive. Valgren's arm tightened as we bailed into the night sky. It reminded me of the first time I'd ridden the dragon when I couldn't yet levitate, terrified because he'd thought it would be fun to drop me from a great height. Like I said, Bluescale's sense of humour is questionable. Valgren put on a burst of speed to avoid the spinning wings.

Less than two seconds later, there was a flash, and Bluescale was jerked to a stop enmeshed in a sparkly, contracting net. My heart pounded as I remembered being caught in a similar trap by Napoleon, a name I'd christened my pig man captor. Using my magic and Bluescale's quick action, we'd escaped Napoleon's dungeon.

Bluescale's shocked emerald eyes locked with mine a second before he vanished.

"What the . . ." It'd been so fast, I could think of nothing to say.

"Something followed us through the opening!" Valgren made a magical gesture. "We need to warn Angus!"

After a brief sensation of movement, we stood in the castle study. Angus looked up from a dusty tome decorated with intricate drawings and leaned back at the look on Valgren's face.

"What's happened?"

"Bluescale was netted after we passed the barrier." He tipped his head towards me. "Barely missed us."

"Did ye see who it was?"

"No, but the person most threatened by the dragon is Myrador. Maybe he found out Raven and I were picking him up today."

Angus tapped his chin. "It's possible." He pushed back his chair and rose to pace, hands behind his back. "Some o' the Cathasach birds have returned wi' disturbing news. The number o' cellar slugs is growing fast."

"How do they multiply?" I asked. "It can't be the regular way. There are too many already."

"When we can answer that, lass, we'll have the problem half-solved."

Valgren grasped my hand. "If you can get others to look for Bluescale, Raven and I'll stone-walk to see if we can determine the extent of the infestation."

Angus nodded. "I'd appreciate that. I'll send a Cathasach te King Dorian. He'll have te keep a watch on Altaria, so he'll be too busy te help us, but Talon, Frost, and I will track down Bluescale."

As Valgren and I sank through the stone floor, I tossed my bag onto a chair. Everything I needed was on me – and with me.

Beneath the castle, a familiar subterranean landscape took shape. When we got deep enough, we changed to horizontal movement, feeling for the scent of cellar slugs. They didn't have an actual smell; it was more a scent/feel which, for some reason, reminded me of rot and gasoline. I realize there isn't any gasoline on Cumulos, but that's what they smelled like. Who the hell knew where they came from?

Valgren dissolved individual slugs we came across but was seeking groups. Clusters seemed evenly distributed – which meant there could be more than we'd feared. After a night spent crisscrossing subterranean Cumulos, I began to yawn and stumble. Valgren raised us from the ground, brushed back a lock of ebony, and gave me a light kiss. "Time for bed," he whispered.

In a flash, I was in my bed in the castle tower. I peeked beneath the blankets. Naked. I heard a soft chuckle and he was gone. Valgren would keep looking, fueled always by Gaia. A smile tugged at my lips as I turned over and closed my eyes. I had a worrying thought about Bluescale until I realized that, after a few hours of his incessant babble, his captors would most likely return him.

***

I was cross-legged on a low wall that surrounded the courtyard fountain watching the morning sun inch its way down crystal walls. Wherever it touched, rainbows sprang to life. Brown bunnies grazed on hanging flowers, noses twitching, little jaws at high speed. I sipped a post-breakfast coffee and sighed with contentment. The hunt for Bluescale and the slugs would resume soon enough.

As a flutter of tiny wings caught my attention, my heart sank. Please let that be a bird!

A high voice dashed my hopes. "What're you doing out here? Don't you have work to do? I could use some of that coffee. Hope you didn't put sugar in it!"

I sighed. "Good to see you too, Scarlet and, if you have a cup, you can have some of my coffee."

"Tip it over. I can drink from your cup."

"No, you can't."

"Yes, I can. I'll show you!"

"You're not sticking your tongue in my coffee, Scarlet! I don't care how small it is! Get your own cup!"

She fluttered in front of me, arms crossed, mouth in a pout. "You are *so* selfish!"

"You should remember that. Don't ask me for stuff, and don't expect me to be your personal slave."

"I do things for you!"

"Name one."

Her face worked, eyes narrowed. "I don't know why I keep helping Cumulos. I should let everybody stumble along without me."

"You should. I have to go now," I said, sliding to my feet. "As always, nice talking to you, Scarlet."

Angus must've asked her for help in finding Bluescale. Not on my team, I hoped. As little wings fluttered into the castle, I consoled myself with the idea that every paradise has its snake. I glanced at my new wind-up watch then trudged up the stairs to Angus' study.

As it was still early, I took the opportunity to study (read snoop). I love the library. I'm pretty sure I could be happy there for the rest of my life. Bookshelves lined the tower all the way to the ceiling. Non-magical people need not apply for membership as levitation skills were necessary to reach beyond the third row.

I floated to the topmost level where ancient cracked tombs were stored. I wouldn't remove any for fear of damaging them, but I perused titles: *Black Magic for Master Mages; Dowsing for Anything; Uncommon Uses for Newt* (cookbook perhaps?); *Flight of the Magi;* and on and on. In the peaceful silence of early morning, sunbeams pierced the topmost windows to cast a warm glow.

So, I was surprised to hear a soft sound from below. To my astonishment, a pig butt stuck out from beneath Angus' desk. As I stared in disbelief, I saw Napoleon cast sneaky looks over his shoulder as he stuck something to the desk's underside.

A boiling heat started in my belly. I'm pretty sure I could've given the devil himself a run for his money in a contest of red-eye syndrome. As I dove towards the pig, I pulled out my wand and shaped a spell that would've turned the sneaky little bastard into bacon.

In retrospect, I realize I should've shut up and sneaked up – or called Valgren – or Angus – or Talon or . . . okay, I see where I had better choices, but haven't you ever done anything on impulse? Second-guessing is a bit like introspection. It neither helps nor ends well.

My bellow echoed off the walls. "Napoleon, you rotten bastard!"

He rammed his head against the bottom of the heavy desk and emitted a piercing squeal. If you've ever surprised a pig, you'll know what I mean. I let fly the spell, but he scrunched under the desk and spoiled my aim. A lot of thumping went on which ended with his little pig feet and fat butt sticking out of a space that was too small for him. I experienced glorious satisfaction as my feet touched the floor. I shoved Angus' chair to the side and took careful aim.

Somehow, Napoleon reversed his position and flopped onto his back, head sticking out from beneath the desk, little pink eyes staring up at me. Yellow-coated teeth bared in a weak, fake grin. He had nowhere to go.

I should've noticed when his eyes slid to the left, but I was too involved with my revenge. The spell was almost ready to fly when I experienced the most curious sensation. My legs folded, and I sank to the floor.

A gravelly voice snarled at Napoleon as the pig man scrambled from beneath the desk. If I could've moved, I'd have thrown up from the stench as he stepped over me. If they could sew tunics, why the hell couldn't they make pants?

Sticky teeth and tiny pink eyes returned to my field of vision. "We'll meet again, White Raven!" he snarled.

Great. Another threat. What had I ever done to him?

In seconds, the room was empty. I peered around as best I could, but there was nothing to do but wait. I suppose I should've been thankful I could breathe and that they hadn't taken me to Napoleon's dungeon. At least now I could tell Angus he should check his desk – and everywhere else for that matter.

Despite the fact I'd come out somewhat the worse for wear in the encounter (some might even hint I'd lost), I'd learned something valuable. The enemy was still using the pig men. I wondered what the most recent promise had been.

Time passed. My nose itched. My ear itched. My back needed scratching. Arghh!

An eternity later, a pair of size fifteen feet stood beside me. Damn. I couldn't even turn away.

"Raven! What happened te ye?" Angus squatted to lift my limp head. "What did ye say? I cannae hear ye, lass!"

I shifted my eyes and groaned.

He glanced down and adjusted his kilt. "Raven, ye worry about the silliest things!" He could be right, but I preferred a certain amount of decorum. With a swift motion, he carried me to a sofa where he placed a pillow beneath my head. "Tis an immobility spell. Twill wear off in a wee bit."

I heard a bird, but it was Scarlet fluttering into the room. "I'll bet you have an itchy nose!" she gloated. "In fact, I'll bet you have itchy spots all over!" As I managed to glare, she propped little fists on her hips. "If you had any friends, they'd probably help you!"

"Scarlet, is that necessary? The lass cannae move."

"I know that! Why do you think I'm taking advantage? After all, she's a hundred times my size!"

"I'm sure ye dinnae need reminding that magic has nothing te do with size."

"She doesn't seem to understand that."

"But you should."

Scarlet narrowed her eyes at me. "I have someplace else to be."

Good.

I felt like a beached whale. I could move my eyes and breathe. That was it. How long did this last? After an eternity, I smelled a verdant forest and knew I could relax. Valgren would take care of everything.

"Raven."

I rolled my eyes upwards. Shit! Dorian in a travelling cloak. He'd probably come through a forest. As if the situation wasn't humiliating enough, I needed Dorian to witness it. I closed my eyes. Perhaps if I concentrated, I could disappear. Unfortunately, I hadn't mastered that spell either.

A warm hand took mine. "Raven, you can't keep running." He glanced down the length of my unresponsive body and smiled. "Especially not right now."

I tried to make my eyes angry, and his smile widened. "Let's have a chat. I'll talk. You listen."

Ha. Ha. Very funny. I heard the study door close and knew we were alone.

"Look at me, Raven." His voice was gentle. "Look at me, please."

When I ran out of other things to look at, I forced myself to meet his melted-chocolate gaze.

"That's better." He smoothed a lock of hair from my forehead. "It's me, Raven. I am and will remain, your friend, no matter what happens in our lives, no matter who comes into them for each other. You don't need to run from me. I understand your relationship with Valgren is important – so I'll stop interfering. I won't bring up our time together if that's what you want, and I can live my life as your friend. None of us knows what the future holds, but the thing I can't handle is losing you from my life. We've been there for each other since we met, Raven, and I never want that to change."

He inhaled a deep breath. "Can you live with that? Will you keep being my friend?"

I'd seldom seen Dorian with his guard down and then, at most, only for a few seconds. Why couldn't he have done this in Denver? Of course, he'd explained all that. When had things gotten so complicated?

Something trickled down my cheek. He smiled and wiped it away. "I'll take that as a yes." He brushed my lips with his. "I have to go. Angus tells me you'll be fine, so I'll talk to you later." With a soft rustle of clothing, he was gone.

At a skittering sound, I rolled my eyes towards the back of the couch – and here I'd thought things couldn't get worse. Cyril crouched there, flickers of sunlight flashing through the crystal that dangled from his collar.

"I hear you've been immobilized," he said, little eyes blinking behind tiny round glasses. I glared, groaned and closed my eyes. "Are you in pain?" he asked. I sent him another scathing look. "Oh. Right. Immobility spell. Can't talk. I haven't seen many of this kind. Appears to be quite effective."

An effort to move my tongue so I could send him away resulted in precisely nothing. I resumed my glare.

"I was hoping you'd attend my classes in the parasitical world of fungi. All sorts of potions and poisons can be made from them."

I wouldn't have wanted him to read my mind at that point. Why didn't he just leave already? It was obvious I was in no condition to take a class in anything.

"Well," he said, blinking little rat eyes. "I'm off to check my mushrooms." And, to my relief, he scampered away.

***

Silence returned. A tingle in my toes worked its way up my body. A half-hour later, I managed to push to a sitting position, head in hands. Angus and Frost arrived as I returned to the land of the ambulatory. Frost, well into her thirties and no longer threatened by my presence, sat next to me.

"You'll be nauseous for a bit," she said, an arm around my shoulders. "Keep your head down."

Considering the rate at which my head spun, there wasn't any danger of me getting up. I nodded and gulped. "What the hell was in that spell?"

"It's a variation of an immobility hex. Quite nasty."

I sucked in deep breaths. "Can you teach me how to do it?"

She seemed surprised by my request. "Who'd deserve such a vile spell?"

"I'm making a list!"

"I see. Perhaps later."

When the shakes had calmed and I'd managed to swallow a mouthful of water, I told them my story. At my claim that Napoleon had been sticking something beneath his desk, Angus got on hands and knees to look. I turned my head away from the view and waited to hear what was there.

"Ach!" he crowed. "Here's the wee thing!"

"What is it?" I asked.

He extricated himself from beneath the desk and came over, peering at his palm. "Tis a wee bug."

"You mean a listening device?"

"Aye, ye could call it that."

He held it so I could see, and I jumped clear over the sofa. "It's a bug!"

He looked confused. "Aye, lass. Tis what I said."

"But . . . I meant . . . you know . . ."

"Electronics dinnae work on Cumulos, remember. But this fellow does pretty well the same job."

"How?" It looked like a centipede with hard-shelled segments along its back. As Angus pushed it closer, I jumped back. "Eww! That's close enough!" *I can't believe I sounded like such a girl!*

"They'll need te return te retrieve the wee beastie. It cannae transmit like a radio, but a good mage can cast a spell te get the information stored in its various bits o' shell."

"Are there more?" I envisioned the floor alive with insects.

"He's nae likely te have many o' these. They're verra rare and expensive te boot."

Thank heavens for small favours. "What are you going to do with it?"

"Add it te my collection o' course. Shame te waste it."

Embarrassed about my girlish panic, I said, "You know, I'm feeling better. Maybe I should look for Bluescale."

"We spent most o' yesterday scanning, but even the Cathesach birds failed te find anything." He paused and looked into my eyes. "Ye realize, lass, that Bluescale would be a great addition te Myrador's army."

My back straightened. "Bluescale would never work against Cumulos! Mydryth already tried that!"

"He could promise the return o' Bluescale's brother, Frederick."

"Isn't he dead?"

"Dead is nae always permanent." *Funny, I'd always believed it was*. "Under the right circumstances, the dead can return te life."

I felt a chill. "That would be a powerful motivator for Bluescale."

"Aye, lass. It would."

Chapter 7

Wind snapped my cloak as I hovered above Cumulos. Telepathic calls to Bluescale had been fruitless. Where could he be? Was he alright? I couldn't imagine the dragon betraying us for any reason, even the return of his brother. It was possible the dragon wasn't even on Gaia. After all, I'd been abducted by the pig men to a planet with two suns and, to this day, I've no idea where I was relative to Earth. Although Angus had sent Bluescale to the rescue, we'd both been captured, I for the second time. The pig men are persistent critters.

The sun grazed the western horizon as I settled to the Cumulos courtyard where Valgren, in sleeveless tunic and soft leather leggings, stepped from a covered walkway. My windblown hair became smooth when he stroked it and, as his lips brushed mine, my broom hit the paving stones with a clunk.

His lips curved. "Am I distracting you?"

I mumbled, "The broom will be fine." From the corner of my eye, I saw it shoot into the castle. If brooms could have attitude . . .

Valgren kissed me again, warmer this time then pulled back. "It's not a good idea to get on the bad side of your broom."

"I'll apologize later . . . wait a minute; is that even possible?"

He chuckled. "A subject for another day. I wanted to see you before I left. Not only is Cumulos being attacked by cellar slugs, but some areas of Gaia as well. I need to see to it."

"And you'll be back when you're back?"

He smiled. "I'll keep Angus informed."

I traced his lips with my fingertips. "Thanks for waiting to say goodbye."

There was the whisper of wings as Moonlight, Valgren's great white Pegasus, sailed into the courtyard. Valgren vaulted to his back and, in seconds, they were clearing the castle walls. At a squeeze of the heart which I preferred not to examine, I decided this would be a good time to get an update from the others.

The study was empty. Feeling intrusive, I scanned a mysterious thick volume on Angus' desk as I kept a wary eye out for more spy bugs. As I pushed his leather chair out of the way, my heart leaped at a loud thump and what sounded like curses in a strange language. I grabbed my wand, prepared to incinerate anything with a snout.

Talon emerged from beneath the desk rubbing his head. "Can't you speak when you enter a room?" He gestured towards my wand. "Put that thing away before you hurt somebody!"

"I normally don't speak to empty rooms," I retorted. "You could've said something!"

As he pulled himself erect, I tried not to stare at his bony legs and strange clasping toes which seemed to belong on a bird. At realizing I was being was less than successful, I took refuge in resentment.

"How was I to know you'd be crawling around under there? What were you doing anyway? The last person I caught was planting bugs!"

He moved with an ungainly motion around the desk. He was quite clumsy on the ground. Perhaps that's why he floated in a lotus position looking for all the world like a fuzzy meditator – with attitude. He got his legs twisted up and perched on the back of a life-sized statue of a Pegasus.

"I was looking for more bugs. It could've laid eggs."

"Oh, god! Do they reproduce?"

"Are they alive?"

"I guess."

"Then they reproduce."

I blanched. "You mean there could be more?"

"I was ensuring there weren't. At least from eggs. It's possible their numbers grow from some other method as well."

"Good. That's . . . very good. Thanks."

"I didn't do it for you."

"Didn't think you would. Thanks anyway."

Footsteps approached from the hallway, and Angus burst in. "Ah, you're here! Glad te see the two o' ye. How did the wee bug hunting go, Talon?"

Talon rubbed his head, adjusted his goggles, and scowled. "Well enough until I was interrupted!"

Angus was good at ignoring pointless distractions. He turned to me. "I take it ye've had nae luck contacting Bluescale?"

"Nothing. And I can't imagine what could interrupt telepathy."

"Dorian's coming te help since he's got the slug-hunting organized on Altaria. We were thinking, since ye have telepathic rapport with the dragon, ye might have better luck finding him with the Mirror o' Grodonon."

My stomach clenched. "Dorian's coming here?" *If I'd been an introspective person, I might've noticed I was more worried about seeing Dorian than I was with having to use that infernal scrying mirror again.*

"Aye, lass. He'll be here soon."

Ack! I wasn't ready for this in spite of his speech about undying friendship. In my experience, you can't shove stronger feelings under the category of friendship for any length of time. It causes all sorts of awkwardness. I have to admit, memories of my night with Dorian all too often caught me unawares, and I was beginning to realize the question wasn't so much could Dorian go back to friendship, but could I?

"Don't look so horrified, Raven," drawled Dorian as he strolled in. He was in casual royal attire (if there's such a thing). "I don't bite." *Actually, I remembered some quite delightful nips* . . . As a flash of intimacy lit his smile, I swear he read my mind.

Angus flicked a look between the two of us. He did a quick eye roll, shook his head, and turned to his desk. He must've wondered how one person could generate such ongoing interpersonal kerfuffles.

"It wasn't about you, Dorian," I said. *Liar.* "I remember how scrying with the Mirror of Grodonon didn't go so well last time." *True*.

"Ye may've had a close call scrying Mydryth when he was stealing unicorns, lass, but twas a great help."

Memory of the grasping shadow of the evil mage made the hair on the back of my neck stand up.

"We'll nae be looking for Myrador or the pig men, Raven; we'll be scrying for Bluescale. Should be safe enough."

I remembered him saying the exact same thing when Mydryth nearly got me. Not so safe.

I tried not to notice how delicious Dorian looked nor his warm glance, but every cell in my body went on alert as he reclined next to me. I'm here to tell you bodies have no sense of decorum whatsoever. Dorian's nearness had my body humming like a choir.

He leaned close to whisper. "Relax, Raven. I'm not going to attack you." Anything I said at this point would only make matters worse, so I refrained from comment.

Frost glided into the room and chose a chair near Dorian. She didn't have to be in her active phase to notice a gorgeous man. He gave her a polite nod. *Don't gnash your teeth, Raven. It's bad for them.*

Angus removed the felt cover from the Mirror of Grodonon. You see, the scary thing about this particular scrying mirror is that it creates a two-way portal between you and whatever you're viewing. If it turns out to be something nasty, that something could shoot right into your lap. Now you see why I'd rather eat mold than use it.

The object was balanced on its own pedestal, the top of which was shaped like the claws of a ring which suspended the mirror. A thin ridge around its edge bounded the film of water that Angus poured from a carved copper chalice.

My trepidation must've been obvious because Dorian said, "I can give it a try. Raven shouldn't take all the risk."

My ears perked. This sounded like a better plan.

"Ye can try, but Raven has better rapport with Bluescale, and we don't want te warn the piggies. We may need te be verra fast."

My heart resumed its former level. Rats! I stood with a sigh. "What do you want me to do?"

"Thank ye, lass. As ye gaze into the mirror, visualize Bluescale. Reach for his essence. How does it feel when you're communicating?"

"He's usually irritating the hell out of me."

"Is he nae your friend?"

"Well . . . yes. But he's an irritating friend."

Angus decided not to pursue this conversational line. He cleared his throat and gestured to the scrying mirror. "I'll stand by ye, lass, te break the connection if necessary."

I eyed the ominous mirror. I didn't doubt Angus' sincerity, but perhaps I had more faith in the unknown enemy's strength. To make matters worse, Dorian was inches behind me squeezing my personal space. How on Earth was I supposed to concentrate?

The pressure eased as he moved to the side and, by the look in his eyes, I knew he knew. I felt like such a juvenile. It didn't help when Frost snuggled against him. At least the mirror would force me to think about something else. Talon hovered near my right shoulder with the expectation of failure clearly written on his face.

"Are ye ready lass?"

The tightness in my throat prevented speech, so I nodded. The obsidian surface gazed up at me with an I-dare-you look. At least that's how it seemed. I may have been anthropomorphizing a smidgeon. I cleared my throat and stepped closer. Why did these stupid things have to be black? Why not a bright blue or perhaps a cheerful pink? Always black. I noticed my thoughts had wandered, so I reined them in. I wanted to get this over with – and there was always the remote chance it might work.

As I peered into the void, the others stilled. Everyone knew scrying took concentration. *Relax. Relax.* I wasn't relaxed. Visions of a clawed hand kept interrupting – and the sight of

Frost brushing a generous breast against Dorian's arm didn't help. At least he had the grace to look uncomfortable.

Think about Bluescale – which didn't help because he was the least relaxing creature I'd ever known. More deep breaths. Think about how he made me feel . . . on second thought, think about our friendship, how I'd felt when I'd thought he was going to die. The black was absolute, and my eyes were going crazy from trying to focus on nothing – like a camera lens searching for an invisible subject.

There was a flick of blue – and it was gone. I tried another telepathic call. "*Bluescale, are you there?*" Nothing. Was that a pink pig eye? "*Bluescale, answer me!*" I leaned closer. Something flickered in the darkness. My eyes crossed, and a pounding started in my forehead. With a sigh of defeat, I lifted my head just as a tongue of flame shot from the mirror.

The stench of singed hair filled my nostrils. My hands flew to my face where, to my horror, my hair and eyebrows felt sticky. As I howled in dismay, a powerful hand grabbed my wrist, there was an awful spinning sensation – and I opened my eyes on a grey seashore.

Chapter 8

The rhythmic swish of waves and the screech of shorebirds didn't help my nausea as I rolled onto my belly. I pushed semi-erect to balance on wobbly knees. That had been the worst trip yet. Hand to forehead, I looked around for a clue as to where I was. A chilly wind blew from the ocean towards a beach of volcanic rock and black sand. An overcast sky made everything grey and dull.

A spot of red was Angus face down in the sand. Relief flooded through me when he groaned and moved his fingers. With a resigned sigh, I tottered over and tugged his kilt to a more modest level. If Angus was here, who else . . ? As I looked around, my solar plexus gave a painful contraction.

Dorian? Stifling a cry, I scrambled to him and dropped to my knees. Also face down, he was terrifyingly still. I rolled him over and tried not to panic at his pallor as I pressed my fingertips to his jugular. At the strong thump of a heart, tears of relief stung my eyes.

"Damn! Tha' was a rough one! I feel sick te me stomach!" Angus used a boulder to pull himself upright.

I spun on him and snarled, "What the hell did you do?!"

"When the flames came through, I used the tunnel it made te transport us. Didn't have time te ask a by-your-leave, but I grabbed ye and Dorian. Bluescale must be here; and he's angry or he would'na be shooting flames. Maybe he escaped."

I scanned the sky. "If Bluescale's in the midst of a battle, where is it?"

Angus surveyed the beach. "It may be quiet at the moment, but the dragon must be nearby. Ye'd best get Dorian awake."

Dorian's breathing was even, and he looked so peaceful, I slapped him hard across the face. Perhaps my relief at his being alive added passion to my action, but I hit him hard enough to leave red fingermarks. Fortunately, there weren't any mirrors in the vicinity. If Dorian couldn't see it, I didn't need to tell him, right? Maybe Angus wouldn't give me away.

Dorian groaned as I helped him to a seated position. "God, I feel sick!" he groaned. "What happened?" He rubbed his cheek. "Why does my face hurt?"

"No time for questions," I said, looking away. "We've got to get off this beach."

As I helped him to his feet, we heard a clatter of hooves. A dozen pig men galloped towards us on stubby, fat ponies. I imagined Napoleon was somewhere in there but, since they were almost identical, I couldn't tell. If not for their lances and the mage riding in front, I'd have collapsed from laughter. They looked ridiculous. Each wore a sort of military tunic with fringed epaulettes along with a peaked military hat. How do you take fat pigs in trouser-less costumes riding chubby ponies seriously?

I got a degree of satisfaction at Dorian's expression of incredulity. "What in hell's name are those?"

"I'll explain later," I said, grabbing his arm. "We need to get out of here."

"Are you serious? I'm not running from them!" He pulled out his wand.

I tugged. "One word – magic!"

"Oh."

Angus was a receding red dot as we sprinted towards ragged cliffs in search of a cave we could defend. I promised myself as I bolted across sand and scrub brush that I was finished with this scrying bullshit. It was somebody else's turn.

Dorian informed me his levitation spells didn't work either as he pulled me to my feet after I'd stumbled over a root. I refrained from mentioning I'd been so focused on our pursuers that I hadn't even thought of levitation. I must be the dumbest mage in history.

Hoof-beats clattered onto a line of shale which bordered the sandy shore, and a spear glanced off a rock inches from my foot.

"Raven, stop screaming! You'll need that air to run!"

I don't know what he was talking about. I never scream. I put on a burst of speed as an arrow landed a pace from my left foot. We leaped a line of boulders that had fallen from the cliff over the centuries and charged towards a narrow, dark slash in the granite cliff.

Angus was well ahead, going strong, and headed towards the same destination. Considering how fast he was running and the fact he didn't wear underwear, I wondered . . . well, never mind.

It was all I could do to keep up with Dorian, and a strip of sand before the cliffs made my legs feel like they'd gained twenty pounds each. Gasping for air as I slugged through it, I cursed myself for using levitation and my broom instead of walking or, better yet, running. If I survived this, I was going to start working out. I ignored a sharp pain in my leg that was yet more proof I needed to get fit.

Angus dove behind a boulder in front of the cave, pulled out his wand, and started deflecting spears and arrows. As we charged past, he ducked in after us, made a swirling motion, and a watery film sealed the opening.

As I struggled to get my wind back, I noticed Dorian staring at me with a strange expression, like he was trying to smother a laugh.

"What's so funny?" I might've sounded a bit waspish, but I was in no mood for his sarcasm. Just because he was barely breathing hard and I could barely breathe was no reason to make fun.

"Nothing," he said, his lips quivering.

"It's *not* nothing! I know you, Dorian!"

"It's just . . . you know; the fire and all . . ."

Oh God! I'd forgotten all about it! I felt my hair. Sticky and frizzy all over the front! My voice was distressingly high. "Is it all burned off?"

He seemed uneasy, like there was no good answer. "Well . . . not all of it. Your eyebrows will grow back and . . . I hear bangs are in style."

"Bangs? I need *bangs*? I have to cut my *hair*?!" My voice attained another octave.

"Not all of it . . . just a little, you know . . . trim here and there. It'll be fine – in time."

"In time? How *much* time?!" Shakespeare would've called my cry a wail of anguish.

He gestured towards the cave entrance through which we could see milling ponies and pig men. "We have bigger issues right now. Could we table the hairstyle discussion?"

In spite of my distress, I saw his point. My breakdown would have to wait. I collapsed onto a rock then shot vertical at an excruciating pain. What the . . . something stuck out of my leg! What on Earth?

Dorian heard my gasp, looked down, and the colour drained from his face. "Raven . . ."

Blood ran from both sides of my thigh – injuries connected by an arrow.

"Dorian . . ?" I was barely conscious of him reaching for me.

* * *

Black shadows flickered along the cave wall. I was covered by Dorian's velvet cloak, and it took a few seconds to realize my leg burned with a great deal of enthusiasm. As memory flickered, I groaned. Shot by a pig man! I'd need gallons of disinfectant!

My companions murmured by a small fire over which hung a tiny copper pot. Dorian glanced up at my groan and hurried over, smoothed my scorched hair back, and smiled. "Welcome back. We removed the arrow and cleaned the wound. You should be alright, but you won't be running foot-races for a bit."

I moved my tongue around to clear out the feel of cotton. "Was the arrow poisoned?"

"No. But it was dirty."

I frowned. "Then how did I get unconscious?"

"Umm . . . you fainted."

I snorted. "Don't be ridiculous! I never faint!"

Without missing a beat, he continued, "Of course not. You decided to take a nap and, while you were napping, Angus and I removed the arrow and dressed your wound."

I could see him resist a smile. "Don't make fun of me, Dorian! I've been shot!"

"Wouldn't think of it." He glanced at Angus who stirred whatever was in the pot. "Angus is brewing a healing potion. Should be nearly done."

I struggled to a sitting position. "How long . . ?"

"An hour. The pig men are still outside, but there might be other entrances. We need to get a move-on."

Angus brought the pot which was wrapped in a leather bag. The brownish steam it gave off looked ominous. "Ye gave us quite a start, lass. Have a go at this. Twill make ye feel better. Careful now, tis hot."

I took a sniff and almost blacked out. I'd no idea anything could smell so awful. It was worse than the putrid odour you get from cut flowers forgotten in a closet.

My lip must've curled. "It does nae taste sae good," said Angus, "but twill heal and stop infection."

As I recalled the sticky yellow coating on Napoleon's teeth, I took a deep breath, held my nose, and swallowed all of it – several times.

"Keep it down, lass. There's nae enough for another batch."

Thank god! I'd rather die than drink more. When at last the retching eased and my awareness extended further than my stomach, I noticed activity at the mouth of the cave. A stubby mage in a brown cowl stood, arms raised, on the far side of the protective shield. His wrinkled and folded face reminded me of a Chinese Pug, and a wide, mobile mouth produced the strangest chant I'd ever heard. It altered between deep bass and frantic coyote howls.

"How long has he been at that?"

Dorian glanced at the strange little mage. "Half-an-hour. We should leave before he gets lucky."

I bent my knee to get up and gasped at the pain that shot through my leg. "Ugh . . ." I gritted my teeth and flicked a sour glance at Angus. "I thought that disgusting potion was supposed to fix this!"

"Twill be an hour or so before ye feel better."

"Meanwhile, I'm supposed to run like this?"

He gestured towards the cave entrance and the frantic mage. "He may be incompetent, but chance alone says he'll get through eventually. Be better if we're not here when he does."

I grimaced and held out my arms. "Help me up." As they pulled me to my feet, I sucked in a breath. "Son of a . . !" I bit my lip.

Dorian slid an arm around my waist. "Are you okay?"

I glared. "What kind of a stupid question is that, Dorian?! Of course, I'm not okay! I've been shot!"

I felt him draw a deep breath. "I realize you're in pain, Raven, but that's no reason to take it out on me. I'm trying to help."

I wasn't ready to let it go. "You'd be cranky too if you'd had an arrow through your leg!"

As the mage reached a high, warbling wail, Angus sent a wary glance towards the entrance. "Can we finish this on the way? I'd like te put some distance between us and the piggies. We dinnae know the extent o' this cave or how far we'll need te go."

With an arm around my waist from each side, I was half-carried into absolute blackness. I hate dark, confined places. Why am I always in them?

"Well?" huffed Dorian as we skirted rocks by the pale light of his wand.

"Well, what?"

"Are you going to apologize?"

"For what?"

"For snapping at me."

I stared at him for a beat. "Don't be ridiculous! I've already admitted I'm cranky. Why should I apologize for it?" Dorian gave a grunt of impatience but fell into silence as we hastened deeper into the cave which seemed to extend forever. I tried not to imagine the cockroaches that probably infested it, not to mention – rats! I hate rats.

As time wore on, the tunnel branched and we started to climb. That was all I needed – more pressure on my leg. Finally, I called a halt. "I need to rest. Set me on that rock, please."

Both men were breathing hard and, to tell the truth, I felt guilty they had to carry me. It must've been an hour. I wanted to try some weight on my leg but didn't want it bleeding again.

Dorian held his wand aloft. "The cliff was high but, if we stay at this angle, we should reach the surface soon."

"Agreed," said Angus. "It should nae be much farther."

I massaged my thigh, careful not to disturb the makeshift bandage made of scraps of my shirt. I tugged at a now very short top held together by one small button. I didn't see why they couldn't have used one of their shirts. After all, they were bigger. More cranky thoughts crowded in until I decided I'd had enough. Even I couldn't stand my attitude.

With a sigh, I pushed to my feet and carefully put weight on the wounded leg, surprised to find it didn't feel that bad. I took a step. Another. Wow! Miracle of miracles! I could walk! Dorian watched as I winced over to him.

"All right already, I apologize."

"For what?" he asked with feigned innocence.

I rolled my eyes. "I formally apologize for being cranky just because I had an arrow stuck through my leg and you expected me to run. Such a little thing should never have made me cranky."

His eyes smiled. "You might want to inspect that apology."

I couldn't help it. A laugh burst from me, and I settled onto the stone next to him. "How the hell do we get into these situations?" I gestured to our surroundings.

Angus held up a hand. "Listen!"

We froze. The chink of stone and echoes of clumsy pursuit came to us. Damn! The pig men had gotten in! I sprang to my feet, decided a little thing like holes in my leg wasn't going to affect my speed, and charged ahead.

Dorian trotted alongside. "Seriously," he said, "are you okay to run?"

"Seems the potion has kicked in. My leg's a little stiff, but I think I can make it to the surface."

"Any chance of contacting Bluescale?"

"I've been trying. I'll keep at it." I wouldn't consider the ebullient dragon might be dead.

A familiar sizzle brought me up short. No! That incompetent twit couldn't possibly have created snake-light! The sizzle came again. I hate it when I'm wrong.

I gauged the width of the tunnel. Too narrow. Snake-light could shoot across it with enough power to fry us all. Dorian and Angus skidded to a stop, unable to hear the dangerous hiss.

"What's wrong?" panted Dorian. "Do you need us to carry you?"

The surface couldn't be far, but our magic was spotty in this place. Did I dare stone-walk? I'd have to take them both. Could I do it? We'd be trapped in a stone coffin if I screwed up.

The sizzling grew louder. "Take my hands!" Dorian and Angus looked like they thought I'd lost my mind. At their hesitation, I bellowed, "Now!" As they grabbed my hands, I squeezed them hard. "Now, don't let go!"

I stepped into solid stone, dragging them along. Dorian had done this before, but it was new to Angus. He had all sorts of magical powers, but stone-walking wasn't amongst them. His eyes widened in the dimness.

"Run!" I yelled.

We sprinted through seams of minerals and trickles of water until I found my target – the tips of tree roots. We had seconds before the sizzle caught us. Angus and Dorian could now hear it as well, correctly assessed it as threatening, and tugged at me in their urgency. I lifted my thumbs to indicate I wanted to go up. As we rose, the hair on my arms lifted in response to the proximity of the snake-light.

My lungs were ready to explode from exertion, and I'd almost given up hope when our heads popped into a meadow surrounded by gigantic trees. With a frantic heave, I pulled the others into the air, and we sprinted towards some hanging vines. As I bellowed instructions to get off the ground, we each grabbed one and climbed like monkeys.

I was able to produce a weak levitation spell to help me along though I noticed Angus and Dorian were far above me. I glanced down as a scorch-mark formed in the grass. A thick tendril of snake-light shot into the air, snapping and searching for its prey. With a final flash of disappointment (or so it seemed), it sank from sight.

The three of us hung for what seemed like ages, nobody willing to set foot on the grass. I surveyed the gigantic branches above which, under current conditions, seemed safer than the meadow. Valgren had assured me that, unlike lightning, snake-light couldn't run up trees. Since I didn't plan on touching the ground for a long time, I resumed climbing.

The others disappeared into the leaves above. As I neared a branch the size of a normal tree trunk, powerful fingers wrapped around my wrist, and I was airborne to be caught against Dorian's chest. It felt nice there with his hands on my bare midriff. He touched a finger to my lips then pointed down and to the left. There was movement at a gash in a rock wall.

Two pig men stepped out followed by the cowl-clad figure. Others huddled in a bunch. They seemed worried.

I felt Angus press against my back making me the middle of a man sandwich. I was confused until I noticed an invisibility shield enveloped the three of us.

Our pursuers scanned the sky. Some skulked behind trees but they all stayed close to the tunnel entrance. Something had them spooked, but I was pretty sure it wasn't us.

A sharp whistle sounded from above, but the heavy canopy made visibility impossible. The pig men leaped in place then shoved at each other in a blind panic to squeeze back into the narrow cave. The mage cleared them from the entrance with a blast and scuttled to safety first. Those that could move rolled to their feet and, considering how fat they all were, the process involved considerable difficulty. Some took two or three tries.

The whistle became deafening. A pig man grabbed the hoof of an unconscious companion and yanked him into the hole as a searing blast of flame scorched the rock. An enormous blue-green form shot past.

Bluescale? I sent a telepathic message. "*Bluescale!*"

There was silence as the giant figure shot into the sky. Then, "Raven? What're you doing here? Don't tell me you need rescuing again!"

Funny how fast the big bag of wind could irritate me. "*I'm here to rescue you! Dorian and Angus are with me.*"

"Why would I need rescuing?"

"How about the fact you were shrink-wrapped the last time I saw you?"

Dorian looked down at me. "Was that Bluescale?"

I nodded. "He'll be back in a minute."

As the whistling sound returned, Bluescale's membranous wings shot out, and he braked to a stop to flutter gently. He scanned the trees. "Where are you?"

I slid from between the two men as Angus removed the invisibility shield. "Here, Bluescale!"

He twisted his sinewy neck into a sharp bend. "What're you doing up there?"

"Looking for you. Why haven't you answered my calls? We've been worried!"

He settled his massive hind end to the singed grass and stretched front legs towards us. "Come down from there. I'll get a crick in the neck!"

We stepped onto his clawed feet and were lowered to the ground. As I eyed the scorched grass with suspicion, I asked if he was the reason the pig men were so afraid to come out of the cave.

"It's because of what I had for breakfast," he said with an enigmatic expression.

Sometimes Bluescale makes no sense. "What does your breakfast have to do with anything?"

He rolled emerald eyes towards me, no doubt in anticipation of my reaction. "I had bacon – lots . . . of bacon."

It took a heartbeat before I got it. "Euww!"

He grinned. "Napoleon isn't smart enough to hold a dragon. It seems the evil mage, Mydryth, has a twin brother by the name of Myrador. Napoleon made the teensy mistake of assuming I'd believe Myrador would bring my brother, Frederick, back to life if I helped him take Earth. Like a lot of people, Napoleon forgets dragons are the ancient keepers of wisdom. If the dark mage is anything like his brother, he'd never keep his part of any agreement. Assuming he'd convinced me to accept the deal, Napoleon made the mistake of turning his back on me for a few seconds."

I blanched. Although I found the little guy disgusting, I balked at the idea of Bluescale eating him. "You didn't . . ."

His sigh was accompanied by a belch of black smoke and a shake of his head. "I tried, but he hid behind some of his minions who performed the ultimate sacrifice," he grinned, "as well as provided me with breakfast!"

My head swam with visuals. "Could we change the subject? How did Napoleon get away?"

He gestured towards the cave into which the pigs had scuttled. "This area's riddled with tunnels. The pig guys hide in them a lot since they brought me here. Bet they don't go after a full-grown dragon again!"

"Looks like they bit off more than they could chew," said Dorian. "Good for you, Bluescale. Teach them a lesson they'll not soon forget."

Angus picked twigs from his kilt and straightened the fabric. "I'm glad te hear ye escaped the pig men, Bluescale, but did ye learn anything about the cellar slugs while they had ye captive?"

"One of the pigs who joined me for breakfast was quite knowledgeable about Napoleon's organization, and I managed to convince him to explain the plan. Although they don't know we have Mydryth trapped as a water bug, it seems Mydryth's twin brother has taken charge."

"How did you . . . never mind. What's their plan?" I asked.

"Myrador makes these tiny black . . . *spots* that suck."

"What do you mean, 'they suck'? They're not good?"

"They're powerful vortices that suck in everything around them."

"Did he by any chance call them *black holes*?"

Leathery eyebrows rose. "That's it! Black holes!" He lowered one brow. "What's the difference?"

Only a universe of difference. "It doesn't matter. How does he make them?"

"He's got these miniature tornadoes in jars, and each one makes a black hole. He stabilizes the hole, puts it onto a cellar slug, and has the pig men deliver them."

"Why doesn't the black hole swallow the cellar slug?"

"Myrador puts a coating on them that isn't attracted to the hole, but they suck everything else into themselves. Wherever the slugs are, matter disintegrates. And they reproduce at a fantastic rate. Theoretically, if there were enough of them, they could swallow the planet leaving only magic. But Gaia would set a limit eventually."

"Why would they leave magic?"

"Different energy."

"Wouldn't Myrador be risking the welfare of his own brother?"

"More for him."

"Are you serious?"

"You've seen the man?"

"Umm . . . good point."

"Where's Myrador now?" asked Angus. "We've got te stop him."

"My breakfast buddy told me he was going to Cumulos to check on things."

I looked around at the others. "Sooo...how do we get back?"

My question was met with blank stares.

Chapter 9

I spun on Angus. "You're saying you've no idea how to get back?"

"These things happen, lass. Dinnae worry. We'll figure it out."

"We'll figure it out?! Like in the spyder world where we were on the lunch menu? I don't remember things working out so well there! You were tied up like the rest of us! In fact, Dorian and I managed our escape!"

"I don't lay claim te knowing everything, lass. As a matter o' fact, experiences like this have provided some o' my best education."

"If you survive!"

"There's that, but sae far tis been pretty good."

"*Sae far?!*"

"Raven," said Dorian, "blaming Angus won't help. We've found Bluescale. We know where the black holes come from and how they work, so we've made progress. We'll find a way home where we can hunt up a counter-spell." He raised a brow at Angus who shrugged.

"Nae doubt there's one somewhere in all o' my books. Might take a bit o' hunting."

Pressure built in my skull. This was obviously one of those times when the male mind jumped its track. I was about to explode when I heard somewhere in my head, "*Relax. They can't help themselves. By some miracle, they've survived the centuries. It'll be fine.*" A bit of sanity from my subconscious. Happens once in a while.

I was doing an eye-roll when a flicker of movement caught my attention. Then another . . . and another.

"Hey, guys!" I hissed. But they were engaged in planning a way home. "*Guys!*"

"What is it, lass?" Angus sounded a wee bit impatient.

I lifted my chin to the forest, not wanting to make it obvious. "There are people in the trees – quite a few I think."

"I can clear out the leaves so we can see," offered Bluescale. He sucked in a gigantic breath.

"No! Don't blast them! We need to find out who they are. Maybe they can help."

"If I removed the leaves, you'd know right fast who they are."

"Yes, but you'd incinerate them! Not a good way to win friends, Bluescale. Don't do anything. I'll find out who it is."

"Wait, Raven," said Dorian as I strode away. "I'll go."

"I'm less threatening." As I moved out of earshot, I thought I heard Dorian mutter something that included "stubborn and bull-headed", but I might've misheard. He knows I'm neither.

Below the huge branches, I halted and looked up. "Hello," I called. "We mean you no harm. We're just looking for a way home."

After a lengthy silence, a male voice floated from above. "What about the dragon?"

"The dragon is our friend. He won't hurt you."

"He kills pigs."

"Were the pigs your friends?"

There was a pause. "The pigs are nobody's friends."

"They'd trapped the dragon, but he escaped. He just wants to return home with us."

"Then you'll leave our forest?"

"We will."

"You'll take the pigs?"

"Umm . . . do we have to?"

Thin ropes fell from the trees, and a dozen forest denizens slid down in silence. Men and women were dressed in olive green, the tallest shoulder-height to Angus. They had bows and quivers slung over their shoulders and short-swords – standard stuff for the magical realm. A man and woman of equal height approached while others watched my companions, bows drawn.

"I'm Fortean," said the man, "and this is Raine."

I introduced my companions and, when they realized Bluescale wasn't going to hurt them, the younger forest-dwellers swarmed over him, stroking his scales and chattering. One trotted over to deliver a staccato burst in a singsong language.

Fortean coughed and seemed embarrassed.

"What is it?" I asked.

"This is awkward, but they're asking if the dragon would take them for a ride."

I raised my brows at Bluescale who pricked sensitive ears towards us.

"Sure," he said. "It'll be fun!" His enormous fangs glittered in the sunlight in a dragon grin.

I didn't like the look in his eye, his dragon sense of humour much too liberal for my comfort. "A nice *quiet* ride." I raised singed eyebrows in emphasis.

He gave me his "spoilsport" expression as he instructed them to get between his backplates. After they'd settled, he shook out his wings, took three great strides and, with a rush of wind, swept into the air.

Raine sent an uneasy glance at the receding dragon. "It will return them unharmed?"

I followed her gaze and crossed my fingers. "He will. He's not as dangerous as he . . . used to be."

As I followed Bluescale's progress, I noticed Raine trying not to stare at me. What could possibly . . . I groaned and touched my hair. Crap! Why was there never a mirror when you needed one? I sighed and answered her unasked question. "I got my face too close to a fire."

Fortean canted his eyes towards the diminishing dragon.

"It was an accident," I said.

Dorian was trying hard to resist a smile. "I have a mirror, you know."

"What? Why didn't you tell me? I've been running around with a scorched face . . !"

The smile won. "It's not like a mirror will fix it."

"Let me have it!"

He dug into a pocket. "Sure you want to know?"

"Of course, I want to know!" If it was so bad he didn't want me to see it . . . I flipped open the little round mirror.

With a pained expression, Dorian covered his ears. "Now you know why I didn't want you to see it!"

My face was smudged with soot. Sparse remnants of eyebrows and lashes looked pitiful, and my hair – the green streak was frizzled and singed. A sob caught in my throat.

Raine stepped forward. I couldn't help but notice her hair was long, straight, and black – perfect. "I will try to repair the damage if you'd like," she offered.

"The only thing that will fix this," I wailed in helpless despair, "is to shave my head!"

Raine touched the singed areas. "It may not be so bad." But her expression didn't fill me with confidence.

"Since the damage is'nae painful, I'd prefer not te fix it with magic til we get back te Cumulos," said Angus. "I understand lassies have sensitivities about their appearance, but our magic may be limited in this place. Besides," he added, "tis nae se bad."

I saw Dorian cover his eyes as I turned slowly to face Angus. "Nae se bad? *Nae se bad?!* How'd you like to walk around with your little pink curls fried?!"

Angus lifted his chin. "They're nae *pink*, lass, they're *red!*"

"Raven," said Dorian, stepping between Angus and me, "maybe we should find a place to wait for Bluescale. Fried hair won't kill you. The pigs will. We don't want to forget about them."

God! Why did the guy have to be so logical? I didn't want to hear about pigs. I wanted to fix my hair!

When Raine learned I had telepathic communication with Bluescale, she invited us to their village. Using my less-than-perfect levitation skills, I struggled up a vine to the first heavy branch while our new companions flew up hand-over-hand. In single file, we trotted along the wide branch to an enormous trunk that was wrapped with a narrow set of stairs. Since there was no railing, I assumed falling off was not an issue for them.

So, here's one of those irrational things with which we all come supplied. I was comfortable flying on a broom; I wasn't even too bad levitating, but open-sided stairs gave me the willies. Might've had something to do with the fact I'd been pushed off a set in the recent past.

I felt Dorian's presence enter my space followed by a steadying hand on my bare waist. Sometimes I swear the man can read my mind. Other times . . . well, not so much. I straightened my spine. How would it look to our companions if they knew I was afraid of heights? This was their equivalent of a highway.

A warm breath brushed my ear. "Watch the back of the person in front of you. Don't look over the edge."

The impulse to assure Dorian I wasn't afraid followed by a haughty toss of the head died with a crash. I'd have to demonstrate bravery some other way.

I lost track of how many times we circled the tree before thick foliage camouflaged the two hundred feet to the ground. From time-to-time, narrow wooden walkways led into the soft green light to disappear into lush vegetation. At the thought of using one of the swinging, narrow boardwalks, the stairs took on a new sense of solidity. Boardwalks joined the trees, and intersecting branches were often close enough to step from one to another. I noticed delicate rope ladders looped from one level to another, but my head spun at the thought of climbing one.

My thighs had set up a serious protest when we emerged into an area clear of leaves though a thick canopy still obscured the sky. Dwellings were scattered throughout, some hanging in space, others tucked into places where two or more branches diverged. Pyramid-shaped sleep pods hung from branches connected by narrow, swaying walkways.

We stepped onto a platform constructed between two enormous branches in the centre of which was a spacious thatched roof supported by poles. Woven mats covered the floor; others were rolled to the edges of the ceiling from which they could be let down to keep out wind and rain. Benches and high-backed chairs were draped with brightly-coloured throws which were as soft as thistledown. With great relief, I collapsed into a chair.

"Are you alright?" asked Raine. No doubt my flushed face and labouring lungs puzzled her. Everyone else's breathing, including Dorian's, was normal. I'd tried the spell that helped me with the stairs at Cumulos but without success. It was clear my magic was unreliable in this place.

"I'm fine, but a drink of water would be nice."

She opened a spigot, and rainwater trickled into a wooden cup. As I took it, I looked around for a diversion to stop everyone from staring at me. "This is an amazing place!"

As Raine settled onto a wide bench into a position reminiscent of Talon, I wondered if I could twist my legs that far. I rubbed my thighs. Not today.

As the others selected places to settle, Raine and Fortean explained their community was situated between the upper and lower canopies to avoid predators. Large carnivores skulked in the shadows on the ground, and giant raptors hunted the skies.

Apparently, two hundred men, women, and children occupied the local area. So far, we hadn't seen young children but, no doubt they were hiding until given the all-clear by the adults.

"We appreciate ye taking us into your home," said Angus. "We'll nae be here long. Though we gathered important information by coming here, we've got te return te stop the pig men from destroying our realm. We'd appreciate any help ye can give. Have ye any idea how the pig men travel between worlds?"

Fortean and Raine exchanged a glance. Fortean leaned forward, elbows on knees. "They have a talisman in the tunnel, but they guard it well. We were hoping to use it to send them back to whatever world they came from."

"Maybe Bluescale remembers something," I said. "Let me ask him." I closed my eyes. *"Bluescale! Can you hear me?"* Silence. *"Bluescale?"*

"Woo-eee! Just pulled out of a spectacular dive!"

"Don't you dare scare those people! You promised a quiet ride!"

"Hey! It was their idea! They're asking me to do it again."

I counted to ten. *"Just don't drop anybody!"*

"These guys aren't afraid of falling at all – not like somebody I could mention."

I chose to disregard the slur. *"They may not be afraid of falling, but they can't fly. Remember that."*

"That's why I took them so high. Gives me time to catch them if they lose their grip."

I'd have been praying by then if I'd been a religious person. I changed the subject and asked if he remembered how he'd gotten there.

He'd regained consciousness trussed in the net. Napoleon had strutted and bragged for a while then waved a glowing blue disk. The next thing Bluescale remembered was awakening in the forest. Unfortunately for the pigs, the net they'd chosen had been susceptible to a steady application of heat. Not a good choice for restraining a fire-breathing dragon.

"Blue glow?" Angus stroked his chin. "I've an idea tis a travellers' talisman – rather hard te come by. If we can relieve Napoleon o' it, I can get us back te Cumulos. Normally, I don't take what does'na belong te me but, since the piggies have been using it te kidnap and attack the innocent, I think I can see my way te relieving the wee scoundrels o' their prize."

"The pigs hide in the tunnels except when they collect water from the stream," said Fortean. "Probably won't come out again today with the dragon hunting."

"I wonder why they haven't left?" I mused.

"Myrador probably told them not to return without Bluescale dead or alive," said Dorian. "If he's dead, he can't be used against them."

As torches flickered to life throughout the surrounding foliage, Raine glanced up. "The sun is setting. You can sleep here tonight as dangerous creatures stalk in the darkness. The pigs would be the least of your concerns, and they're shrewd enough to hide as well." She turned to a quiet man who sat next to Angus. "Please bring food for our guests."

He nodded. "Yes, your highness." He vanished into the gathering evening.

"Are you royalty?" I asked.

She looked blank.

"He called you, 'Your Highness'."

As she shook her head, perfect hair flowed in a cascade. "He uses a title that relates to height from the ground. We've no such thing as royalty here. Fortean and I live at a high level and B'lin uses the term as a form of respect as we're leaders of the people. Leadership is not inherited. Those who are capable of leading *lead*, no matter their lineage."

Bluescale's booming voice crashed into my head. "Coming in for a landing!"

Thank the stars for small favours. *"You didn't drop anyone, did you?"*

"Just a little one – but I caught him. Everybody's fine. We're friends."

I closed my eyes. Don't say anything, Raven. They're all safe and sound. *"We're with the forest-dwellers in the trees. Can you find a safe place to stay until morning? Raine says the forest floor is dangerous at night."*

There was a pause as, once again, Bluescale pondered the depths of my naivete. "I'm one of the *reasons* it's dangerous, Raven!"

Right. *"Great. See you in the morning then."*

Dorian cocked a brow. "Bluescale?"

I nodded. "They're back. His passengers should be up soon."

"All of them?"

"Hard to believe."

* * *

Torches filled deepening shadows with sparkling, living light. A few insects buzzed but, to my surprise and infinite relief, mosquitoes didn't exist there. Bowls of aromatic stew served with black bread were delivered by two younger versions of our hosts. After discharging their duties, they retired to a dark corner of the platform to watch the alien visitors, a rare event in their world.

I hadn't realized how famished I was until I bit into thick bread slathered with something like butter, and I must admit my conversational skills suffered as I focused on the task at hand. After mopping the last of the soup with a morsel of bread, I groaned with satisfaction and leaned back in my chair.

"That was delicious! Thank you for a wonderful meal."

Our hosts seemed pleased as Dorian and Angus echoed my sentiments. When the last of the bowls had been emptied, the junior pair gathered them and disappeared into the darkness.

Now that I had the opportunity to broaden my focus, I noticed night sounds echoed throughout the forest. Strange bird calls, rustlings, and an occasional abruptly-silenced cry made the hair stand on the back of my neck. I'd have been worried about Bluescale if I hadn't suspected him of being the cause.

I'd smothered a third yawn when Raine suggested it was time to retire. We could all sleep in one of the hanging platforms. Angus flicked a glance between Dorian and me then asked if he could sleep on the bench he occupied.

"I'll be fine here. Tis verra comfortable," he said, pushing his fingers into the surface. "And I'm an early riser, so I'll nae be a problem in the morning."

I felt like strangling him.

"Of course." Raine gestured for Dorian and me to follow.

Oh boy! Not a good idea! As we approached one of the swinging walkways, my feet froze with such suddenness, Dorian ran into my back.

"Sorry," he mumbled. "Why did you stop?"

I stared at the swaying, wooden path that lead to a pyramid-shaped enclosure which hung from a gnarled branch. Raine had almost reached the sleeping platform, her light footfalls setting the bridge to swinging. Although I instructed my feet to move, somewhere along the line a powerful censor disagreed.

Dorian gave a chuckle. "Close your eyes, Raven."

Of course, I turned to look up at him. "What?"

"Close your eyes."

"Why?"

"Just do it, please."

"Dorian, I'm not walking over that thing!"

With a swift motion, he slung me over his shoulder like a sack of grain, and we were over the dark abyss, bridge swaying beneath. Abject terror kept me from uttering so much as a squeak. In spite of my horror, I was relieved that Raine was occupied with lighting an oil lamp so didn't witness my humiliating entrance.

Dorian set me on my feet then held a finger to his lips to forestall the impending tirade. He made a head gesture towards Raine knowing full well I didn't want to share my fear of heights. I had to settle for silent expressions of fury.

As the lamp caught the flame, I was chagrined to discover only one sleeping platform. Raine wished us a pleasant night, showed us how to tie the door, and disappeared into the night. I rounded on Dorian but, before I could get a word out, he closed the distance between us.

"Don't," he whispered, cupping my face.

"Don't what?" I demanded.

"Just don't." Then he lowered his lips to mine, and my brain jumped its track. I've no idea what I'd been planning to say.

He was warm and sensuous, his outdoor scent mixed with spice that filled my senses to the exclusion of everything else. I could've handled pushy male chauvinism, even deliberate seduction – but not this gentle vulnerability.

Sometimes in Denver I'd fantasized about what it would be like to be kissed by Dorian, but the reality had been more mind-bending than anything I'd imagined. I blamed our one incredible night on marijuana smoke so, in my book, it didn't count as my fault. If I were to blame anybody, it would've been Talon. He'd been the one burning the stuff, and Dorian and I had been caught in it.

But, what a night! The parts I could remember still gave me warm flushes. Of course, I'd bolted like a jackrabbit the next morning, and I've admitted to avoiding him ever since.

This thing with Valgren was too confusing. Even though the Rider had been clear there'd be no commitment between us, I still had this ridiculous notion that a woman could only have a relationship with one man at a time. And I was comfortable with that idea. It seemed ethical. Of course, it hadn't been too long ago that premarital sex had been viewed as unethical. Now, you were weird if you didn't indulge. Sigh.

My head spun when Dorian's lips left mine and nuzzled my neck. Warm, gentle hands slid to my naked waist to pull me against him.

He straightened to look into my eyes with an intimate smile. "I didn't plan this but . . . I keep remembering . . . I'd like to do it right – with a clear mind." His chocolate eyes were deep black in the light of the lamp. "I'm sorry for the way it happened, but it was still pretty amazing."

I swallowed. "It wouldn't have happened at all if we hadn't been under an influence."

"We're pretty good at staying away from each other."

"It's always something, isn't it? First the danger to me. Now, Valgren."

His gaze turned serious. "Raven, if I thought for one instant you were committed to Valgren, I'd wrap myself in a blanket and go to sleep, but neither of us can deny this attraction we feel for each other." He caressed my face with his fingertips. "Now we're in a magical world, there's not so much keeping us apart. I can handle the competition of another man; I couldn't handle putting you in danger."

He smoothed my hair back. "Raven . . . I'll stop if you ask me to."

As his eyes locked with mine, a fluid warmth suffused my body. I may have questionable ethics but . . . well, maybe I'll leave it at that. I rose on tip-toes and slipped my arms around his neck. I'd think about the repercussions tomorrow.

After a kiss that I'll remember for the rest of my life, Dorian carried me to the sleeping platform where the coverlet seemed to have been woven of dandelion fluff. When he slipped in beside me and gathered me into his arms, I was transported to a world that was warm, sensuous, and wonderful. I hope no one was watching in the darkness because I expect our platform swung for quite a while.

Chapter 10

The sun burned horizontal shafts through the forest as we waited for the pig men to make their way to the stream. Bluescale was hidden behind a grove of evergreens awaiting my signal.

After twenty boring minutes, a porcine snout emerged to sniff the air. With furtive glances at the sky, a half-dozen pigs scuttled to the stream, canteens in hand. Of course, the last to emerge was Napoleon who fidgeted and scanned the clouds. I recognized the baby-poo colour of his fringed epaulettes. Coward that he was, one of the others carried two canteens – and Napoleon paced in safety before the cave. Probably had told them he'd guard it – as if a cave was going anywhere.

I wondered where the squat mage had gone. Maybe he'd had enough of dragons and decided to go home – or maybe Bluescale had gotten him. I didn't want to know.

As I squatted on a branch and remembered my captivity by the repulsive pig man, my blood began to warm – and then to boil. I wasn't letting that fat little bastard intimidate me! I grabbed a vine and slithered down it in plain sight. Dorian hissed a warning followed by vile curse words I'd never heard him use. Without a backward glance, I strung a particularly sharp arrow and strode towards my prey.

"Napoleon, you disgusting pig! Move and you're dead! I haven't had pork in weeks!"

He gave such a violent start, he tripped on a rock and toppled over. In a flash, I was astride a boulder, bow stretched to the max. "I'm willing to bet this arrow will pierce any protective spell!"

Napoleon grunted and rolled from side to side in an effort to right himself. He was half-way to his feet when I bellowed, "Stay!" Like he was a bad dog.

He subsided onto a low rock, little pink eyes burning with rage. "How dare you point that thing at me? Do you know who I am?!"

"Do you know who *I* am?"

He thinned myopic pig eyes. "You're that human with the dragon. I should've killed you!"

"You should have."

"There are soldiers in the cave! All I have to do is yell!"

"Good try, Napoleon. All your minions are getting water."

"Why do you call me Napoleon?"

"Human history tells of yet another fat little murderer who figured he was important. We don't remember him with great fondness."

The sides of his snout lifted in a snarl to reveal the sticky yellow teeth that gave me the willies. "Earth will remember me. And I guarantee it won't be with fondness."

"Myrador will have you for breakfast!" I thought about that for a beat. "Perhaps literally. You're too stupid and greedy to realize he's using you. *Sit down!*"

He'd pushed to a half-crouch, no doubt in an effort to puff out his chest. He lowered back to the rock, pink eyes redder by the second.

"Try it, Napoleon. Make my day!" I sent a mental apology to Arnie.

The murderous red became calculating, and his snout morphed into a smarmy fake smile. "Perhaps we can make a deal. You seem to be friends with the dragon, and we need him to free the others from the streams. With swarms of dragons on our side, the Earth will fall."

"Napoleon, do you know anything about human military weapons?"

"Why would I care about them? Humans are a bunch of non-magic idiots!"

"All the dragons in the world would just be target practice."

"Magic can overcome any human weapons!"

"Is that what Myrador told you? Never mind. You talk too much. Give us your travellers' talisman, and I might let you live."

He straightened. "Over my dead body!"

"That is acceptable." I tightened the bow string. My arrow never wavered. In a perverse way, I realized I was hoping he'd move so I could check him off my list but, of course, he'd be replaced by another who looked just like him. As his gaze flicked behind me, I shifted my focus long enough to see Dorian with a loaded cross-bow. Odenai Castle had all sorts of gadgets.

The pig's eyes widened. "You're of the Royal Family of Altaria!"

"Good observation, Napoleon," he said quietly. I've learned Dorian is at his most dangerous when exceptionally calm. "I'd be happy to kill you and take the talisman but, unlike you, I don't kill for fun."

Napoleon's voice had gone up a notch. "My men will be here any second! Drop your weapons!"

"Your soldiers have had a run-in with the locals. But you're right; the survivors will be here shortly."

Soft, padding footfalls approached as the forest-dwellers prodded three pig soldiers ahead of them. "These cowards curled up on the ground and wouldn't fight," snarled Fortean with disgust.

With a sense of unease, I looked behind the group. "There were others."

"Not anymore," said Fortean.

Oh.

Angus wiped a sword with grass. "I hate it when I have te kill something. Makes a mess o' my blade. I'll have te polish it when I get home." Napoleon had paled several shades. His soldiers shuffled pointed hooves in the dust and looked at the ground. "Now," said Angus, sheathing his weapon. "Let's discuss the travellers' talisman."

Napoleon lurched to his feet. "I need it to get home!"

"Ye are home."

"What? You can't do that! There's nothing here!"

Angus glanced towards the forest-dwellers. "Ye might nae want te insult your new neighbours."

Raine scowled. "They're not staying here!"

"Well, now, it looks te me like you're nae welcome anywhere, but first things first." He made a hand motion, and Napoleon's tunic fell to the ground.

Napoleon tried to cover his belly with his hands. "You people are *sick*!"

Considering all he wore was a tunic, I couldn't grasp his point. After the tunic levitated to Angus' outstretched hand, he examined the pockets then tossed it to the ground. "Tis nae here. Ye'll need te be giving me the talisman – now!"

Napoleon's piggy ears shot up on either side of his cap which was now his single garment. As he made a mad dash for the cave, I could almost bring myself to shoot him.

With a curse, Dorian shot past me to slam the fleeing pig to the ground. There followed a lot of thrashing, dust roiling, and ear-splitting squeals. I'd have to remember to thank Dorian. I'd have had to spend the rest of my life in a shower if it'd been me.

Napoleon put up a pretty good scrap, but it was embarrassing. Naked pig wrestling. At last Dorian tied Napoleon's arms behind him, jerked him to his feet then handed the pig to Angus. He stalked into the cave, dusting himself off.

"You can't have it! It's mine!" screamed Napoleon, struggling against the mage's massive arm.

"Ye'd best be standing still if ye want te live," growled Angus.

The other pig men stared at the ground, embarrassed by Napoleon's nakedness. It was all beginning to feel icky although I couldn't for the life of me figure out why. Maybe embarrassment is contagious.

Seeing that Angus and the forest-dwellers had the pig men under control, I followed Dorian into the cave where I paused to let my eyes adjust. Eeuw! What a mess! Stuff was strewn everywhere. Dorian had started at one side and was working his way around, searching every item he came to. Yuck! I took a deep breath and, making an effort to control my revulsion, started at the opposite wall, gingerly lifting things with the toe of my boot.

Dorian chuckled. "If you want to find anything, Raven, you're going to have to touch stuff."

"Are you sure? I'm doing pretty well this way."

He grinned. "Sometimes you're such a girl!"

"And that's a bad thing?"

His smile warmed. "Sometimes it's a great thing."

Heat blasted through me. I ducked my head and returned to the search. Pinching things between thumb and forefinger, I shook garments and blankets.

Five minutes of revulsion later, I heard Dorian's whoop of triumph. "Found it!"

I dropped a blanket like it was on fire and wiped my fingers on a rock. Dorian examined the disk-shaped item then slipped it into a leather pouch. "Hope Angus can make it work," he said.

We found Napoleon clothed but his hands were tied. Angus examined the amulet. "Aye, tis a talisman of excellent quality. Now, I wonder where the wee piggies got this? Perhaps from Myrador so they could trap the dragon? He'll not be verra happy te find they've lost this wee treasure along wi' the dragon." His ice blue gaze pierced Napoleon who fidgeted. "Ye've got yourself into a real pickle now, haven't ye?"

Napoleon lifted a whiskered chin. "Myrador will take care of you!"

"Aye, he'll try. I've a feeling he'll take care o' ye as well, but maybe not as ye expect."

Oops! I'd forgotten Bluescale. After a mental summons, a blue streak shot by, did an aerial roll, and skidded to a stop in a cloud of dust. The pig men paled.

"Aw, guys! You brought breakfast!" The dragon licked his lips and grinned as he waddled up. As the pig men fell over each other to get away from the enormous teeth, Bluescale shot a bolt of flame into the air. "Well-done or rare?"

"Didn't you go fishing this morning?" I asked.

"Of course. But fish isn't pork."

"Bluescale, can we change the subject, please? Nobody here's going to be eaten. Besides, we've got the travellers' talisman. We can go home."

"D'ye think ye could give us all a ride, my friend?" asked Angus. "The travellers' talisman will open a doorway big enough for everybody."

Fortean ensured us the pig men would be terminated if left in their world – and Bluescale refused to let them sit on his back. He looked down his long snout. "The only part of me they'll ever touch is my tongue!"

It seemed we were at an impasse. Then I remembered how they'd captured Bluescale. When I presented the idea of using the net, the pig men didn't think much of it. Seemed it was uncomfortable.

Fortean and Raine notched arrows into their bows. "Fine. We'll kill them," said Fortean.

"No!" squealed Napoleon. He scrunched his eyes and darted behind Angus.

Angus reached back, grabbed the pig by his tunic, and held him at arm's length. "I dinnae care for the likes o' ye standin' behind me!"

Napleon's eyes were closed, and tears dripped down his snout.

Angus rolled his eyes. "For god's sake man, have ye no pride?"

Napoleon opened a hopeful eye. "Would it help?"

"Nae, it wouldna' help, ye daft twit!" As Angus dropped him in the dirt, the forest-dwellers took aim.

A chorus of squeals erupted. "We'll ride in the net! We'll ride in the net!"

I was relieved to hear this as I had no desire to witness their deaths. I turned to Bluescale. "Will you carry them as cargo?"

He snarled. "This may strain our friendship, Raven, and the net had better be long!" I think he was. . . kind of joking.

It was decided we'd drop them in Australia's western desert where they could enjoy some blistering sunshine. Perhaps their illustrious leader would rescue them.

Dorian found a container that held the "seed" of the net which expanded to whatever size was required. He stretched it on the ground and instructed the pig men to stand on it. Wincing, they inched onto the harmless-looking network of sparkling strings.

"This net hurts, you know," whined Napoleon.

Bluescale's snout shot to within inches of Napoleon's face, and he roared, "*I know!*"

The four of them shot to the middle of the net and, in an instant, were squeezed into a wriggling, complaining ball.

After farewells, the forest-dwellers stood to the side as we climbed between Bluescale's backplates. As I settled against Dorian's solid chest, memories of the previous night ignited. I'd almost pulled away before I gave myself a mental head-slap. As Dorian's arms came around me, I settled back and waved to our new friends.

Bluescale took three running strides, his mighty wings beat twice – and we were airborne. There was a lot of squealing as our cargo bounced along the ground before it swung into the air. We made a long, slow circle for a farewell pass over the forest-dwellers who waved from below. The vine used to tie the net to Bluescale's neck must've been too long, or perhaps the dragon didn't notice the pig men were being dragged along the tops of evergreen trees. Screams echoed as we made a dive towards the meadow in a last salute to the forest-dwellers. I heard a thump and Napoleon's curses. At Bluescale's ripple of laughter, I decided not to jeopardize my comfortable position by speaking up. After all, I could be downgraded to coach.

When we were high enough to see the edge of a blue ocean to the left, Angus extracted the travellers' talisman and muttered an incantation. A black dot appeared in the distance and shot towards us, expanding until it became a bronze disk on edge.

Bluescale looked back over his shoulder. "Straight through," said Angus. When nothing changed as we approached, I stiffened against Dorian. "We're going to slam into that thing!"

"It'll be okay," he said. Then he nuzzled and kissed my ear. "You could be a little more trusting."

I'm such a sap! How could one little kiss make me relax? Who knows? But it worked.

As Bluescale's nose was about to connect with the bronze surface, the disk transformed into a metallic ring with a view of an ocean below. As we sailed through, there was a dull thud and more curses from the pigs. Guess the net was a bit long or Bluescale's aim was off.

When Angus intoned something, the scene shifted to a reddish desert. Bluescale dove towards the coast which was bordered by parallel rows of dunes. Ten feet from the ground, the net opened followed by four thumps and loud squeals as our cargo skidded down the sandbanks.

"Normally I'm a bit politer," said Angus from behind us, "but I dinnae think this lot deserves it. Besides, if I had te talk te that Napoleon again, I cannae guarantee I would'na kill the wee bastard myself!"

We were in complete accord.

Bluescale executed a steep turn, made a feint towards the pig men who scrambled out of the way then, with a guiltless laugh and mighty strokes of his wings, carried us into the sky towards Cumulos.

Upon our arrival, I noticed the cloud island floated over grey skies that spread over the Pacific. There were advantages to living above the weather. That raised a question. Did I live here? What about my life in Denver? I couldn't think of a single person who'd be devastated if I disappeared. I'd been mostly single (well, off and on) since I'd met Dorian. Life was simple and safe in Denver –where I'd now die of boredom.

I'd have to be careful not to put too much stock in the previous night. It'd been wonderful for sure, but Dorian was still a king – and I still a bastard. I'd been born not only on the wrong side of the blanket; the blanket had belonged to a mere human. My magical father was a mystery and might remain so and, though it was clear Dorian was attracted to me, even I had sense enough to realize kings married for political reasons.

As I sighed and snuggled close, his arms tightened. "What's on your mind, Raven?" he whispered.

I turned to look at him. "I'm so confused."

He gave me a light kiss. "I understand."

And I believe he did. It's quite marvellous when you consider he's a man.

Chapter 11

Talon perched on the Pegasus statue, the pages of a dusty book flipping by themselves at belly height. Frost, draped in a comfortable armchair, perused a hefty leather volume which was etched with intricate carvings of reindeer, red sleighs, and holly leaves. Did that mean . . .? *Focus, Raven!*

Dorian and I shared a couch, our feet on footstools, heavy books on our laps. An occasional quiet snore drifted from Sin who was curled next to me.

I was in heaven at the opportunity to peruse such wisdom. Although my search was for info on cellar slugs, I kept being distracted by other fascinating stuff. Did you know you could slow or accelerate age, move in time, materialize stuff, cause flowers to bloom . . ? The list was endless. No wonder mages got caught up in their work!

"Look at this! Here's a picture of an early flying snake. They existed!"

Dorian slanted a glance at me. "Predecessors to dragons, Raven."

"But *not* dragons. How did they change?"

"Evolution?"

"If you ever took a good look at the theory of evolution, you'd know chance can't explain half the stuff."

"Like magic?"

"That's one example. And look at this! Do you know why electricity doesn't work with magic?"

"Raven?"

"What?"

"I'm trying to read."

"Oh. Sorry." I remained silent for a full minute. "Do you know how mages can live indefinitely?"

With a grunt of exasperation, Dorian surged to his feet and moved to the furthest chair in the room. Some people resent being informed.

Scarlet, who'd been reading along with Angus from a position on his shoulder, fluttered to Dorian, her expression smug as she passed me. I heaved a sigh and stroked Sin's wide back which caused a furious onset of purring. I bet if he hadn't been so damn fat, he could've batted her right out of the air.

Angus slammed his book closed with a gesture of frustration. "I dinnae see how, in this entire library, there's nary a thing about the wee beasties other than they're a rare infestation and damned hard te get rid o'!"

"My mages are at work on this too," said Dorian. "And they've got colleagues in places I've never heard of."

"I'll talk te some o' the other mages. Maybe some o' them knows o' the slugs." He surged to his feet. "I'll be back in a day or two. Unless ye want te help Cash in the tunnels, there's nothing much te be done til I'm back."

With a glance at me, Dorian said, "I'll update my soldiers and mages. We know the pig men have spent time in the Caves of Cynbel, so I'll have a couple of apprentice mages give the caves another sweep."

And just like that, Dorian, the king, emerged – and Dorian, the lover, became a memory. I'd known it would happen but . . .

"I'll come with you," said Scarlet.

I had the unworthy wish she'd run into one of the quick, slim, fit cats of Odenai. I stroked Sin. I didn't want to see her dead, just humbled. Maybe a nice long scratch . . .

My pleasant daydream was interrupted by Angus asking my plans, and I wasn't quick enough to stop my gaze from darting to Dorian. "I'll . . . give Cash a hand."

I didn't want to be in the castle when Dorian left so took a short flight to brood beside a lovely pond. I was indulging in a wave of self-pity when movement caught my eye, and Dorian floated to the grass. Crap!

"How'd you find me?"

"There are only a few places you go when you're unhappy, and Cumulos isn't that big." He looked around. "This is one – calm and peaceful." He set his broom against a gnarled willow tree. "We need to talk."

I hate it when people say that. It usually ends as badly as introspection does.

I followed him to a grassy bank where he stuffed his hands into his pockets, walked to the shore, and looked over the pond. When the silence became long, he turned and paced to me. His dark eyes were troubled. Stopping inches away, he said, "I'm sorry. I've been selfish."

This was not what I'd expected. "Excuse me?"

"I took advantage of your attraction to me – of our attraction to each other. It wasn't deliberate; I just . . . wanted to be with you again." He stroked my cheek. "I may be a king, but I'm also a man, Raven. Maybe I haven't worked out how to balance the two." He tucked a strand of hair behind my ear. "But it's not fair for me to complicate your relationship with Valgren when you've been clear he's important to you."

He huffed out a breath. "So, I'll back off." He gazed into my eyes. "For now. But, be warned, if I sense a weakening of your resolve, I'll move in like a shot."

This conversation felt like the break-up of a non-existent relationship. I chewed the inside of my cheek. "I don't regret last night, Dorian. It was incredible . . ."

"But?"

"I need a whole heart to be with you. And your position as king doesn't help. And Valgren is . . ."

He stroked the side of my face. "I know." He leaned forward and kissed me in a way that made my knees weak. When he raised his head, mine was spinning. He smiled. "I can't promise to always keep my distance, but I'll try. I'm heading home. See you soon."

And he was gone.

Chapter 12

Dorian and Valgren weren't on Cumulos, and Angus wouldn't be back for a couple of days, so I decided to return to Denver for a while. Frankly, I needed the rest. Recent events had been a rollercoaster. I'd been sucked into a vortex, shot in the leg as I ran for my life, encountered Napoleon yet again – all of which had culminated in an incredible night with Dorian. No wonder I was bleary-eyed.

I inscribed a message disk to inform Frost so no one would worry. By the use of a transportation spell I'd finally perfected, I soon skimmed above the city which slumbered in the afternoon sun – as much as Denver ever slumbers.

I checked the cloaking spell then dropped towards my balcony, surprised to find I'd missed the place. I pushed open the glass doors and set my broom in an umbrella stand, something I'd bought after I'd tired of the broom slamming onto the floor at all hours and scaring the hell out of me. I couldn't prove it was deliberate, but the broom did seem happier in a stand.

Clothes dropped on the way to my bedroom as I envisioned a long, hot shower. Cumulos had tubs for bathing, but no showers. A waterfall was about as good as it got. When a glance in the mirror gave me a horrific glimpse of my hair, I seized a pair of scissors. Dorian was right. Bangs would cover the singed areas. Around a lump in my throat, I selected a handful of green and made a careful cut. At least I couldn't make it worse. A few eyelashes remained, and I could draw in half-an-eyebrow. I cringed at the realization that Dorian had made love to me while I looked like this. It was a good thing the lamp light had been dim.

After I'd repaired some of the damage, I climbed into the shower, lathered my hair three times then towel-dried it and collapsed with a groan onto my bed – which I discovered still carried the sweet scent of woodland flowers. Guilt attacked with a vengeance, but I fought it off. In the end, I snuggled into the pillow Valgren had used and fell into a dreamless sleep.

When I awoke, it took a few seconds to realize I was in my cozy room in Denver. I couldn't remember the last time I'd slept so long. Maybe I'd just turn over and get a few more winks; you know, because I could.

"I'm hungry!"

My eyes shot open. Surely not . . . I bolted upright and brushed hair from my eyes in a panic. Please let it be the residue of a nightmare! At the flutter of tiny wings, I closed my eyes and repeated, "She's not real. She's not real."

"She *is* real!" snapped the irritating voice.

I opened an eye. Sure enough, Scarlet hovered at arm's length. A vein throbbed in my forehead. That kind of blood pressure first thing in the morning could be hard on the heart, but I was beyond caring. I fought off the blankets, staggered upright, and pointed to the balcony.

"Go! And tell Dorian I don't need help!"

She propped little fists on her hips. "It's a good thing I don't take your cranky morning attitude personally. Dorian said you were like this."

My mouth opened but I was so insulted, nothing came out. Dorian said that? Why would he . . . Wait a minute! How would he know? I narrowed my eyes. "He did not say that!"

She crossed her arms, stuck out a lip, and turned her back to me. "Did too!"

I growled and stomped to the kitchen where I jerked open drawers and hunted under cutlery. She fluttered behind. "What are you looking for?"

"A fly-swatter!"

"What for . . ?" Her jaw dropped. "You need me!"

"Like I need a disease!" I pushed spoons around. "Where the hell is it?" *It'll give you some idea of my level of frustration to note I was looking in food utensil drawers for an icky fly-swatter. As if!*

"Look-it," said Scarlet as she settled cross-legged onto a cookie jar. "Since you're up, why not make us breakfast? It'll put you in a better mood." My stomach growled on cue. "See? You're hungry."

"It's not hunger making me cranky!"

"I'll assume that's the hunger talking. Pancakes and eggs would be good, and I've acquired a taste for coffee. I take cream and sugar."

I leaned on the counter, my nose level with hers. "I am not your servant!"

"Of course not." Without missing a beat, she said, "The coffee could drip while we continue this conversation, and there are probably eggs in the ice-box."

"The fridge!"

"What?"

I ground my teeth. "It's called a refrigerator!"

"What?"

"The ice-box!"

"Don't be ridiculous! That makes no sense." She waved a tiny hand. "I believe the coffee's in that canister."

"I know . . ! Where the coffee is!"

"Then what are you waiting for?"

It was a good thing I couldn't find the fly-swatter.

An hour later, I collapsed onto the couch and propped bare feet on the coffee table. Scarlet sat on a stack of DVDs drinking coffee from a doll's teacup, childhood memorabilia I hadn't had the heart to throw away. Big green eyes rolled towards my feet next to her. "Is that necessary?"

"Is what necessary?"

"I'm trying to eat. I can't do that beside your smelly feet."

"You're done eating, and they're not smelly!"

"I'm not finished my coffee, so I'm not finished eating."

"My table. My feet. Your problem."

She threw me a narrow-eyed look then fluttered to the kitchen counter where she dangled her legs over the edge.

I heaved a sigh. "So, tell me exactly why you're here. I'm sure it's not because you miss me."

"Dorian said I had to."

"You always listen to Dorian?"

Her eyes widened. "He's king of Altaria! You expect me to argue?"

"You argue with everyone else," I mumbled.

"What?"

"Never mind. Why did he send you?"

"When Frost said you'd gone home, he was afraid Myrador might follow."

"Myrador isn't going to bother me here in Denver. Probably couldn't even find it."

"Why not?"

"Magical people don't spend a lot of time in North America, and this building is filled with humans."

"I doubt the mage is afraid of humans. He can ensure they don't see him."

Hmm. Probably right about that. "So, what can you do against Myrador?"

"Remember what Angus told you?"

"What specifically?"

"Size doesn't matter."

"I doubt he believes that."

"What?"

"Never mind."

"Is it always so hard for you to focus?"

My feet thumped to the floor. "I'm going shopping. Make yourself at home while I'm gone, or you can leave if you like." I stomped to the bedroom to dress.

She fluttered after me. "See what I mean? One second we're talking about Angus, and the next, you're going shopping – whatever that is."

I stared. "You've never been shopping?" I stripped off my nightshirt and inserted my head into a light top.

"No. Is it fun?"

"You'd hate it. You should stay here."

"Dorian says I have to stay with you . . . what did you say?"

I made an effort to loosen my jaw. "I said he probably had good intentions."

"What was that about the road to hell?"

"Never mind. I'm dressed and I'm leaving." I grabbed my purse, ensured I had money, and hustled to the door.

"I'll give you a rash!"

I jerked to a halt; chewed the inside of my cheek. "How bad?"

"Bad. Itchy. All over your face. Should highlight your scorch marks."

If I'd been a gorgon, she'd have turned to stone. "How am I supposed to take you shopping? You're a pixie for chrissake! People will see you!"

"Not if I don't want them to."

"I suppose that means you want me to carry you."

"Wear something with pockets."

I looked down at my tank top, sighed, stomped back to my room, and added a light shirt with large pockets. Scarlet slipped into the left one where she promptly disappeared. I heard a muffled, "smaller pockets!". After helping her out, I dug into my closet for something else.

"Look, Scarlet," I said as we hit the sidewalk, "if you don't stop complaining, I'm going to drop you into a garbage receptacle! I'm a woman. I have breasts. I don't care if you don't like touching them. It's the safest spot, and I'm not changing again. You could've stayed in the apartment!"

A pair of pedestrians rolled their eyes my direction and gave me a wide berth. Great. Now people thought I was arguing with myself. "Be quiet, Scarlet! People are going to think I'm insane!"

I walked three blocks to a multi-storeyed mall. The lower floor had food kiosks, so I took the escalator to women's apparel. Scarlet's big green eyes got the size of golf balls when she saw the racks of clothes.

"Who makes all these garments?" she asked.

"Children in sweatshops."

"What's a sweatshop?"

"Hopefully, a temporary way of doing business."

"You can get all these clothes?"

"Not all, but I can buy any I want."

Her eyes rolled up at me. "Then why do you dress the way you do?"

"Shut up, Scarlet!"

Over the next two hours, I tried on clothes, and Scarlet got into the spirit of the thing. As I paid for a third outfit, I noticed she looked sad. "What's wrong?"

She plucked at her green tunic. "I wish there were clothes my size."

I scanned her tiny form. "Maybe there are." I grabbed my bags and headed for a toy store where, half-way to the back, I found a section filled with Barbie dolls.

"What do you think of this?" As I presented a packet of Barbie clothes, Scarlet practically salivated – and I must admit I was starting to have fun. I drew the line at ten outfits, paid for them, and headed for the food kiosks. All that shopping had made me hungry. I found an isolated table behind a support column where we shared a hot dog and pop.

"See, Scarlet? No Myrador. Just a nice afternoon of shopping."

"I like this shopping thing. Can we do it again sometime?"

"I'll think about it." I dumped our paper plate and plastic utensils into a nearby waste receptacle, gathered my bags, and headed home.

As my key scraped into the lock of my apartment, I felt an odd chill but, in anticipation of divesting myself of heavy bags, I ignored the whispered warning. As I pushed the door open with my foot, a hand grabbed the front of my shirt, jerked me inside, and I was thrown onto the living room floor. The door slammed and locked.

Chapter 13

A weedy-looking man stared over a hawk nose. Dark hair was combed straight back from a receding hairline, and the condescending sneer was familiar. Myrador. Damn! I caught a whiff of something awful and snapped my head around. A patched and bandaged pig man strutted from behind the couch.

"Napoleon, you prick! We should've dropped you from a lot higher!"

An ugly sneer gave me a glimpse of yellow teeth. "Your mistake."

"So," said Myrador in a softly, terrifying voice. "At last we meet." He was dressed in black and carried an outsized wand. *Guess size mattered to him*. He strode to a kitchen stool, perched a hip on it, and flipped back a red-lined cape which once again made me think of a stage-show magician.

"What do you want?" I have a tendency to snarl when terrified.

He tapped the wand against a palm. "You should be more respectful. After all, I hold the chain of the pig."

Napoleon's pink eyes thinned.

"Don't be ridiculous! I eat bacon for breakfast!"

"Ha. Ha." Myrador's tone was flat. Apparently, he didn't appreciate the humour. Most likely Napoleon didn't either.

"So," I said, getting to my feet. I pretended to brush myself off while feeling for Scarlet. A tiny "ouch" confirmed she'd survived. Bet she appreciated that soft cushion now. "So, what's the deal? What do you want with me?"

"Your magic, of course." He scanned my face and hair. "You've fouled a spell or got your face too close to a fire, so you're either clumsy or incompetent. Perhaps both. I'd be doing the world a favour. At least I know how to use magic."

"The magic of a continent is different from yours, Myrador – as your brother found out."

His expression became calculating. "Yes," he said. "Tell me about my brother. Where is he?"

I had such a big mouth! "How would I know?"

"He hasn't been to Wickness in weeks, and nobody's heard from him. I'm happy to have the castle to myself, but Mydryth isn't exactly a trustworthy sort. I prefer to know what he's up to."

"Do I detect a lack of fraternal affection?"

An involuntary shiver shot through me as he bared long teeth. "Mydryth and I have a . . . friendly competition. Keeps our wits sharp." *Along with your knives, I'll bet.* "Now, where is he?"

When I didn't answer, Napoleon growled and stepped closer. I raised one-and-a-half eyebrows in astonishment and pointed at Napoleon. "Seriously? You can't do better than him as an enforcer?" I scrunched my nose. "And how about someone who smells better?"

Myrador seemed almost apologetic. "Pig men don't have messy ethics with which to deal, and I don't need anyone bigger. I'm the most powerful mage in history."

"Hunh. Good help is hard to find even in the world of magic, I guess."

He gave me a pained expression. "Answer my question."

"No."

His eyes widened as if he couldn't believe my level of stupidity. My brain kicked into gear enough to examine options. One: I could fight him. *That was a joke.* Two: I could trick the two of them. *Unlikely.* Three: Run away. *That sounded promising.* Four . . ? Sounded like door number three was the winner.

As I often did on nice days, I'd left the patio doors open. Did I dare? As Napoleon's dirty hands/hooves reached for my arm, I charged for the doorway, snatched up my broom . . . and leaped into space – in the middle of the afternoon – in view of thousands. A couple drinking coffee on their balcony saw me plummet past. Poor things would have nightmares for the rest of their lives.

Myrador was unlikely to pursue me in front of all these human witnesses but, if I didn't get my broom under me in the next few seconds, it would be irrelevant. I still wasn't good at levitating under emergency conditions, not to mention – I should be cloaked. Where was Dorian when I needed him? And, yes, I realize I'd claimed I didn't need him. Things change!

"Scarlet!"

A red head poked from my pocket followed by a shower of sparkling light. Our descent slowed, and I could tell by the watery effect surrounding us she'd cast an invisibility spell. At least we wouldn't be seen, but the sidewalk still approached too fast. I was going to get hurt – a lot – if I didn't get onto my broom.

Less than twenty feet from the concrete, I'd thrashed around enough to get a leg over it. It was almost like it fought me. I'd suspected before that my broom didn't like me – or it wanted a better rider. Perhaps it didn't appreciate being saddled with someone who lacked magical competence. I scowled and envisioned breaking it over my knee.

There was no time for pretty reflection. Myrador wouldn't be far behind. I'd no doubt he could levitate and cast an invisibility spell with perfection.

I got my broom under control and dodged around the crap that infested city streets until I came to the local subway entrance. With a glance over my shoulder, I skimmed down the middle of an escalator that was filled with commuters headed into the bowels of the city. Some took a weak interest in the rush of air before returning to their phones. I don't know what I was worried about. I wouldn't have drawn attention even if I'd been visible. A story might've appeared in one of the less credible newspapers printed next to *Two-Headed Dog Graduates High School!*

As I reached the bottom of the escalator, I scanned the area for a hiding place. Most men will avoid a women's washroom. I spotted one, and my heart pounded as I waited for someone to open the door. When a pack of giggling Asian teenagers emerged, I slipped in to float above the stalls until I found an empty one. I lowered into it in case Scarlet's invisibility spell didn't hold.

Scarlet popped her head out. "Thought you didn't need me!"

"I'm not usually chased by homicidal maniacs!" I growled.

"You'd be a splat on the sidewalk without me!"

"Alright! What do you want? A thank you? Thank you, Scarlet, for saving my life! I'll put it in writing if you'd like."

Her little face scrunched. "Hmm. That wasn't as satisfying as I'd hoped."

"Are we done now?"

The stall door slammed into me as someone tried to open it. "This door's jammed, but there's no one in here," said a woman's voice." She rammed it against me again.

An indifferent voice answered. "Pick another one."

The first woman had a stubborn streak. "I hear voices. Where are they coming from?"

I put a finger to my lips and levitated. This woman reminded me of myself. I just knew she wasn't going to let it go. Sure enough, when she tried again and the door opened, she peered into the stall and looked all around.

"I tell you, I heard two women talking! One had a nails-on-chalkboard squeaky voice."

I felt my diminutive companion stiffen. "Let it go, Scarlet," I whispered.

"You gotta lay off the pot, Alice. The crazy house is looming." The second woman peered into the mirror, added more lipstick, and squeezed her lips together. Bright red ran into vertical lines around her mouth.

"I'm not crazy!"

"That's what all insane people say. Come on. The train leaves in five minutes." She dropped the lipstick into her purse and snapped it closed.

Alice was almost out the door when Scarlet darted in front of her at head height. With a furious scowl, she snapped, "My voice is not squeaky!"

Alice fainted.

Scarlet slipped back into my pocket as I manoeuvred around the paramedics. A train was leaving, and I didn't care where it went so long as it was away from there. I floated over a swarm of heads and ducked down behind the last car where I could hitch a ride without anyone noticing.

The only thing to hang onto was a rim above the back window – which should be enough as my broom could support my weight. The train pulled out, and I'd exhaled a breath of relief when I caught a movement in the air above the escalators. Crap! Maybe Myrador wouldn't notice us. I turned my face into the window and closed my eyes against increasing wind turbulence.

I was almost convinced we'd escaped when a searing pain shot through me. A glance over my shoulder showed snake-light whipping from wall-to-wall. I had nowhere to go. Another flash snapped the middle of my back. It was all I could do to hold on as my broom faltered. Scarlet slumped to the bottom of my pocket and, sure enough, our invisibility spell flashed twice and fizzled out. I hung by my fingers, chest flat against the window as the train gathered speed.

A pair of fourteen-year-old boys stared in stupefaction – mostly at my chest in a thin tank top as the shirt billowed behind. At least they were the only occupants of the car. I glared and gritted my teeth. This would be tough to explain. I mouthed, "Help . . . me!"

They came closer. Curious. Stupid. Fourteen-year-olds should be illegal.

"Help . . . me!"

As they approached the window entranced by my breasts, Scarlet pushed her head groggily out of my pocket. The youngsters, eyes like saucers, fled the car. As my broom slid further, I focused on levitation to take the pressure off my fingers. Scarlet's magic was non-functional at the moment, but at least she was alive.

The kids must've gotten someone's attention as there was a screech of brakes, and my face mashed into the window along with the rest of me. Through the glass of the connecting doors, I saw a grim security guard stomp towards me followed by the excited boys. No doubt he wanted to prove they were lying before calling the cops.

"Scarlet?"

"Wha . . ?"

"Do something, Scarlet! I'll be arrested, and you'll go to a lab. You wouldn't like that!"

She shook her flaming curls and blinked. "What the hell was that?"

"Myrador's favourite toy – snake-light."

"Bastard!" She grabbed her head. "Feels like my skull's going to explode!"

The guard squinted like he couldn't believe his eyes. In a few seconds, it would be too late. Sweat ran down my back. "Scarlet! Can you manage an invisibility spell?"

A sparse sprinkle of dust was followed by a faint buzz which fizzled in seconds. The man who stomped towards us was really big.

"Scarlet!"

The guard slid the door aside and stepped into the last car, eyes round. Crap! He could see me.

"Scarlet!" My voice had gotten distressingly high.

More sparkling dust burst from my pocket, and I was relieved to see the watery effect of an invisibility spell.

The guard had been surprised. Now he was astounded. As the train screeched to a halt, he jumped to the ground to walk around behind. He even peeked underneath. As he straightened and removed a peaked cap to scratch a balding head, I prayed he wouldn't touch the train as I couldn't levitate out of the way.

"Son of a bitch!" As the man pulled out a radio and stomped back to the car, I wondered if he'd vindicate the boys or hang them to dry.

Steel wheels ground on steel rails. I pulled my broom up with my toes and sat down with exaggerated care. The broomstick felt kind of spongey, but it was recovering.

Myrador would wait for the guard to leave, but he wouldn't be far. When I was sure my broom would carry me, I slipped along the side of the train, moving up until I reached the lead car. The red-hued security guard faced a conductor who was doubled over with laughter. Poor man. He'd re-think that "honesty is the best policy" crap in future.

I slipped in front of the train as it picked up speed. You know, subway trains are fast – really fast when they're on your ass. The only benefit to the situation was that snake-light couldn't get past it in the tunnel. But if I didn't want to become an oversized bug on a windshield, I'd best get out of there.

The tunnel widened until there were two tracks. Uh, oh! Sure enough, there was a light in the distance – another train coming at us. I wonder how many people who ride the subway every day think about the few inches that separate them from certain death.

The roar of trains and buffeting of wind took all my attention for a time. As the other dwindled down the dim tunnel, I let out a sigh of relief, put on a burst of speed, and looked for another station. I didn't remember them being so far apart. Finally, there was (yes, I have to say it) a light at the end of the tunnel.

At the station, I shot above the heads of passengers and, with a sense of elation, (unwarranted as it turns out), into the open air. Near the top of a ten-storey building, I heard the familiar hiss in time to dart around a corner. Plants on a balcony exploded, showering me with dirt and leaves. Damn! Myrador was closing in!

"I'm open to ideas, Scarlet!" I shot across the street to circle behind a brick church.

"I'm thinking!"

"Think faster! I'm going to try for that office building, but that snake-light is seconds behind us!"

Her little fingers snapped. "I've got it!"

"What?" She climbed onto my shoulder to look behind. As a trail of silvery dust streamed from her fingers, I heard a mischievous giggle.

"What're you doing?"

"Making him groggy. Mages always underestimate pixies – and I love it when they leave themselves open like this. Fool. He'll awaken in a few hours in that alley filled with trash."

There was a distinct *whump* in a dumpster after which Scarlet collapsed into such hysterical laughter, tears streamed down her face.

"Uh . . . thanks, Scarlet. Think I'll go home, lock up, and head back to Cumulos. My apartment doesn't feel so safe anymore."

***

My new clothes looked great hanging in my closet at Cumulos. It's true, I could use a spell to create whatever I wanted, but designers had better ideas. I stroked a silk scarf that matched my eyes and wondered if Valgren would notice. Sigh. *From where do such thoughts come?*

A row of tiny garments hung on a thin wooden railing. Scarlet modeled a mini-skirt and tank top from Barbie's wardrobe which, I had to admit, fit pretty well. If she wasn't ten inches tall, she'd be major competition. She fluttered before a full-length mirror I'd found stored with other old furniture. My opinion is that women need mirrors – it's a fact of life.

"Is this what people are wearing in Denver?"

"Young women wear tank tops when it's warm, and men love women in mini-skirts."

"Hmm," she said, a finger across her lips. "I feel naked. Not that pixies care about being naked, it's just that clothes are warmer."

"Try this," I said, holding up tiny jeans and a knit sweater.

She changed and surveyed the effect. "I should wear white more often. I look excellent!"

Who'd have thought Scarlet and I would bond over clothes?

Chapter 14

"How much damage have ye found, Cash?" Angus was leaned back in his leather chair, feet propped on a corner of his desk.

A bench groaned and weapons clanked. "It's a losing battle in the tunnels," said Cash. "They multiply faster than I can kill them, and yesterday I noticed the holes are bigger. They've a ragged edge to them but nothing in the middle. A black hole is exactly how I'd describe them."

Angus glanced at Talon perched on the Pegasus statue.

"Some of the outlying areas are weakening," said Talon. "The castle is untouched because of protective spells as well as the fact it's made of crystal, but eventually it'll be affected, especially when the ground around it begins to crumple."

"Frost, have there been any reports o' people or animals being harmed?"

Jewels flashed in Frost's dark hair as she turned to Angus. "The holes are still too small, but I expect that'll change soon."

"How much time de ye think we have?"

She lifted an elegant shoulder. "A few days at most. I suggest we bring the villagers to the castle for the time being."

"Will ye take care o' that?"

"Of course."

"Cash and Raven, can ye delay the spread o' the slugs as much as ye can? I've another meeting scheduled with the Mage Council."

"Sure," I said, glancing at Cash. "The bigger slugs are easier to find."

***

After hours of tramping through dingy tunnels, I was taking a break in the sunshine when a roar came from above. I shaded my eyes to search for the source and spotted a dark speck that grew into a familiar sight. Wings flat to his sides, Bluescale blasted straight down. He either had a death wish or enjoyed terrifying me.

At the last second, his wings shot out, and he skimmed the ground, executed a couple of barrel rolls, and let out an exultant laugh. I couldn't help but chuckle. Sometimes I think I'm too serious.

Giant teeth were exposed in a grin, and his tongue lolled like a dog's as he came around a second time, skidded onto the grass, and halted mere inches from me. Perhaps being less than wise, I trusted him to stop before bowling me over – well, not totally trusted. I cringed a little.

He let out a loud belch. I turned my head away, and waved a hand in front of my face. "Bluescale! That's disgusting!"

"The fishing was great this morning!"

"Smells like it. Yuck!" I grimaced. "Could you step back? You're in my space!" I moved upwind.

"Good morning to you too," he said. "Aren't you glad to see me?"

I had mixed feelings about Bluescale. His giant heart was surrounded by a number of disturbing behaviours.

"That's better," I said when I could breathe again. "I am glad to see you. I wanted to ask if there's anything in your communal dragon library about cellar slugs."

He curled his lip. "I don't like slugs. They aren't big enough to eat, and they make a mess."

"These are worse."

After being apprised of the increasing severity of the situation, his rubbery brows rose, and a puff of smoke erupted from his nostrils. "Why don't you fry them all?"

"I'd love to, but that would scorch everything else."

I waited as he accessed the dragon knowledge base. "Nope," he said, shaking a massive head. "Nothing there. What else kills them besides fire and stomping?"

I remembered my mother's complaints about slugs in the garden when I was a child. What had she done? The proverbial light bulb glowed over my head. "Salt!"

"What about it?" asked Bluescale.

"Garden slugs are killed by salt! Dehydrates them. Why wouldn't it work for these? Maybe we don't even need magic!"

"How would you get them all?"

"We could spray or maybe flood the tunnels with salt water!"

"Which you'd get where?"

"There are oceans of it! Bluescale, if Cumulos can fly, why can't it float?"

"Wouldn't float for long if you flooded the tunnels," he pointed out.

I was already running. "I've got to talk to Angus!"

When I barged into the study, Talon and Angus were in consultation with an elderly mage – probably a member of the Mage Council. Abandoning any attempt at good manners, I thrust myself into their midst. "I have an idea!"

Talon adjusted his goggles and tightened his lips which conveyed what he thought of my interruption, so I was surprised to find my suggestion wasn't dismissed out-of-hand.

"Hmm," he said. "You may have something there. Hard to believe."

I wasn't above using guilt. "I saved your life, Talon! You could be nicer!"

Although I had saved his life, there were aspects of the experience I'd rather he didn't remember, like the fact it had been my fault he'd sustained a broken arm, contusions, and a significant amount of fur loss. I don't know which he disliked more – the fact he'd nearly died, or that I'd been the one to save him. And I think he suspected I'd been too solicitous about his injuries. I'm not usually so thoughtful when it comes to him, and he knows that, but I'm the only one with a full memory of what happened, and I wasn't talking.

He scrunched skinny legs into a tighter knot and declined to comment. I returned my attention to Angus. "Can Cumulos float?"

"It can, but it will'na float verra high if its tunnels are filled wi' the ocean. One good storm, and Cumulos would be neighbour te Atlantis. We'll give it some thought, lass. Thank ye for the idea."

Apparently, after the mages had dissected the idea, they'd determined it worthy of pursuing because the next morning, I was summoned to the Cumulos control chamber to get started. Unaware Cumulos even had such a room, I was naturally curious. Talon and Angus were already there and busy with gauges and toggles.

The room was a half-sphere lined with switches and round screens that resembled antique radar. Strange writing was scrawled across metallic surfaces, and a lever as tall as a man dominated the room. The front section was of thick glass held in place by solid metallic supports. Two comfortable leather chairs were bolted to the glass which curved to become part of the floor, enabling pilots to watch below as well as to the front. More chairs were scattered further back.

I sucked in a deep breath at all the space between us and the ground ten thousand feet below. I realize Cumulos floats in the sky but, because it feels like Earth, you forget how high up you are. And I know I can fly; it's just that sometimes my early nature reasserts itself – the nature that says I'll scream all the way to my death. Besides, I'm still not good at emergency levitation. What if Cumulos fell – which is, of course, a ridiculous idea, but still . . .

Angus glanced up from beneath a plaid tam. "You're not still afraid o' heights, are ye lass?"

"Of . . . of course not. That would be silly."

"Aye, it would."

Talon twitched his toes and gave me a knowing look. One of these days, I should help Angus get Talon back home. There had to be a way . . .

"So . . . ah . . ." I said, tiptoeing around the edge of the glass floor. "What's all this for?"

"Tis the control room. When we want te move Cumulos other than wi' the wind, we come down here."

"How big is Cumulos?"

"Ten miles long, five wide, and one deep if ye don't count the top o' the mountain behind the castle."

"And it's made of stone?"

"Aye. Tis like any other island."

"That much stone must be heavy. How does it float?"

"The force that would pull the stone down is reversed. This room controls how much."

"You have anti-gravitic technology?"

"If ye need te call it that. We say Gaia pushes instead o' pulls."

"How do you get Gaia to push?"

"We ask nicely."

I gave up.

"Valgren and Dorian will be here shortly te help."

I must've blanked out at that point because Angus was still talking when my attention returned.

". . . and Valgren can monitor the depth o' the island from here." He pointed to a spot where a bulky metal wheel was fastened to the curved wall. Gauges that looked like fat thermometers were bolted above it at eye level.

"The continental magic o' ye and Dorian might come in handy, and Valgren can communicate with Gaia."

"Can't he just ask her to change the gravitational . . . magic?"

Talon lowered himself to the biggest chair which seemed a bit of overkill, and un-knotted his legs. He has the knobbiest knees I've ever seen. "Gaia has other things to do besides help us give Cumulos a bath," he said.

"Isn't removing the slugs important to Gaia?"

I was surprised when he answered. Must've had an attack of chattiness. "That's why she has people like Valgren."

"Valgren says I'm a Rider."

"He might've said that to please you. It wouldn't be the first time a male has stretched the truth in order to manipulate a female. Riders need to be competent, not just lucky."

I envisioned ripping spindly legs out of their sockets then spun to Angus who examined a row of toggles.

He held up a hand. "Ye'll have te handle your own battles, lass. I've got te check the equipment te ensure this delicate operation does'na drown us all."

He was right. Talon was barely half my height. I could protect myself. Then I recalled the size thing. Much as I'd have liked to throw him down and sit on him as I'd done to Ruthie Savenhoff in third grade, I suspected it would end badly for me. He knew how to do things I didn't even know could be done. I stuffed the steam back into my ears. *Pick your battles, Raven.*

I stomped over to watch Angus poke around the toggles and peered at the illegible script. "Who wrote this?"

"Nae idea."

"Who built Cumulos?"

"I dinnae know that either."

"Can you read this stuff?"

"O' course. Couldn't run Cumulos otherwise eh, lass?" He gave me a wink and a grin.

"But, how did you . . . never mind."

I felt like a two-year-old. Why did everyone always know what they were doing, and I almost never did? Would I ever become one of the knowers? Or was I destined to remain ever the incompetent, confused student?

I tried again. Angus had mentioned Cumulos could sink in a storm. "How will you know if bad weather is coming?"

"I check the weather channels."

My eyes must've bulged. "Pardon me?"

"Well, lass, I'm nae a meteorologist. I could come up with a spell, but it would take time. Tis quicker and easier te check the weather report."

"But . . . but . . ." Sigh. "Never mind."

"Even without magic, humans are getting better at precognition. They call it science, but tis the same thing – a way te observe patterns."

This whole thing between science and magic got more confusing all the time.

"I think I'll go find Cash." I didn't want to be there when Valgren and Dorian showed up. Although I wasn't keeping secrets, I experienced free-floating guilt. Perhaps it was my North American background which sucked up belief systems whether one was conscious of them or not. There's nothing like a religion to make you feel guilty just for being alive.

Cash had a simple philosophy. Protect Cumulos and Basia. That's what I needed – something simple on which to focus. Since the control room was at the lowest point of the floating island, I climbed an interminable spiral of stairs up to the basement of Cumulos castle. From there the spiral was replaced by straight flights which seemed to go on forever. These guys needed to invest in some escalators. Perhaps I should suggest it. Oh yes – no electricity. Damn!

Cash and Basia would be in the gardens. I followed hallways until I came to more stairs. Clear crystal descended in a gentle curve to the atrium. With each step, the air thickened with the scent of flowers and moist earth. I relaxed and inhaled it deep into my lungs. The quiet gurgle of miniature waterfalls filled the verdant silence, and I felt the impulse to recline in a sunbeam on the grass. Cats had the right idea. Resisting the urge, I rambled through shaded trails dotted with wooden benches.

Bunnies with bright inquisitive eyes and twitchy ears hopped across paths to disappear beneath graceful ferns. They were followed by miniature partridges, yellow feet a blur as they scuttled around fallen logs covered with moss. I jumped as a furry individual that looked like a cross between a badger and a rodent crawled from a nearby den before it sniffed the air in a friendly manner and ambled away. It must not have inherited the badger's antisocial disposition.

As I wandered, a voice became audible. Since it sounded like it came from a cave, I assumed I'd found Cash. Crouched beside Basia, his craggy features split into a grin that would've terrified small children and timid adults. Basia was on all fours, hands deep in fresh soil as she pressed around the base of a newly-planted twig. She paused long enough to flash a quick smile that made her eyes disappear.

"Raven! How go the preparations?" boomed Cash.

I assumed a cross-legged position on a bed of moss and plucked at strands of grass. "Even though it was my idea, it makes me nervous, Cash. Cumulos is safe in the sky above the weather, but the ocean is a dangerous place. What if Cumulos sinks, and it's my fault?"

Cash's hand covered my arm from elbow to fingertips. "Angus, Talon, and Frost have a lot of magic, not to mention Valgren, Dorian, and you. Cumulos will be fine. Flooding the tunnels with salt water was a great idea. Myrador will be furious."

Sigh. One more thing for which the dark mage would hate me. When he discovered I was responsible, he'd be after me again. I planned to ask every magical person I knew for advice on how to defend myself against the dark mage. It had been embarrassing to have a ten-inch person save my . . . well, you know. Thankfully, she'd returned to Altaria to be with the Royal Family so I didn't have to listen to her incessant gloating. At times, I thought being Myrador's prisoner might be less painful.

I could imagine her explanation to Dorian of how helpless I'd been and how I'd be dead if not for her intervention. The very thought made me grind my teeth. I don't know which I hated more – the fact that Scarlet had saved my life, or Dorian had sent her to do exactly that. He obviously thought I couldn't look after myself and . . . sigh. I hate it when he's right. As a bout of introspection loomed, I decided to head it off by asking Cash for an update.

The slugs had reached critical numbers. Holes in the tunnels grew by the hour. At the end of his explanation, I had few doubts Cumulos was between a rock and a hard place.

After being informed in the politest manner possible that I was unlikely to be helpful in sealing the atrium, I wandered to a back garden. Angus was engaged in manoeuvring Cumulos to a point above the mid-Pacific as far from human activity as possible but, since I'd no clue how Cumulos moved, I was superfluous in that effort too. Perhaps a flight before the attempt to turn Cumulos into a gigantic ocean-going ship would settle my nerves.

When my broom arrived, I groped for it while watching a pair of yellow birds swoop around a trickling fountain. When

I realized I wasn't connecting, I looked over to see it floating six inches from my fingers. Hmm. Brooms are supposed to anticipate their rider's needs. Mine did all too well, it seemed.

I couldn't see myself telling . . . well . . . *anyone* that my broom didn't like me. How embarrassing would that be? That's like saying your shoes wanted a time out. How did one negotiate such an arrangement?

I snatched it from the air and resisted an urge to throttle the devious little thing. Maybe it would have more respect if I told it I was a Rider of Gaia. Sure. Even I didn't believe that. It wasn't like I thought Valgren was untruthful, more like mistaken. No doubt future events would show a glitch in Gaia's calculations. *Oops! Don't know how that happened. Not Raven! Somebody else. Anybody else!* Keep that up, Raven, and you'll be throwing yourself in the ocean!

I gave my head a shake. It was just a broom . . . a device to which I entrusted my life on a regular basis . . . hmm. Maybe it was a female thing. Frost, now out of her "affectionate" phase, might have some advice. Anything at this point would be helpful.

As I settled onto the handle, I wondered if it would drop me. It held, waiting for a signal like any other broom. Since this little issue affected my enjoyment of flying, fixing it was going to the top of my to-do list – right after the grand extermination event. I gave the signal to rise and, in seconds, floated above the rolling green hills of the island.

I explored Cumulos until stomach growls provided an urgent reminder that suppertime approached. Dorian and

Valgren would be here already. Until an obvious choice presented itself at some point, I'd decided it would be best to treat them both as friends because currently, I was confused as hell, and removing the black holes from Cumulos was more important than my morals (or lack thereof). Besides – I'd faint if I didn't eat soon.

I felt his presence the instant I stepped into the crowded study. How long had it been? Nearly a month? It felt like forever. Dressed in leather leggings and jerkin, he lounged against a lion statue, arms and legs crossed. Long, blond-streaked hair framed a sensuous face that would always be semi-wild. Biceps flexed, a heart-stopping smile flashed beneath moss green eyes – and every cell in my body vibrated.

"Are ye coming in, lass?"

"Huh?"

"You're blocking the door. Cash would like te join us."

I hadn't even noticed an eight-foot giant behind me. I jumped, no doubt turned a deep shade of pink, and stepped aside.

"Thanks," boomed Cash, and clanked to his bench.

Valgren gestured towards a spot next to him. Cursing myself for lack of a spine, I crossed the room. He stroked my hair once, and his hand settled onto my shoulder in an unconscious gesture of familiarity.

Talon rolled his eyes and Frost firmed her mouth. Perhaps now wasn't such a good time after all to ask her advice on anything.

"Are ye alright, lass?"

"Huh?"

"Are ye alright?"

"I'm fine. Why do you ask?"

"Ye've nae heard a word I've been saying."

"Sorry. I've been . . . having trouble with my broom."

"Could ye put that aside for the moment? We'll be in position by tomorrow, so we've nae a lot o' time."

"Of course. I'm sorry." As the scent of forest glades filled my senses, I realized I'd have to live on another planet to ignore Valgren.

"Dorian! Tis great te see ye back."

My heart hit the floor as Dorian strolled into the room, every inch a monarch. His eyes shuttered as he exchanged nods with Valgren, gave me a half-smile then greeted Angus.

Frost adjusted the neckline of her gown. Even though her amorous phase was over, she'd always had an eye for Dorian. What woman wouldn't? As she slid over to give him room, I realized the growl I heard came from me. I felt like a pit-bull guarding two food dishes on opposite sides of a room. Hard to get a good meal that way.

"I appreciate that you asked me to be part of this," said Dorian. "We've gotten Altaria free of slugs so, if we can dispose of them here, that might be the end of it." Then he deliberately sat beside Frost.

An expression of surprise flickered before she leaned towards him with a welcoming smile. It's possible my mouth popped open but, fortunately, nothing came out. If I hadn't known him better, I'd have said he was trying to make me jealous – and doing a damn fine job. *I admit there could've been a certain lack of logic to this. Maybe I inherited a healthy sexual appetite from my philandering father – whoever he is. Maybe this wasn't my fault!*

Then again . . .

The conversations continued. What I heard was salt water . . . blah, blah, blah . . . depth measurement . . . blah, blah, blah . . . tunnel dimensions . . . blah, blah, blah. I figured I'd follow instructions when the time came.

An eternity later, plans were finalized, and the attempt scheduled for early morning. Much to Frost's disappointment, Dorian returned to Altaria after the meeting.

As the others filed out, Valgren threaded his fingers through mine and cupped the side of my face. "Moonlight's outside. The clouds are incredible today."

I swallowed. "Shouldn't we get ready for tomorrow?"

"We have time."

The essence of Valgren engulfed me. In the courtyard, he sprang up onto Moonlight's broad back, an arm curled around my waist. Then he gave a quiet signal to the Pegasus who took a few long strides, giant wings spread, and Cumulos receded behind. Moonlight's thick white mane flowed around me in a curtain of security, and my decision to treat Valgren as a friend died a fast death. I'd have to sort my feelings another time.

Chapter 15

The next morning was clear and, to say I was nervous, was an understatement – more like terrified. Guess I still thought in terms of "heavy". Cumulos, for example, made of stone, must be unbelievably heavy. It was difficult to wrap my mind around the fact that nothing has inherent weight. It was a measurement of Gaia's pull on an object, and Gaia could reverse that pull. Gravity as an unchangeable force was an illusion – a damn good one, but an illusion all the same.

We were in the control room suspended below the gigantic floating island, a calm ocean far below. Angus flipped dials and gave instructions from the main control chair as Talon floated at his shoulder. Valgren and Dorian stood at a series of wheels that controlled valves, and Frost was in a chair bolted to the transparent floor that curved to become a transparent wall. The chair beside her was empty – because I was too chicken to sit in it.

I kept remembering we'd be first in the water, and I've always had this aversion to drowning – silly, I know, but there it is. Valgren had once turned me into a fish to prevent exactly that, but the trauma of the incident that had made it necessary was still burned into my brain. And being a fish? Well, that'd been just too weird. I don't recommend it.

"Are ye ready, lass?"

I wiped damp palms on my pants. "Now?"

He raised thick red eyebrows. "If we're te finish before nightfall, we'd best get started."

I huffed out a sharp breath then crept across the glass floor to the chair beside Frost.

"Tis nay going te break, lass. Besides, ye can fly." Angus watched me in bafflement.

"Tell that to my childhood conditioning!" It seemed I was a bit testy.

"Relax, Raven," said Dorian. "We need everyone to have their wits about them."

"Who put you in charge?"

He raised his brows. "The citizens of Altaria."

"We're not on Altaria."

He heaved a deep sigh. "Raven, you can do this. Just believe in yourself."

I grumbled something unprintable and lurched into the chair. I can be over-sensitive when terrified.

"Alright then, let's get started." Angus got to his feet and grasped the huge vertical lever. His muscles bulged as he eased it forward.

When nothing happened, I experienced relief. "It's not working?" *Hopeful.*

"It takes a few minutes, lass. We'll begin te sink shortly." *That's what I'd been afraid of.* "Watch the pressure gauges, Dorian. Valgren, if ye'd coordinate with Gaia?"

They nodded and fiddled with gauges. That's my technical term – fiddled. I'd no idea what they were doing. As I've already admitted, I hadn't absorbed much of the planning session.

"Here we go," said Angus. Puffy clouds began to lift relative to us, and I had to remind myself that breathing was necessary to live.

We dropped at a steady pace over the next half-hour. Frost watched for ships and planes because we needed to disable the cloaking mechanism before we hit the water. A new island in the middle of the Pacific might raise awkward questions – or invite an attack from paranoid militaries.

At a thousand feet, Angus brought the island to a stop for a final review. This time, I paid more attention. The plan sounded logical. Maybe it would work. My job was to open the valves and flood the tunnels – a terror that had kept me up all night.

When Angus was sure we understood, he pushed the lever until ocean waves expanded. I reminded myself our island ship was five miles long. Those little waves, relatively speaking, weren't going to be a problem. They weren't; they weren't; they weren't . . .

Who'd built this stupid thing anyway? Why couldn't the control chamber have been on top?

Seawater splashed the glass – and we were below the surface, the light dimming. I experienced an almost irresistible urge to hold my breath as thousands of bubbles raced along the glass walls on their way to the surface. Down . . . down.

A sea turtle glanced at us with mild curiosity before turning away through a cloud of jellyfish, and three dolphins peered through the glass at the gigantic new sea creature. They followed us down, swimming in circles, wanting to play. When Angus stopped our descent, it was quite dark, and I didn't know whether to hold my breath or hyperventilate.

"Ye can flood the first tunnels, lass . . . Raven?"

"Huh?"

"Ye can flood the first o' the tunnels."

"Oh . . . yeah . . . um." How did that go again? My fingers hovered over the panel in front of me.

"Start on the left, lass. Fill the first set, wait an hour, pump them out, then go to the second. Do ye nae remember?"

I wasn't sure I could remember my name. "Uh . . . yes." Hand shaking, I flipped the toggle I knew would flood the first set of tunnels. It felt like poking a hole in your own boat. As a low grinding started and the walls shook, my eyes must've become blue golf balls. "What's that noise?!"

"Tis the seals o' the tunnels opening." Angus glanced at Valgren. "How are ye doing with Gaia?"

Valgren was relaxed, arms rested on one of the heavy valves. "Gaia is happy to help. The salt water cleanse will be good for Cumulos. It hasn't been done in a long time."

I swung around. "You mean you've done this before?"

"It's been done before," said Valgren, "but not by me."

"How old is Cumulos?"

He shrugged. "Don't know. Small increments of time are not relevant when you deal with eons."

I supposed so. I returned to staring through the glass as a humungous grey shadow approached. Was it a whale? What if it hit the glass? A gigantic head on a long sinewy neck turned to look at us . . .

"For heaven's sake, Raven! You almost deafened everybody!" Dorian had his hands over his ears.

I was plastered against the back wall pointing into the darkness with a shaky hand. "What . . . what the hell is *that*?" A giant face with reflective eyes looked in at us. Whatever it was had a greyish hide, and hundreds of teeth showed in a mouth that could've swallowed a truck. As it slammed into the glass, a shudder ran through the control room. Although we might've looked like tasty morsels, my little body wouldn't even have constituted a snack.

Valgren, with a delighted grin, slipped an arm around my shoulders as he watched the creature. "It's one of the monsters of the deep. We're lucky to see it."

"Lucky? Are you joking? It wants to eat us!"

"We're fine, Raven. Cumulos was built to withstand a great deal." As he kissed my forehead, I saw Dorian turn his back. If

I hadn't been overpowered by terror, I'd probably have been flooded with guilt.

After an eternity, the behemoth moved away with sinuous waves of its body as flippers the size of a battleship grazed the glass. I don't think I took a breath the entire time.

As Valgren strolled to his station, I scrounged the nerve to return to my chair, eyes riveted to the screen. Dorian, without expression, walked up to me, reached across, and switched some toggles. As he returned to his post, the grinding and shaking began again. Had it really been an hour? I sucked in a shaky breath.

"Thanks, Dorian. I'll be okay now."

In spite of my apprehension, the day progressed until the second-to-last tunnel was being emptied. Maybe it would be all right after all and, in a couple of hours, Cumulos would reclaim her place in the sky. Funny, how you could get to believe an island belonged in the clouds.

It was late afternoon. I was wolfing down a peanut butter sandwich when I noticed Angus had a worried frown. I stopped chewing as an ice-ball formed in my stomach.

"What's wrong?"

"The weather report's been updated."

"To what?"

"A tropical storm is headed our way. Sae far it's nae a hurricane, but could turn into one if wind speeds get high enough. Twill be touch-and-go if we're finished in time, but we need te get all the slugs else today has been a waste o' effort. Only takes a couple o' them te start over."

"What if the storm catches us?"

"Cumulos cannae lift in the middle o' a storm. We'd have te ride it out down here."

The ice-ball in my stomach expanded. "You're joking."

"Have ye experienced a hurricane, lass?"

I shook my head. "British Columbia doesn't get hurricanes, so I've only seen them on television, but they seem scary."

"They are. Cumulos is pretty solid, but we dinnae want te be caught in one, not even a tropical storm if we can avoid it. The winds will damage the surface o' the island."

"Can Cumulos withstand it without breaking apart?"

"Probably."

Probably. My stress level slammed into the red.

"We may as well continue with the flooding since we're nae leaving til we're done. Tis tough te find a stretch o' ocean without boats or aircraft for a full day."

I willed the fat cylinder on my bronze control slab to empty faster. When it reached the bottom, the second-to-last tunnels would be pumped clear. The repetitive nervous tap of my nails on the panel no doubt irritated the hell out of everyone.

An eternity later, a metallic groan reverberated accompanied by a final trickle from the cylinder. One more. I flicked the toggle and metallic grinding resumed. The last set of tunnels were being flooded. I swear I felt Cumulos sink as seawater poured into its basement passageways. It did drop a miniscule amount but nothing like I imagined. I glanced at my naked wrist in a habitual but fruitless effort to check the time.

"It's four o'clock," said Dorian. "We'll be done by six."

I turned to Angus, an unasked question in my posture.

He pursed his lips and shook his head. "The weather report says tis moving fast. It'll be here before we're finished. Dinnae worry, Raven. Cumulos is built o' solid rock, so it'll nae be pulled apart sae easily."

"What about the village residents?" I asked.

Angus switched his attention to Frost. "How many are still outside the castle?"

"The families are all in the courtyard, but animals are still being brought in."

"Could ye ask them te speed it up a little? We'll be cutting it fine."

Frost nodded and left the room with a sidelong glance at Dorian. Grrr . . . I spun to face the front, hoping for a distraction from my temporary insanity – at least I hoped it was temporary. Slouched in my chair, I crossed my ankles over a corner of the control panel and crossed my arms. And no, I wasn't sulking.

"So, what's with the sulking?" Dorian strolled over to survey the underwater view.

"I'm not sulking. I'm waiting."

"If that's what you want to call it."

The room narrowed, and I concluded it might've been because my eyes had become mere slits. "That's what I want to call it!"

"No need to get cranky." He sent me a beatific smile. "Think I'll go help Frost." And he was gone.

The grinding noise was now my teeth. I tried to concentrate on the variety of ocean life that swam past and prayed the monsters of the deep didn't decide on an encore. The day had been stressful enough, and it wasn't over. *I've noticed exhaustion can have a tiny deleterious effect on my sunny disposition.*

I took a deep breath and tried to emulate Valgren who'd taken Frost's chair next to me, his feet propped on the panel, muscular arms crossed. Unlike me, he was completely relaxed. He gave me a quick wink and a half-smile then turned to watch the view-screen as if it were a television show.

Long dark shadows glided through the murk. I was trying to identify them when a killer whale slid past the glass, checking out our glowing fish bowl, I suppose.

Valgren glanced at me. "Isn't he beautiful?"

"Uh . . . sure," I replied, trying to slow the machine-gun staccato of my heart.

Of course, Valgren noticed. He could probably feel my heartbeat. "You'll come to trust Gaia in time, Raven – once you know her."

I noticed Valgren always referred to Gaia as *her*, and I always used *it*. I thought I understood Gaia's nature all too well, and I hadn't noticed compassion in any part of its makeup. More like indifference. I nodded. "Of course."

"Once you're not afraid of Gaia, you'll see a different world."

Was that it? I saw Gaia as dangerous and indifferent whereas Valgren saw compassion and joy? I lived in fear and he in love? It was a good thing I wasn't inclined to be introspective. This could've given me a headache.

"I'm not afraid of . . . well . . . much."

He grinned, leaned to give me a quick kiss then returned to contemplating the sea life.

I felt vaguely insulted. "What was that for?"

"It'll be fun dismantling your walls of denial."

I felt my quills rise. "I'm *not* in denial!"

His only response was to chuckle. No snappy comebacks leaped to mind and, anyway, I'd be willing to bet it was impossible to make the man angry. There wasn't the slightest touch of meanness in his entire makeup. I, on the other hand . . . good lord! More dangerous introspection!

A half hour later, I leaped from my chair and stomped to the back. "I need some air."

"Be careful o' the surface, Raven. The wind's picking up," said Angus as I swept past.

Talon watched as I headed for the door.

"I suppose you're going to tell me to watch out for the wind too!" I snapped.

He stretched fuzzy lips into a short, humourless smile. "I wasn't going to warn you at all. Gaia selects against the . . . well, I hate to use the word, 'stupid', but . . . stupid."

I skidded to a halt. "I am not stupid!"

"The way you're not in denial?"

"Ah, go to hell!" And I stomped out.

Endless stairs later, I found a small door that, for some reason, was difficult to open. Still cranky and not paying much attention, I managed to slip through and, to my shock, it slammed shut behind me. An instant later, I was smashed against the wall by a screaming wind. I stared in horror at a monstrous ocean wave which swept halfway up the hillside towards the castle.

Oh . . . my . . . god! A product of forests and prairies, I'd had little experience with oceans other than flying above them in safety. Now, as far as the eye could see were monstrous grey waves topped with frothing whitecaps. I'd no idea waves could get that big. Ocean liners would disappear into those troughs!

It was almost as if Gaia heard and replied, *"If you think that's bad, get a load of* this!" The skies opened and, in seconds, horizontal rain drove across the island. If this was Angus' idea of the "wind picking up", I'd hate to see what he called a real storm – which I was pretty certain I was about to experience. Getting some fresh air now seemed a mite foolish.

All I could do was to stare into the tempest that threatened the beautiful cloud island. How could I have been so stupid as to suggest such a thing? I was risking everyone's lives, for crissake! This couldn't possibly work! My stomach clenched, and I couldn't look anymore.

Snapping my mouth closed to keep the rain out, I struggled to re-open the door, but it took considerable strain and a generous application of magic to get it to budge. The powerful winds threatened to tear it from my grip. When I finally managed to inch it wide enough, I darted through the opening. The resounding slam that followed nearly tore the door from its hinges.

Grateful it hadn't caught me half-way, I leaned against a wall. As I sucked in great gulps of air, I tried to understand why Angus had agreed to such insanity. He must be as crazy as I was.

When I could breathe again, I pushed dripping locks from my eyes, wrung out my hair and t-shirt, and sloshed back to the control room.

At my arrival, I could see Dorian choke back a laugh. "So, was the air fresh?"

I put a hand to my hair which was whipped into knots and plastered to my head. With a scowl at Dorian, I marched to Valgren with mute appeal. His smile was suspiciously like Dorian's, but he refrained from comment as he stroked my hair and clothing. I noticed Dorian turned his back for that part. In seconds, I was dry and knew from experience that my hair now hung in perfect ebony waves, the emerald streak glowing in the lights. Some singed parts still showed, but I'd eliminated most of them by vigorous brushing.

"Thank you. It was . . . breezy."

Talon scowled as if disappointed Gaia hadn't dragged me to the bottom of the ocean. Frost glided into the room, every hair perfect, and informed Angus that everyone was in the castle. She'd obviously been wise enough not to step outside.

"We should stay in the castle for the duration," said Angus. "The storm will hit soon."

"The storm will hit soon?!" I blurted. "What the hell do you call what's here already?"

"It's just getting warmed up, lass. I'd like te get the final tunnel emptied as soon as we can. All that seawater makes Cumulos heavy."

"Can't you just increase the anti-gravity . . . Gaia's pushing magic?"

"If Cumulos gets too light, it'll be smashed by the wind and waves. If too heavy, it'll sink. We want a stable balance before the main storm hits."

My throat was dry as I regained my seat next to Frost. The sub-oceanic view now felt safer than the surface. I fretted as the fat cylinder neared its goal. A few more minutes. Unable to sit, I rose so I could pace. An air of tension came from somewhere, but it seemed I was the only one who felt it. Was I the only chicken in the room? Sigh. Probably.

I'd plopped into my chair for the fifth time when a timer indicated the tunnels had been sterilized. All that remained was to remove the seawater and wait out the storm. With a sigh of relief, I switched a toggle, and the grind of valves and pumps reverberated for the final time. A half-hour more, and we were done.

Valgren dropped his feet to the floor. "I'm going to see how deep Cumulos is sitting. Might need Gaia to make an adjustment." He glanced at me. "Want to come?"

"Outside?"

I may have appeared anxious because he smiled. "Yes. I'll protect us from the wind."

So, why could he control the wind while I . . . sigh.

The gauge wasn't going to move any faster by being watched, so I thought I might as well do something useful. Resisting the urge to look at Dorian, I lurched to my feet.

"Sure. Let's go."

Ten minutes and many stairs later, we approached a narrow side door hidden in a corner. As Valgren made a hand motion, a spherical ball of translucent blue light appeared and expanded to encompass us. His arm around my waist, he opened the door with ease, and we stepped into hurricane winds. I expected to be slammed against the wall or worse, whipped away like a soap bubble.

Strangely enough, neither of those things happened. Howling wind whipped nearby bushes, and branches flew past, but we were unaffected. I'd have to put this bubble thing on my growing list of things to learn.

As we lifted from the ground, I was horrified to see the damage being done to Cumulos' beautiful trees and gardens. Massive waves driven by a furious tempest surged up the slope towards the castle, withdrew and surged again with a deafening roar. Huge oaks were stripped of leaves as their branches whipped the ground.

The village was far enough up the slope to escape the raging ocean though it was pummelled by the deluge. If the buildings had been made of wood, they'd have already been gone. As it was, the little stone houses looked like a collection of tortoises huddled on a mountain slope. Former footpaths had become torrents that carved gullies into the hillside as water gushed to the sea.

I had to shout to be heard above the din. "So, where's Gaia's gentleness now?"

"Sometimes a good scrubbing is in order," said Valgren with maddening calm. "Cumulos will be spotless after this."

It looked to me like the cloud island was being destroyed.

"We'll go higher," he said. "Cumulos is doing an adequate job of riding the waves."

The ocean thrashed in fury as far as the eye could see – which wasn't that far considering the horizontal curtains of rain. Still – terrifying. Since I like to find the silver lining in situations, I imagined the storm kept Cumulos safe from the prying eyes of boats and aircraft – about the only good thing I could come up with.

In a few minutes, we were high enough to see the extent of the island. Regardless of how bad it was being battered, Valgren had such an air of confidence, I began to settle down. I wasn't in charge and couldn't fix anything, so I might as well relax.

Then from my lily-livered subconscious erupted the realization that my well-being was dependent on a teensy bit of magic, meaning if that blue bubble popped, we'd be sucked into the vortex below.

I swear Valgren's telepathic. He stroked my hair and nuzzled my neck. "We're fine, Raven. The storm won't get through the spell."

He slid to a seated position taking me with him, an arm around my shoulders, his attention on the raging winds below. "Isn't Gaia magnificent?"

I guess that was one word for it. Another was "petrifying".

I gnawed my lip as, for some reason, Talon's words returned out of the blue, and I had to ask. "Valgren . . . you once said I was a Rider of Gaia. Were you just . . . you know . . . joking?"

He lifted my chin to look into my eyes, and the scent of forest and wildflowers filled the bubble as moss-green sank into my soul. “Raven, I’d never tell you such a thing if it wasn’t true. You were born a Rider. Just because you lack an upbringing that would make it easier doesn’t change that. Everything you need is within you here.” He touched my chest with his fingertips and my heart fluttered. “I’ll help you bring it out. I know who you are.”

“But Talon says . . .”

He brushed my lips with a fingertip. “Talon is a creature with a nasty disposition who comes from another planet. He hasn’t a clue what being a Rider is about. Trust me. You’re all you need to be. You will learn to trust yourself.”

“Was my father a Rider?”

“Your father must’ve been magical but was not necessarily a Rider.”

“Where do they come from?”

“Riders?” At my nod, he said, “It varies, but Gaia ensures there are enough for her needs.”

“Were you born in the normal sense? Do you have a mother?”

“Gaia’s my mother, but I wasn’t born as you understand the term. A long time ago, I woke on a bed of moss in a most fragrant forest. The glade was carpeted with wildflowers, and sunshine slanted through the trees. I remember listening to the lovely forest music of a dancing stream.”

“Guess that explains why I always smell wildflowers and forest when you’re near.”

A brow went up. "You do?" At my nod, he said, "Now, that's interesting."

"Why?"

His smile broadened and he kissed me. "Never mind. We'll talk about it another time."

I was determined not to let him distract me, difficult though it may be. "Were you fully grown when you awoke?"

"I was. Somehow I knew how to care for Gaia and that she'd care for me."

"So, you just . . . materialized?"

He shrugged. "Humans materialize all the time. We call them babies. Why would it be so different to materialize fully-grown?"

Good point.

We were high above the island and rising. "Where are we going?" I asked.

"To see the extent of the storm."

That sounded better. I'd rather wait it out from above – far above. Tropical storms and hurricanes weren't so scary when seen from a couple of miles up. They looked like graceful galaxies swirling along the Earth giving no indication of the devastation they wreaked on the surface.

Greyness vanished as we broke through to sunshine and blue sky. A commercial airliner droned too far away to be a danger. The view blurred, and we floated near the blackness of space, the globe of Earth clear to see. It was the first time I'd been high enough to view our beautiful blue-and-white ball afloat in an endless sea of black, and it was immediately obvious how stupid our schoolyard disagreements were. Embarrassing. Travellers through the neighbourhood most likely ensured we remained confined to our self-created hell until we grew up.

As if in answer, two pulsating blue lights streaked across the blackness, made a right-angled turn, and disappeared.

I grabbed Valgren's arm. "Did you see that?"

"What?"

". . . never mind."

"The storm's pretty extensive, so Cumulos won't be out of it for a few hours yet."

Although I'd have been happier to stay where we were, I said, "We should go back. The others might need us."

As our sphere dropped, Valgren said, "Since we've cleared the tunnels, the rest is a matter of riding out the storm. Cumulos is well-balanced and solid enough to handle even hurricane-force winds and waves. It should be fine."

Sure, it should. Whatever could go wrong . . ?

Chapter 16

I was calm until we reached the island and I saw uprooted oak trees tossed like match sticks on the furious ocean. I hoped Angus and Valgren knew what the hell they were talking about when they said it would take more than a tropical storm to damage Cumulos. Some days, I felt like taking notes on all the things they could do.

The travelling sphere made opening a side door effortless and, after he'd ensured the door was latched, we trotted down the stairs to the control room where Angus and Talon presided over gauges and dials.

I glanced around. "Where are Dorian and Frost?"

Angus answered over his shoulder while tapping the side of a gauge. "Helping the villagers with their animals.

The courtyard is safe, but the animals get excited with the wind and rain. They're used te mild weather, so tis a shock for them."

Cumulos usually floated above most of the clouds which made weather a non-issue, and the magical folk created gentle rain as needed. No wonder the animals were upset. They must've thought their world had come to an end.

"Do they need help?" I asked.

"Hard te say. Why don't one o' ye stay te monitor the island depth and the other check upstairs? By the way, how does it look from above?"

Valgren rested an arm on a control lever. "Ocean's pretty wild but, if it doesn't get worse, Cumulos will be fine. It was overdue for a good cleaning anyway."

"Thanks for checking, Valgren. I'll be glad when we've returned te the clouds."

Before anyone could say another word, there was a deafening *CRACK!* As we spun to the view-screen, we saw a monstrous figure covered in thick scales had slammed into the glass. Both ends of the creature lost in the distance, its hide looked like it had been coated with giant turtle shells. I thought it was big enough to swallow a house without a hiccup and, as I moved to Valgren's side, I wondered why Gaia would have need of such a creature.

It was a good thing the glass was strong . . .

With a stab of terror, I realized that, like a rock pitched against a windshield, a circular web of lines had formed. No one spoke as a jagged streak snaked across the glass, and a thin fan of water sprayed onto the floor.

Four streaks of energy pulsed from outstretched palms, converging at the crack in an attempt to fuse the glass. But the pressure of the ocean was enormous.

"Raven!" bellowed Angus. "Get Dorian and Frost! We'll need them both!"

I tore out of there like I was on fire. Casting a levitating spell on the fly, I was at the courtyard in seconds.

Pandemonium reigned as villagers struggled with anxious farm animals. Near the fountain, Dorian stuffed an uncooperative rooster into a wooden crate. After a lot of squawking and flapping had gone on, Dorian snapped the latch then brushed feathers from his coat. He gave me a half-smile as I raced up. "That guy thinks he's bigger than he is."

"Dorian, where's Frost? There's been an accident in the control room! The glass is about to burst!"

Dorian materialized a message ball, tossed it, grabbed my hand, and we shot through the hallways. At the wide doorway to the control room, we skidded to a halt. Angus and Valgren, ankle-deep in rapidly-rising water, poured beams of energy into the fissure. Talon floated at head height adding a purple stream to the mix. The sound of crackling energy and the distinctive smell of ozone filled the room.

Dorian and I blasted as much energy as we could summon, and the water slowed, but the great pressure of the ocean created new cracks. Desperation shoved my brain into gear. I'd been in no-win situations before. A vision of Bluescale and

I tearing through the tunnels from Napoleon's dungeon came to mind. Other images flooded to my mind's eye – useless stuff.

No wonder I was lousy at magic. I couldn't focus for more than a few seconds. For god's sake, Raven, think!

I shifted my attention to a new crack that shot from the original circle and moved my energy to follow, trying to generate enough heat to melt the glass. But an entire ocean cooled it at the same time. Thin fans of water shot from the new fissure. I wished I had magic staples to pull it all together . . . or a . . . *net* . . . Those goddamn nets were constantly being used against me. Maybe they could be useful for a change!

Sometimes I'm astonished at how smart and how dumb I can be at the same time. You'd think that would be a contradiction but, in my case, it was business as usual.

"Angus! Remember the net Napoleon used to catch Bluescale and me?" He grunted and nodded, veins on his forehead pulsing, his attention on the cracking glass. "It was incredibly sticky *and* it contracted! If we could make some, maybe it would hold the cracks until the storm is over!"

"De ye . . . know . . . how te . . . make it? Tis rare knowledge I have'na found yet."

"Me?"

"Yes, lass."

"Um . . . no."

Valgren shifted focus to me. "I can make the net, Raven. We'll have to wait for Frost to take over for me though as it'll take a few minutes."

Come to think of it, what the hell was keeping the witch? Before I could get up a good head of steam, there was a flash and she materialized. An expression of astonishment tinged with a dash of fear crossed her face.

Valgren glanced at her as she waded into the deepening pool, long dress billowing behind. "Frost! Here!"

They switched places and Frost's beam of blue joined the rest. As water inched up my thighs, I realized there had to be a hole at the bottom where we couldn't see it.

I tried to see what Valgren was doing as he climbed shallow stairs towards the door. I promised myself to learn how to make that net so the next time I met Napoleon, I could turn him into a pig-in-a-blanket.

Valgren tipped his bead back, closed his eyes, and extended his arms as if to catch something. His stance reminded me of the first day we'd spent together when he'd stood on a rock to pull werewolves from the bushes. His sword had flashed in the sunlight, and honey-streaked hair had lifted in the wind as he'd propelled them through a spinning pentagon. I'd been mesmerized by the image and, even now, with all this fear coursing through me, I responded to the memory.

"Raven!"

"Wha . . . what?"

"Your aim is off, lass!"

"Oh. Sorry."

I turned my back to Valgren. The water had crept to my waist, and I wasn't sure I could maintain a spell while treading water. The big doors could be sealed but, to adjust the depth of the island, we had to be *in* the control room. *Note to self: Next time you have the bright idea of giving an island a bath, resist the urge to share.*

Our sealing spells were now going through seawater which didn't work well. It was only a matter of minutes – perhaps seconds. There was a deep rumble, and the big doors behind us closed with a resounding slam. I spun in disbelief to Valgren, but it was Angus whose arms were raised, the remains of a spell trickling from his fingers. His face was drawn as he turned to me.

"We cannae let the water into Cumulos, lass. Twill sink the island for sure."

"But . . ."

"We'll either solve the problem or die in the attempt. Cumulos must survive."

There was a new gushing sound, bubbles streamed outside the glass, and I was on tiptoes to keep my chin above water. I spun in desperation to Angus. "What do you need me to do?"

"Valgren's nearly completed the spell. The webbing's beginning te form. If ye can dive, take one and use it te patch one o' the holes, but be careful you're nae pulled into the ocean. We've nae time for a rescue."

I was treading water, the ceiling getting closer by the second. Valgren stood on a raised landing, eyes closed, water to his chest. Golden tendrils twisted like snakes around his torso. With a few swift strokes, I was next to him, resisting the urge to touch for fear of distracting him. After three tries,

I grasped a twisting tendril, sucked in a deep lungful of air, and dove.

At first, I couldn't see any damage but, as I was about to need a breath, I saw where a chunk of glass had broken away. I pushed the end of the tendril against the edge where, to my astonishment and relief, it stuck. It was evident the netting would stretch forever, and I was soon engaged in crisscrossing the strings across the hole, smoothing it to form a solid patch. After currents threatened to pull me into the dark expanse, I twisted a tendril around my waist and stuck it to the inside of the room.

But I was running out of air. There was a flash of movement and Dorian was beside me with two more tendrils. The world was going grey when he pulled me to him, placed his lips to mine, and exhaled wonderful air into my starving lungs. Then he pointed his thumb upwards and shoved me towards the surface where I sucked in great heaving gulps of a diminishing air supply.

There was no time to rest. I grabbed more netting and dove again to join Dorian and Talon who worked furiously. Frost and Angus were patching a crack that threatened to burst. If it did, we were done. The glass would collapse.

There was another good-sized jagged opening. As I reached across it to secure a strip of netting, a powerful vortex sucked at me. Before I could brace myself, it had popped me out of that hole like a cork from a bottle.

With mounting horror, I drifted away, my struggles useless against the inexorable pull of the ocean. The glass was obscured by netting, so it was unlikely anyone would see me. I glanced at the cord around my waist. Maybe I could pull myself hand-over-hand. Would it hold?

My lungs screamed for air.

It was too far . . .

A dark shadow crossed the distant glass. There was a jerk on my waist, and I was pulled against the current. I could do little to help but, an eternity later, strong arms pulled me through the fissure and someone blew air into my lungs. Then I was pushed to the surface. As my face broke the water, I sucked in great gulps, frantic to breathe. I was shaking, nauseous, and tears streaked down my face to swirl away with the water.

"Hold this! Stay here!" A pale Dorian wrapped my fingers around a metal bar and dove away.

There was no time for self-indulgent fear. After replenishing my lungs, I followed. Netting filled the water to such a degree, becoming caught in it had become a danger. After gluing a new safety-line, I stuffed the sticky material into the hole – which was four feet across. Currents sucked at it, and pieces drifted into the depths.

Our furious actions finally got the opening closed. When the patch had been strengthened to the point we thought it would hold, we turned our attention to smaller leaks that weakened the wall and threatened to let in the ocean. We were making headway, but the water was close enough to the ceiling I had to tip my head to draw a breath. My heart pounded, and my vision deteriorated from holding my breath for so long. I was running out of time in so many ways.

I'd grasped another clump of netting and was about to dive when a sudden roar filled the room. Terror shot through me. The glass must've collapsed at last! Dorian's head popped through the surface next to me. At my panicked expression, he mimed the pump had started.

I glanced at Valgren who was in the highest position in the room next to the doors, eyes closed, golden tendrils twisting around him. The water was to his chin.

Air hissed in through a vent as water was pumped out. Since the water level was dropping, it was clear we'd made progress. That didn't mean the wall wouldn't collapse though. It was badly damaged, and I'd no idea how long the webbing would hold. I carried on reinforcing every crack I could find, easier now the water level had dropped, so we could identify the leaks. There was no conversation as everyone scrambled.

An eternity later, the last of the water poured into a drain leaving the room draped in golden strings and seaweed. Valgren still hadn't moved, and netting continued to form. I lurched to my feet and staggered to him. Considering there was enough netting to seal the entire room, I thought we had enough.

At a nod from Angus, I stroked Valgren's cheek and whispered his name, worried about the shock of jerking him from such a deep state. Netting draped us both. Since he didn't respond, I stood on tiptoes, pulled his head down and kissed him.

I knew he was back when his arms went around me, and the scent of flowers and forest arose. When he opened his eyes, the material stopped forming.

"Thank you," he said. Then he smiled and looked around at the devastation. "Guess that's enough netting."

I peeled it off his shoulders as he did the same to me. He glanced down with a half-smile at my soaked clothing and, with brief strokes of his hands, my hair and clothes were smooth and dry.

"Thanks," I muttered.

Angus adjusted a sagging kilt. Talon looked like a stray dog, purple fur plastered to a skinny frame and pot belly. Frost, of course, was ravishing even in a soaked gown. Dorian glanced at me, collapsed into a chair, and closed his eyes. I leaned against a wall, viewed the disaster, and took my first real breath in hours.

Chapter 17

The room felt small with the view-screen covered in webbing. Angus grabbed a string of seaweed that draped a control lever and dropped it into a pail where it made a sucking/squishing sound. Talon was on a hunt for sea urchins or other such dangerous creatures that may have gotten in.

I stared at the wreckage. "After all this, those damn slugs better be gone!"

As Valgren dissolved the last piece of excess netting, he closed his eyes for a few seconds then looked at me. "Gaia says Cumulos is clear. Despite our near escape, this was a good idea, Raven – probably the only thing that would've worked."

"Aye, lass. I haven't had time te thank ye properly. The net idea saved Cumulos – not te mention, all our lives."

It was Valgren who did it," I said, "not me."

"I might not have thought of it in time," said Valgren. "I've never needed it."

"I'd appreciate it if ye could instruct me in creating the net," said Angus. "Tis nae in my books, so I'll write one for it."

As Valgren nodded, Dorian stepped forward. "Do you still need me? I'd like to return to Altaria. With Myrador still on the loose, I don't like to be away too long."

He caught my eye and my heart stopped. He wasn't going to mention saving my life. And how do you thank someone for such a thing?

"Of course, King Dorian," said Angus. We're most grateful for your help. It wouldn't have gone sae well without you. But the rest o' us should have nae trouble lifting Cumulos. The storm is spent."

Dorian gave me another wordless glance, nodded at Valgren, and strode from the room.

We decided to get cleaned up and have a sandwich before taking on the task of raising the island. The sun would set soon, and it was safer to return to the skies under cover of darkness.

After a bath to wash away the salt, I met Valgren in the kitchen where he poured me a coffee. I took the cup along with a plate of sandwiches and plunked onto a sofa where I scarfed it all down. I awoke sometime later snuggled against Valgren's chest. Since I didn't remember going to sleep, I narrowed my eyes at him.

"You were tired," he said.

I decided not to pursue it, as being in Valgren's arms was my absolute favourite way to wake up. All too often, I was alone.

The others had joined us while I'd been asleep. Angus and Frost were back to normal but, though I tried not to stare, Talon looked like he'd been blasted by a commercial hair drier. Purple fuzz made him look like a stuffed toy. It almost made me want to pet him but, since I valued my appendages, I refrained. When I caught him making surreptitious motions to flatten his fur, I realized he probably thought being fluffy made him look helpless and cute – not something to which he aspired.

After another sandwich and two cups of coffee, I was ready for the ascension – more than ready. I wanted Cumulos safe in the clouds.

The sun had set an hour earlier when we trooped into the control room. Now that we knew what we were doing, it wasn't long before the disturbed ocean was roiling below. I heaved a sigh of relief as I peered over Angus' shoulder at a miniature view-screen which showed excess water poured from the island in hundreds of waterfalls.

The biggest concern now was being spotted by humans. Civilian aircraft or ships weren't a problem as no one would believe them anyway, but military planes were a different story. They tended to target anything new in their skies. A miles-long floating island would qualify as a threat and, considering the beating Cumulos had just sustained, I wouldn't bet my life all its spells were functional.

Tired of staring over the mage's shoulder as the Pacific sank, I slanted a look at Valgren. "Does Gaia have any input on this?"

He gave a final twist of a dial and flicked a toggle. "She is calm. Cumulos will lift easily now the storm has passed."

Although I experienced a lessening of anxiety, I'd be fully relaxed only when the ocean was far below.

Valgren glanced at me. "Don't worry, Raven. Gaia isn't about to let one of its floating islands sink into the ocean."

. . . *One* of its floating islands??

***

Sunshine created a pattern across a patchwork quilt. A muscular arm tucked me against a warm body. I lay quiet, luxuriating in the feel of Valgren, preternaturally aware of the soft sound of his respiration, the touch of his breath against my neck.

Any time I woke with Valgren asleep against me, I was awed that such a thing could happen. None of my magic came close to this simple thing. Remembering how he seemed to know what I thought and felt, I hoped he was asleep. Those feelings made me too vulnerable and smacked of the desire to possess – and Valgren was not a man anyone could possess. Deep down? I didn't want to limit his freedom. I didn't like limits myself. So, there I was in another confusing situation. I was a contrary woman.

Warm lips pressed against my neck which caused my own to curve into a smile. "Good morning," he murmured, tightening his arm.

"Mmm . . . good morning, yourself."

He shifted onto an elbow and turned me onto my back, moss-green eyes gazing into mine. "You are so beautiful," he breathed. Sleep-tousled hair framed his face as he stroked my cheek before lowering his lips to mine. Valgren's kiss never failed to fill me with magic and wonder. Sometimes I thought about what life would be without him but could never bear to follow the thought to its conclusion.

As he lifted his head, I wrapped my arms around him. "It seems Cumulos is safe for another day," I murmured. "I'll bet we could find all sorts of activities to keep us occupied this morning."

"What did you have in mind?" he asked with a sensuous smile.

"I'll follow your lead."

***

"Moonlight and I are going on a mission for a few days," said Valgren. "Would you like to come along?"

We were shoulder-to-shoulder, elbows rested on the balustrade that encircled the tallest tower of Cumulos.

"Where are you going?" Which was a stupid and irrelevant question. If Valgren wanted me to go anywhere with him, I was going!

He smiled. "Somewhere you've never been."

"Ahh . . . a mystery place."

"Sort of. No humans have been there."

"Are there magical people?"

"A few."

"When do we leave?"

He chuckled. "I knew I could count on your curiosity."

"Curiosity?" I arched a brow. "Maybe I just wanted to spend more time with you."

His smile broadened. "I was counting on that too."

The sun was high when Moonlight sailed into the courtyard and trotted to us with a nicker of welcome. Valgren was dressed in what I thought of as his Gaia attire: soft leather leggings and boots, greenish tunic. A bow and sword were in slings along his back, and various pouches hung from a woven belt.

I was in similar apparel minus the sword. My wand was pretty much my best defence since anything sharper constituted a danger to myself and others.

After greeting the Pegasus, Valgren turned to me. "You'd better ride in front. The sword and bow will be uncomfortable. Besides," he smiled, "I like you there."

I kind of liked me there too so didn't argue. He lifted me onto Moonlight's broad back and sprang up behind, an arm around my waist. At a murmured word, Moonlight galloped across the courtyard. As mighty wings unfurled, he made a final long stride – and we were airborne. He made a tight bank, gained altitude, and we sailed over the castle wall. My fingers were wrapped in his long, silvery mane as I struggled against residual anxiety from a longstanding fear of heights.

Valgren's arm tightened. "You can let go. I've got you."

Just once, I'd like to do something that would blow his doors off. I wanted to be the one sailing in and saving the day. People would say, "Wow! Isn't she great?" Instead of, "It's okay; I'll keep you from falling off a perfectly safe Pegasus." It was embarrassing.

"Thanks," I said, loosening my fingers and changing the subject. "How far is this place?"

"An hour across and one down using time compression."

"Excuse me?"

"You'll see. It's a beautiful flight."

He was right about that. We crossed the south coast of Australia and out over the ocean on a cloudless day. If I remembered my geography correctly, the only thing to anticipate ahead was a lot of ice. Nevertheless, Moonlight's mighty wings continued to stroke until a land mass appeared on the horizon. Of course. Tasmania. I'd forgotten it was even there. Guess it was time to brush up on my geography.

Moonlight tipped a wing and, after a stomach-stopping descent, we skimmed mountainous terrain filled with the musky scent of rain forest. A sharp left brought us to the crystal waters of a river that tumbled from the mountains in terraced increments. Moonlight's powerful wings lifted us over a ridge that was part of a circular wall – an ancient volcano.

The Pegasus dipped, this time to the right, and flew towards an escarpment bordered by trees. We wove through the aromatic canopy, branches whipping past in a blur until we burst from the forest a stone's throw from a jagged opening.

Before I could react, we were winging through a darkening tunnel. I'd had my fill of tunnels recently, so this was a bit of a disappointment.

I'd come to the conclusion Moonlight must have the navigational ability of a bat when I discerned a glow in the distance. Since it intensified as we approached, I wondered if the tunnel walls were covered in the same luminescent moss that Talon, Dorian and I had found in the gnome burrows.

I was wrong. The light came from a cylinder-shaped hole the size of a village that went straight down. As I sucked in a sharp breath at the bottomless hole, Valgren tightened his arm. "It's okay, Raven. Moonlight knows what he's doing."

Our mount began a long, slow spiral that reminded me of a hawk on a summer breeze. We sank . . . and sank . . . and sank. I was dizzy when we reached the bottom where a wide opening appeared in the side. Dipping into it, Moonlight swooped along an ever-brightening cavern.

One second we had stone walls on either side; the next, we were above a sparkling blue lake surrounded by hills and forests. A sun-like ball hung in a greenish sky.

Wow! Who knew?

Valgren's lips touched my ear. "Your mouth is open."

I snapped it closed. It might give you some idea of how astounded I was that I didn't even care. "What . . . what is this place?"

"It's called Winderine. Life forms are different here than on the surface."

"Why are we here?"

"There have been rumours about spyders, so we're here to take a look."

"It's . . . it's stunning!" *You can comprehend how awed I was by the fact that it didn't even register Valgren had said we'd be looking for spyders.*

Trees were more than double normal size; mushrooms were as tall as maple trees, and rose-coloured moss covered the ground in a soft carpet. A band of silver sand encircled the tranquil lake. Birdsongs filled the air as their composers swooped along beside us, curious about the newcomers.

"They can see us."

I felt Valgren's nod. "There's no need to hide. Humans don't come here."

"Nobody's found it by accident?"

"The presence of a human causes camouflage to activate over the entrance. Also, few people climb this far into the mountains."

"It's sad, isn't it?"

"What?"

"Humans are seen as such a scourge. Why are they that way? I've known lots, and they're not evil."

"Individually, they aren't evil. Put them together . . ."

"I wonder why that is."

"Gaia sometimes hints there's an evil energy on the planet that controls humanity. Maybe one day we'll know. The only thing I'm sure of is Gaia wouldn't have humans without a good reason."

I sighed. "I suppose." I seemed to be slipping into philosophizing. That wasn't me, and I didn't want it to be me. I've noticed philosophy makes life complicated, and I'd prefer to enjoy the ride.

The underground world seemed to go on forever. "How big is this?"

"I haven't explored the whole thing. This system consists of networks of country-sized caverns, but there are layers beneath this one, some of which I haven't visited."

That was mind-boggling. "There are things about Gaia you don't know?"

"Lots. I know what I need to know when I need it."

"What if you wanted more?"

"Gaia would tell me if I asked, but I don't need it all in my head since it's always available."

"Your own personal data bank."

"Something like that."

Moonlight descended until his hooves sank into silver sand. Wings folded as he galloped along the shore. As he slowed to a stop, I realized we were beneath a fifty-foot mushroom with darkened irregularities along a thick trunk. Our mount chuffed air through his nostrils then dropped his head to graze.

Valgren vaulted to the ground and reached for me. When I slid into his arms, he lowered his head and kissed me until all that mattered was Valgren. Then he pulled back, flashed his gorgeous white smile, and grabbed my hand. "Come with me!" He reminded me of a child with a secret to share.

The irregularities in the mushroom stem turned out to be doors and windows. He swung open the door and motioned me ahead to a small foyer and spiral of stairs. We ran up the stairwell to an open area with oval doorways along the curved walls. Circular holes in the ceiling were covered by a thin membrane that allowed natural light to filter through.

"This is beautiful, Valgren! Who lives here?"

He stripped off his belt and weapons, and hung them on a hook on the wall. "I do. I made it so I had a place to stay when I was here."

One wall opened to a balcony that overlooked the sparkling clean lake and picturesque mountains in the distance. Butterflies with twelve-inch wingspans explored giant flowers as dozens of colourful songbirds fluttered. Cascades of gigantic blooms hung from the roof, and the aroma of flowers was heavy. I'd never expected such a beautiful place could exist.

"This is absolutely stunning, Valgren! There are no words . . ."

"There's more," he said, taking my hand and leading me through an oval doorway. He stopped inside the room and awaited my reaction.

Flower-covered vines climbed along the walls. A trickle of water flowed from somewhere in the ceiling into stair-stepped cups then through a hole in the floor. The room was dominated by a giant pea pod that had been adapted to become a bed filled with soft, woven blankets. A skylight was centred over it.

"You should hear Gaia's lullaby when she rains onto the skylight," said Valgren.

I couldn't quite smother the pang I felt. "Your women must love it here."

There was silence for a beat. "I wouldn't know."

I looked over my shoulder. "What do you mean?"

"I've never brought anyone here. It's my private retreat, the place I go if I'm injured or exhausted or just want to enjoy Gaia."

I knew for a fact he could be injured, had almost died saving Bluescale – perhaps had. "I didn't know you could get tired."

"It's been known to happen." He watched me, waiting.

I expelled a breath. "I'm sorry, Valgren. My human upbringing reared its ugly head for a minute. I'm okay now."

He stepped towards me, lifted my chin. "It's possible to love without possessing. As a Rider, you will learn this. Don't worry. It'll take time." He gave me a light kiss. "How about a refreshing swim? We'll pick fruit for supper and take a stroll. There are a few other places I'd like to share with you." His lips curved, and he shook his head.

"What?"

"I've never wanted to share this with anyone, yet I find myself anxious for you to like it."

"How could anyone not love it, Valgren? It's wonderful!"

He stroked my hair back. "It seems Gaia was right again."

"What do you mean?"

"Nothing." With a swift motion, he shrugged out of his tunic. "Race you to the lake!"

Chapter 18

The delicious scent of almost-coffee drifted to my nostrils. I pushed back tangled masses of ebony and emerald as Valgren entered the room wearing only leather trousers, honey-streaked hair delightfully mussed.

"Good morning," he said as he perched on the side of the giant peapod and offered a wooden mug. "Not quite coffee, but it's close."

When I noticed his appreciative gaze wander over me, I pulled the sheet up. Now, is that stupid or what?

Valgren laughed, gave me a quick kiss, and wandered to the balcony to gaze at the stupendous view. After a tentative sip, I found it was quite agreeable – a little woodsy but pleasant overall.

"We're going to meet some people this morning," said Valgren. It's a long hike but quite beautiful. You'll enjoy it."

"We can't fly?"

He turned to face me then leaned against the balcony railing, legs crossed at the ankles. "This way we're closer to Gaia."

Note to self: Exercise is healthy. "You're right. I'm getting lazy with all this magic stuff."

"Fortunately, this 'magic stuff' can help you stay healthy without exercise, but I love to explore Gaia."

I threw the blankets off and surged to my feet. "You're right. Let's go."

Valgren's warm green gaze scanned me. "There's no hurry."

***

Sometime later, I followed my companion along a winding footpath. The warble of songbirds and the heady scent of flowers filled the air and, from somewhere, came the gentle gurgle of a stream. Soft loam muffled our passage as I tiptoed past gigantic purple flowers being pollinated by bees the size of hummingbirds.

Maybe flying wasn't such a bad idea after all. Could I even levitate here? I was relieved to find my magic worked as well as it ever did when I lifted a couple of feet.

An hour later, we came upon a rocky outcropping that overlooked a valley. Valgren slid to a sitting position, legs dangled over a two-hundred-foot drop, and pulled out a package wrapped in waxed paper. He broke off a chunk of a thick green substance and handed it to me.

"Gaia's special food. You could live on it." He leaned onto an elbow, bent one knee, and scanned the view as he chewed.

The dark green stuff had the consistency of a soft granola bar and gave off a musky scent. I nibbled at the edge but, like the coffee substitute, it was surprisingly good. Wouldn't want to live on it, but it was good for travelling. "What is this?"

"Blue-green algae. Most perfect food on the planet."

I stopped chewing. "Algae?" He nodded. "Isn't that pond-scum?"

"That's a distant relative."

"How distant?"

He slanted me a look. "Distant enough."

Yes. Trust issues. I had to admit, I did have a few of those – well, a lot of those. But I'd trusted Valgren with my life before and would again.

"Sorry. Habit."

"Bad habit," he said with a curve to his lips.

I bit off a big hunk of the bar and chewed. "Better?"

He smiled and returned his attention to the view of a beautiful valley. A half-hour later as I wondered why we weren't moving on, there was a soft rustle in the bushes. Valgren didn't seem to notice. When it came again, I was about to point it out when he touched a forefinger to his lips.

Branches near the ground swished, and an orange-skinned man who was less than four feet tall stepped onto the path. He wore a loin cloth, a heavy leather necklace, and looked like he was made of rawhide. A woven headband kept thick, orange curls in check, and coal-black eyes stared at me.

"Hello, Jed," said Valgren without turning around.

"You must have eyes in the back of your head, Rider," said the little man in perfect English, eyes still on me.

"She's taken," said Valgren in a mild tone, still without looking.

"Can I borrow her?"

"No."

"Why not?"

"She'd kick the crap out of you."

He straightened to his full height. "She's just a woman!"

Valgren turned to face the newcomer. "You might not want to tell her that."

"Why not? She may be an Amazon, but she's still just a woman."

I could feel pressure build inside my head. So much for wanting to meet the locals.

"I've got things to trade." Jed walked around me in a circle, checking me out as if he were interested in purchasing a new horse.

I didn't want to make enemies of Valgren's friends, but enough was enough. "Keep talking like that, little man, and I'll crush you like a bug!"

His eyes widened. "She doesn't have much for manners."

"Don't say I didn't warn you," said Valgren.

"A wrestling match with her could be fun." He stepped close and ran his fingers over my thigh.

"Don't count on it!" I snarled and, springing like a cougar, kicked his short legs from beneath him. I rolled him onto his belly but, before I could secure a hold, he'd slithered away. I managed to grab an ankle to drag him back but somehow, he landed on top of me. I kicked him over my head, did a back somersault and landed on his chest. Before he could respond, I flipped him over, slammed him onto his belly, and yanked an arm between his shoulder blades. Considering I was more than double his weight, I imagine my knee felt less than pleasant where it ground into his spine.

He howled and squirmed but, when I grabbed him by his leather collar and began to twist, he shrieked for help.

Valgren swallowed the last of his snack and cleaned his fingers on the grass.

"Apologize or we'll find out if you can fly!" I banged the little man's face into the dirt to make my point. The cliff face was a bare six feet away.

"I'll never apologize to a woman!" he yelled, spitting out loam.

"Good. I like option two better anyway!" I grabbed him by the loincloth and wide leather necklace and lifted him like a sack of grain.

"Valgren! Do something! She's crazy!" he choked. It was like trying to hold onto a maddened cat.

"Maybe you should apologize like she asked. By the way, *can* you fly?"

"Okay! Okay! I apologize already!"

"For what?" I grunted as I struggled to keep hold of him. The toes of my left foot were over the cliff edge.

"For anything you want!" he screamed. "I'm sorry you're just a woman!" I twisted his loin cloth. "No! No! I meant . . . I meant, I'm sorry for what I said!"

"So, we're done with this misogynistic crap? I've got a short fuse when it comes to disrespect!"

His head was over the ledge, the whites in his eyes showing as he twisted to catch my eye. "Yes! I'll never do it again!"

I glanced at Valgren who watched with a broad grin. After resisting the temptation to toss him, I dropped the little man onto the path where he landed with a thump. I stuck a finger in his face. "Don't expect leniency from me ever again!"

"Okay! Okay!" He scrambled away and adjusted the loin cloth. "You could've really hurt me, you know!"

"Don't tempt me," I snarled.

"Now that's over with," said Valgren choking back a laugh, why don't I make introductions? Raven, this is Jed, a Tasmanian Giant Pixie. Jed, this is White Raven, a mage from the Americas."

"A mage? I thought she was just your . . ." My blistering scowl brought him up short. "Never mind."

I stared at Jed. "This guy's some kind of giant?"

"Giant pixie," said Valgren.

"That explains the disposition – and I already know one pixie too many!" I turned my attention to Valgren. "Why doesn't he look like Scarlet? And where are his wings?"

"Except for their predisposition to rub people the wrong way, giant pixies are different from Scarlet's people. Jed, for example, can't fly."

"I can make him fly," I growled.

As the pixie edged towards the bushes, Valgren rose. "I need to go with Jed for a bit. There's a nice pool a short walk ahead. I'll meet you there in an hour." And before I could respond, they'd vanished into heavy foliage.

I looked around. So, here I was, alone on what might as well be a strange planet. As a pair of scarlet butterflies with two-foot wingspans fluttered past, I suppressed a squeak of surprise. The last thing I needed was for Valgren to rush back to protect me from butterflies.

Hand on my chest, I inhaled deep breaths. I could to this. The trail was clear. I'd just beaten the dickens out of an admittedly tiny man, but I was pretty tough.

I realized I was once again failing to trust Valgren. He'd never leave me in danger. Then again, Gaia was all one big happy family to him. I'd noticed several less-than-friendly aspects of Gaia that would kill me given half a chance. I sighed, shook dirt from my hair, squared my shoulders, and headed up the trail. Now that I had time to think, the whole incident with Jed was embarrassing. How had I gotten worked up enough to attack a man – especially such a little one? I was a big bully.

I found the pool which was kept filled by a stream that tumbled down a ravine. I swished my fingers in it. Clear and cool. It seemed to be a quiet spot. Maybe I had time for a quick dip. Dirt was working its way into the waistband of my pants, and it would be nice to rinse my hair. I shook my head and a shower of loam flew out. God knew what crawly things could be in it.

I stripped, rinsed my clothing, hung it on branches, and dove into the pool. It wouldn't take long to clean up.

The temperature was perfect. I paddled about, floated on my back, eyes closed, black mane floating about me like a halo. Like most Canadians, I enjoy the warmth of sun on my skin, a rare event in northern climes. Although reluctant to leave the pool, I also didn't want Jed to catch me naked so, with a sigh of regret, I squeezed excess water from my hair and waded towards the edge.

I hoped my clothes had dried a little. Now where had I . . . Son of a . . . My clothes were gone!

I heard a masculine chuckle. A man dressed like Valgren lounged on a flat rock, my clothing hanging from his fingertips. Longish hair was a rich black. Laughing dark eyes sparkled with humour, and perfect teeth gleamed in a broad grin. He appeared to be the exotic product of African and Asian parentage. Wow!

I however, wasn't about to let that get in the way of a good head of steam. How dare he? "You could at least have the decency to look away!"

He shook his head. "Not a chance. It's not every day a man comes across such a wondrous sight."

"Give me my clothes!"

He waggled them on his fingers.

"Why didn't you leave them where they were?"

He raised an eyebrow.

Of course. Stupid question.

"I'll dry them for you," he said. Without waiting for a reply, he ran a hand over them and the dripping water was gone.

Was I the only one who couldn't do that?

I wasn't about to beat the stuffing out of *this* guy. He was tall and strong . . . and I was short on time. Any minute now, Valgren would return, and I'd be naked with three men – one of which was Jed. Although my jaw flexed from grinding my teeth, I realized I had little choice. Actually – none.

I waded from the water with as much dignity as I could muster and tried to ignore his evident pleasure. I took two long strides on the grass, grabbed my clothes, and sent him a glare that should've burned his soul. I heard another chuckle as I stomped behind a tree to dress.

I was tying the strings of my tunic when I heard masculine voices. Peeking around the tree, I saw Valgren embrace the newcomer like a long-lost brother. Even Jed greeted him as an old friend. *Raven behind the eight-ball yet again.* Who the hell was this guy? Realizing I wasn't going to find out by hiding in the bushes, I adjusted my clothing and stepped into the clearing.

Valgren gestured me forward with a broad smile. "Raven, I'd like you to meet a fellow Rider. This is Arwin."

I scowled. "I should've known."

"Should've known, why?"

I returned Arwin's amused chuckle with a stony look. "Remember when you'd changed us from fish back to human form?"

Valgren looked confused at the change of subject. "I do."

"Remember when I asked you to turn your back?"

He grinned. "I remember that well."

"And did you?"

"Of course not! I'd have had to be crazy!"

I gestured towards Arwin. "Meet your twin!"

Valgren gestured between Arwin and me. "You mean he . . . found you bathing?"

"He stole my clothes!"

I don't know what I was expecting. A normal human male would've been pissed, but Valgren threw back his head and laughed. "All Riders appreciate the finer works of Gaia," he chuckled finally. "He can't be faulted for that!"

My mouth dropped open. To say I was flabbergasted would be an understatement but, before I could say a word, Jed burst out, "I knew I shouldn't have left! *I knew it! Knew it! Knew it!*" He stomped his little feet in the dirt.

A target for my rage. In a single motion, I picked him up by his loincloth and threw him screaming into the middle of the pond.

"Raven," soothed Valgren. "Take a breath. You're not in Denver. Arwin was paying you a compliment."

"A compliment? How in hell is that a compliment?"

"Would you rather he turned his back in disgust? He came across a beautiful woman bathing in the woods. It's normal for a man to want to get acquainted."

I sucked in deep breaths trying to process the logic – and, damnit, it did make a certain amount of sense . . . I think. What did I want? Valgren to be jealous? Wasn't this better? Arwin hadn't harmed me. In fact, if I examined the situation without wounded pride, he seemed like a nice guy.

Screams came from the middle of the pond, so I spun to an easier target. Jed bobbed, nose barely above the water. It seemed he could neither fly *nor* swim. "Don't piss me off any further, Jed! You're already on thin ice!"

He raised a hand. "Can I ask a question?"

"Fine! Whatever!" I snarled.

"What is ice?" I turned my back on him.

Valgren stepped close and, as his special aroma enveloped me, I heaved a deep sigh and looked at my feet. "You must think I'm insane."

He tucked a strand of hair behind my ear. "You've a mountain of cultural conditioning to overcome. It's not an easy task to change habitual thoughts and feelings. It may take years."

"Years?" I was mortified at the wail in my voice. "Am I that dense?"

He radiated an infuriatingly understanding Valgren smile. "There's no rush. It's your destiny, and there's all the time in the world."

"Valgren, don't you ever get angry? Are you never upset?"

He shrugged. "There's little to be upset over. Everything always works out in the end."

I turned to Arwin. "Is that true? Things always work out for Riders?"

"We're part of Gaia, so we're always home," he said. "Gaia takes care of us."

"If you're always safe, what about challenges? Aren't you bored?"

They exchanged a look. "We can be hurt, Raven; as you know, even killed," said Valgren, "but Gaia will reform our bodies if she wants. Our . . . essence remains alive. It's immortal as is yours."

"How many times have you died?"

He shrugged as if it didn't matter. "Half-a-dozen or so. It's not the most pleasant experience, so we try to avoid it. Of course, the first time is unsettling."

Unsettling! It was obvious I still lived in a different world than the Riders, and I wasn't convinced I'd ever make the transition.

A voice drifted from behind. "Can I come out now? This is kind of deep."

I remembered Jed was bobbing on his toes to keep his nose out of the water. Valgren made a hand motion, and Jed floated to the path. As his feet touched soft loam, he sidled away. Good. I wanted him afraid of me. Maybe it would teach him some manners.

He peeked from behind Valgren with a worshipful gaze. "I *love* strong women!"

Then again, he was a pixie. "We're leaving him here, right?" I inclined my head towards Jed.

"Communications with the locals will go better if Jed introduces us. Everyone knows him," said Valgren.

"Bet they don't like him."

Jed straightened to his almost four feet. "Everybody loves pixies! I'll grow on you, wait and see!"

"Like a fungus," I snarled. I turned to Valgren and Arwin. "Why are we here?"

"There are reports of spyders in the area," said Arwin. "Nothing definite, but enough to warrant a look."

I recalled Valgren saying something similar which, for some insane reason, I'd ignored. My voice might've wavered. "Spyders?"

"These are bigger and more aggressive than the ones you witnessed."

"So . . . *worse* than the spyders I've already met?"

"Arwin and I'll be there, Raven," said Valgren. "We'll keep you safe."

And there I was again – in need of protection. How girlie can you get?

Jed looked insulted. "I'll be there too!"

"Of course, Jed," said Valgren. "I'm sure we can count on you."

I was pretty sure of what I could count on from Jed, and it had nothing to do with fighting spyders. I rolled my eyes at Jed's puffed up "I-told-you-so" look.

"We should get going," said Arwin.

We settled into single file, Arwin in the lead. Valgren was behind me followed by Jed. We followed a stream that danced over coloured rocks and, after an hour's hike, the trail dropped into a verdant valley.

The surface of the Earth has nothing to compare with the stupendous beauty of that place. It was breathtaking. Flowers were everywhere. They hung from trees, peeked from beneath rocks, and covered hillsides. Small fuzzy creatures stirred blossoms as they passed along invisible paths beneath a floral ceiling. Crystal streams tumbled over sharp rocks to create waterfalls that disappeared into greenery far below, and the gentle breeze smelled like a flower shop on Mother's Day.

I was gaping like a tourist when Arwin came to such an abrupt stop, I rammed into him. As I apologized and stepped away, he gave me an amused glance and smiled. "No problem."

We stood in silence for long enough that I started shifting from foot-to-foot. I was about to ask what we were waiting for when the trees rustled.

"Briar!" yelled Jed. "Come on down! The giants won't hurt you . . . well . . . maybe keep away from the female!"

With a start, I perceived a wizened man with pale blue skin was perched on a branch. He skittered down the tree and trotted over to Jed who puffed with self-importance as he performed introductions. The newcomer, dressed in a loose tunic of woven material, was taller than Jed but didn't reach my shoulder. He had a pointed chin, sharp cheekbones, and pale fuzz covered a triangular head. I noticed neither Jed nor Briar carried weapons. Must be a safe environment but, if spyders moved in, it wouldn't be safe for long.

Briar was a member of a tribe of fays. Shy creatures who preferred their own company, they were seldom seen even by Riders. It made me wonder if the fairy tales my mother read to me as a child had some basis in fact.

I felt eyes on me and noticed Briar watched me from the corner of his eye. I must have looked enormous.

Jed punched him on the shoulder. "Pay attention, Briar! There's work to do!"

Sadly, I believe the little man was jealous.

Valgren and Arwin squatted to be at eye-level with the diminutive men. Spyders had been seen farther up the valley, and Briar had been selected to guide us to the last known sighting.

After two hours of following the fay, I wondered why we weren't flying but kept quiet because I didn't want to sound like a whiner. As we approached a cliff edge that overlooked a swamp, Briar pointed to the far side. The sighting had been near a cave over there. Arwin levitated to check it out while Valgren and I waited with the others. If it was safe, we'd transport our guides.

As I sank onto a rock to rest, Jed planted himself next to me.

I rolled my eyes towards him. "You still can't fly, Jed."

With a glance at the cliff edge, he scuttled away to join Briar. As Valgren took Jed's place, I slid over to make room for him. "Is it really possible for spyders to invade this beautiful land?"

"It's possible for spyders to invade any part of Gaia. Myrador and Mydryth know her weak points."

"At least Mydryth's out of the way. If we could get Myrador to join his brother . . ."

"That would simplify things, but spyders are dangerous on their own without anyone's help."

I noticed our diminutive companions kept glancing at me. Valgren leaned close and whispered, "Would you like help with Jed? He's never seen such a beautiful giantess."

"Are you going to beat him?" Hopeful.

"Something better." He smiled, and forest scents enveloped me as inviting lips lowered to mine. As always, time stood still and, in seconds, I'd forgotten all about our audience. Sometime later, the warm softness pulled away, and I opened my eyes. He ran the tip of a finger over my lips and smiled. "That was nice."

Nice? I'd melted into a puddle!

"Hey!" A rude little voice I was beginning to resent almost as much as Scarlet's broke into our interlude. "What's going on here?"

Valgren answered without taking his eyes from mine. "I should think that would be obvious, Jed."

"Well . . . well . . ."

"She's taken, Jed. Find your own woman."

"Everybody knows Riders don't take *a* woman!" Accent on the singular.

"Things change." He kept his eyes locked on mine.

Jed and Briar went into hysterical paroxysms of laughter, their shrill cackling like nails on chalkboard. "Good one, Valgren!" choked Jed. "Good one!" They punched one another and rolled on the ground in a paroxysm of mirth.

As the idea of shoving them both off the cliff gained in appeal, Valgren gave me an unconcerned smile. Guess there was no point in trying to change fays and pixies into something else.

Ten minutes later, Valgren stood at the edge of the cliff and scanned the far side of the swamp. As he tipped his head, I could tell he was listening to Arwin. He nodded a couple of times then turned to us.

"We can go. I'll carry Briar since he's heavier."

I blanched. "You expect me to carry this . . . this . . . chauvinist *pig*?!"

"Only way to get over the swamp. You can behave for that long, right, Jed?"

Jed looked like he'd won the lottery. He bounced around on his toes, white grin flashing. As Briar climbed onto Valgren's back, I shot Jed a threatening scowl then scrunched down. He scuttled behind me and, in seconds, strong arms and legs clamp on. I hadn't piggy-backed anyone in years.

I scowled at Valgren. "Let's get this over with!"

As we levitated, I flattened to a horizontal position hoping Jed would sit up straight. No such luck. He was plastered to me like a second shirt. As we floated off the cliff edge and over the valley, he clamped tighter.

"Jed!" I choked, "I need to breathe!"

"Oh. Sorry." I sucked in a deep breath – which was good because I needed it to scream.

"Get your hands out of my shirt, Jed, or I'll rip your arms off!"

Groping hands slid away.

"What am I supposed to hang onto?" he whined. "There's only your neck or your . . ."

"Don't even think about it," I snarled. "Sit up and hang onto the collar of my shirt. Other than that, touch nothing!"

Things went well until I felt exploring fingers on my derriere. I dropped my shoulder, and Jed fell screaming into space. Before he hit the ground, I grabbed him by an ankle and jerked him skyward.

"We could've done this the easy way," I growled, "but no, you can't keep your hands to yourself. Well, this is 'Plan B'. Enjoy the flight!"

Jed's arms and his other leg wind-milled, and he continued to squeal as we floated over the marsh. Valgren deposited Briar and, seconds later, I dropped Jed in an ignominious heap on the ground.

He scowled as he scrambled erect. "You could've hurt me, you know!"

"Good! Keep your hands to yourself!"

Valgren stepped over to Jed, grabbed him by the loincloth, and lifted him with one arm until they were eye-to-eye. "Remember what I said about Raven?" His voice was dangerously soft.

Jed looked worried. He nodded.

"You disrespect her again, and you'll deal with me." The force of the words, though quiet, were like blows.

Wow! He *could* get agitated!

"I won't. I promise." Jed's obsequious smile looked strained.

Valgren held him a minute longer to ensure the message sank in before lowering him to the ground. As Briar watched the exchange from a safe distance, I got the feeling the harassment was over.

Thank you, Valgren. But why do guys need another guy to clue them in? A woman demanding respect was seen as a come-on. It was evident I'd have to get a lot meaner.

Valgren motioned to a faint trail I hadn't noticed. "Briar, you lead. I'll bring up the rear. Should be less than five minutes."

He was right. A few twists of the trail and there was Arwin perched on a rock in front of a cave. He slipped to the ground. "I'm pretty sure there are spyders in this cave. Something feels off."

My skin crawled at the memory of the creatures. And these were bigger than what I'd experienced. According to

Arwin, they were six feet long and strong enough to pick up a man.

"So . . . do you need somebody to keep watch at the tunnel entrance?" I asked. Ever hopeful.

Arwin's glance held a hint of humour. "The spyders are in the tunnels," he said, "not out here."

"Ah . . . so you're saying you don't need a guard?" He beamed a full-on smile and shook his head. He knew exactly what I'd been trying to do. Damn!

Chapter 19

"Briar," said Arwin, "can you show us where the spyders were?"

Briar's pale blue face paled further. "I'll take you close enough to find them." He straightened, gave an audible swallow, and marched into the dimness.

We trundled along behind and, as natural light faded, Valgren and Arwin manifested glow-spheres. I was memorizing turns when Arwin halted. This time I was prepared and screeched to a halt (metaphorically speaking) a couple of inches from his back. At his downward gesture, we all froze.

The back of my neck itched as my hair stood up, and an involuntary shiver rippled through me. Supernatural terror hovered at the edges of my self-control as images of being shrink-wrapped by giant spyders flashed to my inner sight.

My subconscious communicated with terrifying clarity what it thought of my current situation, pointing out how stupid I must be to put myself in such a position – *again*. I imagine it was disappointed in me and about to file for a transfer.

The abrupt pitter-patter of tiny feet faded towards the entrance. It seemed Briar had resigned. The whites of Jed's eyes were almost luminous in the light of the glow-spheres, but he held his position. For a long while, nothing moved except twin trickles of sweat: one down my back, the other between my breasts. Was that a skittering sound? The scrape of a fallen stone?

As Valgren and Arwin extended the diameters of the light-spheres, I had to bite my lip to keep from screaming as countless reflective eyes, four to a set, stared from the blackness.

"So," murmured Valgren. "Seems the reports are true. That's unfortunate."

As if on cue, there was a loud scuttling . . . and the eerie eyes charged.

***

Someone screamed as the Riders made circular motions, palms out, and a solid translucent sphere enclosed us. In seconds, dozens of hairy claws were all over it, and gigantic eyes peered in from less than an arm's length way.

Valgren pushed my face into his chest. "It's okay, Raven. They can't get in. We want to observe them."

Since the screaming stopped, I admit it might've been me. When I'd gathered enough courage, I peeked at a sticky liquid that ran along the surface of the sphere. "What's that?" I barely recognized my voice.

"Sure you want to know?" asked Valgren. At my nod, he said, "It's acid. It paralyzes then dissolves its prey."

Already sick with fear, this tidbit didn't help.

Valgren and Arwin concentrated on the activity of the spyders. The sphere rolled a bit from time to time as the spyders pushed against it, but the Riders were undisturbed. Perhaps I was overreacting. I peered again at the spyders trying to get at us. Nope! Definitely not! If anything, I was holding together fairly well.

"Raven! Where are you?"

I nearly jumped through the top of the sphere. *"Bluescale?"*

"Have you gone deaf, girl? I need to follow your thoughts. Speak up!"

"What are you doing, and where are you?"

"Valgren sent a message that you guys needed me, but I can't get a fix on his position. Says you're with him."

"Unfortunately."

"Hear you have an infestation."

"To put it mildly." I peeked at the acid that ran along the sphere, smeared by hairy, sticky feet, and reburied my face in Valgren's chest. *"We're in a cave filled with giant spyders. Are you close?"*

"Not far. I see the cave entrance. Let Valgren know I'm coming in. Gonna get hot in there! Better get behind something!"

I relayed the message and had a bit of a hissy fit that Valgren hadn't informed me he'd called Bluescale.

"I told you we'd be fine," he said with maddening assurance. "I wouldn't put you in danger, Raven." He nodded at Arwin who watched us. "Dragon's on his way in. Better shore it up."

In seconds, the sphere thickened until the spyders were grey shadows.

It'll give you some idea of how distracted I was that I never noticed Jed was wrapped around my leg. He said later it had been to protect me. Right.

I felt a dull reverberation followed by a brilliant orange flare. I wasn't happy with being on the receiving end of Bluescale's jet-propelled flames but, at the high-pitched screeches of incinerating spyders, my fear diminished. And, yes, I had zero compassion for the creatures considering what they'd had planned for me.

A huge shadow that emitted flares of light passed us and continued down the tunnel. I assumed it was Bluescale having a blast (no pun intended). Hunting was his favourite pursuit. Normally, I didn't like to think about that but, today, I hoped he got every last one of them.

When silence returned, I asked if we could vacate the tunnel. Valgren pointed out the flames would've used up all the oxygen. *Of course.* We had two choices. Stone-walk or wait for the air to freshen. Arwin hoisted Jed onto his back, the sphere collapsed, and we stepped into the coolness of the underground where at least there weren't any spyders.

When we emerged beside the tunnel entrance, I sucked in huge amounts of fresh air and brushed imaginary spyders from my arms. "My god, that was creepy! I'll have nightmares for a month!"

Valgren put an arm around me. "I can help with that."

No doubt.

A sliding sound preceded the emergence of Bluescale. Covered with soot and dirt, a wide grin stretched his snout, and smoke drifted from his nostrils. As he gave a mighty shake, I ducked away from the cascade of dust.

Jed stepped from behind Arwin, eyes as big as saucers. Guess he'd never seen a real live dragon before.

Bluescale caught sight of him and spun around until he was nose-to-nose with the little man. I think the only reason Jed didn't move was that he was paralyzed with fear.

"Raven!" burst Bluescale. "You shouldn't have! You brought me a snack!"

If Jed hadn't been orange, he'd have blanched pure white. Instead he turned a sickly beige.

Without missing a beat, I said, "Thought you might be hungry after all that killing."

Big green eyes rolled over at me. "Can I really eat him?"

I pasted on a thoughtful look. "What do you think, Jed? I might not be able to stop him. After all, I'm just a woman, and he's a fully-grown dragon. He might not listen to me."

Jed spun to Valgren and Arwin. "Can't you guys control her?"

"Wrong answer, Jed," I said, and walked away.

Both Riders crossed their arms in silence. Bluescale licked his snout then sniffed at Jed as a dog would a special treat before wolfing it down.

When Jed realized the Riders weren't going to rescue him, he screamed, "No! No! No! I'll do anything you want! Call him off! Call him off!"

I turned around. "You think a mere *woman* can control a dragon?"

"Yes! I believe you!"

I watched him with narrowed eyes. "I might consider letting you live on one condition."

"Anything!"

"If you ever touch me again, my friend Bluescale will come back to collect on his snack. Do you understand?"

"Okay! It's a deal! It's not like you're so special anyway!"

I felt like slamming my head against a tree.

"Well?" asked Bluescale, tongue lolling in hope.

"Sorry, buddy. You'll have to settle for fish. Probably tastes better anyway. Jed looks kind of stringy."

The dragon swung his nose close to Jed and sniffed as if inspecting food. "Preheating would fix that – long, slow roast."

Ugh! I couldn't continue. "Forget it, Bluescale. You're not eating people – even someone as disgusting as Jed."

"I'm hurt you'd lead me on like that," grumped Bluescale. Then he smacked his lips. "You've made me hungry."

I gestured to a nearby lake. "Have some fish. We'll wait."

"Good idea!" He leaped into the air with a mighty blast of wings. "Hope there's trout!"

Arwin propped a foot on a log, forearm on his knee then looked at Valgren. "I'll pass on the spyder info to the other Riders. You staying around?"

Valgren nodded towards the lake where Bluescale was having a great time diving. "We'll stay a day or two then take the dragon back with us."

Arwin and Valgren conversed about their work, and I was relieved when Jed recovered from his fright enough to join them. I sat on a log, enjoyed the stunning panorama, and watched Bluescale's antics. When he returned twenty minutes later, scales glistening, he gave a violent shake. I sucked in a breath and shot him a glare. It wouldn't occur to him to do it where he wouldn't soak the rest of us.

Oblivious to my ire, he crouched beside me. "Ready to go?"

He reminded me of a dog who'd been promised a walk. All he needed to complete the image was a leash dangling from his mouth.

The Riders still chatted nearby but, with Bluescale's return, Jed eased to the edge of the forest where he kept an eye on the dragon. I glanced back at the Riders in time to see Arwin clap Valgren on the shoulder in a friendly fashion, send me a wave and a suggestive wink then fade into the forest. I wondered if all Riders were so . . . you know. If I was a Rider like Valgren suggested then maybe that was why I was so . . . never mind.

"Jed," said Valgren. He gestured towards Bluescale. "Would you like a ride home?" He levitated to Bluescale's back to settle between the rows of backplates.

Bluescale eyed the pixie with a wide grin. "Can I consider him take-out?"

"What's a take-out?" asked Jed with a cautious look at the dragon's gigantic canines.

"It means you should walk home," I said. "It's a nice day."

Jed looked confused. "It's always a nice day. They're all the same."

"Lucky you," I said. "There are places where Gaia is less than kind; places where this breeze gets strong enough to rip trees from the ground."

As Jed went into a paroxysm of laughter, I maintained an unwavering gaze. His laugh reduced to a weak cough. "You're kidding, right?"

"Are you coming, Jed?" I levitated to the dragon's back.

Jed scanned Bluescale again. "I . . . think I'll walk. There's a trail around the swamp."

"Good choice." As I settled against Valgren's chest, Bluescale gave a tremendous flap of his wings, and we were airborne.

As I watched the wondrous scenery, a niggling thought kept interfering with my enjoyment. Finally, I squirmed around to face Valgren. "So, what was all that stuff with Jed? I thought Riders didn't get jealous or possessive."

His lips quirked at the ends. "You mean when I told Jed you were taken?" At my nod, he said, "In order to communicate, people have to be at a similar level of understanding. Jed's comprehension of male/female relationships is that women could not, in any way, be equal to men. In his world, that isn't a belief; it's a fact."

I may have curled my lip. "Is that's why he's such an ass?"

Valgren's smile broadened into a grin. "Your point of view is broader than his. You've been exposed to different cultures and ideas through direct experience, books, movies – even your time in other magical realms."

I raised my brows. "So, his behavior towards me is acceptable because he doesn't believe I'm his equal?"

"It's not acceptable, Raven, which is why, after he'd taken liberties with you, I needed to dominate him. At his emotional maturity level, he understands the force of a stronger male. To him, females are property. Once he saw you were protected by a powerful male, he backed off."

"Christ! That's so . . . infantile!"

"In North America, men owned the bodies of their wives until the mid-twentieth century. Women were property to be used and abused as they saw fit." He took my hands. "You can't break through belief systems using facts. Beliefs are entrenched through emotion. Those types of concepts don't change unless shattered by an upset strong enough to break the emotional bonds that support the belief. If the suffering is sufficient, a new concept might replace the old."

I gazed steadily into his eyes. "So, you're saying you weren't serious. You weren't really jealous?"

Valgren squeezed my hands gently. "I'm saying I had to go to Jed's level of understanding to get him to respect you.

Since he's incapable of coming to our level, I had to go to his. I could only do that by dominating him. Do you understand?"

I was chagrined to realize a part of me had wanted Valgen to feel possessive of me. Perhaps I had more in common with Jed's emotional maturity than I'd thought. Yikes!

"Thanks, Valgren," I said. "That makes sense. I get it now." Then I turned away to face the front. As I leaned against his chest, I hoped he didn't feel my deep sigh.

Chapter 20

I suppressed a jaw-cracking yawn. It had occurred to me on more than one occasion that magical people got up far too early. I'd like to know who wrote the rule that says you can't sleep until you wake up. I suspect a streak of masochism in people with this unnatural urge to leap wildly out of bed in the morning. It can't be normal.

"Tired, Raven?" asked Dorian. He was leaned against a corner of Angus' desk.

My eyes watered as I stifled yet another yawn. "What makes you think that?"

Valgren's hand rested on my shoulder. "Hunting spyders has entailed some short nights over the past few days."

Dorian's fleeting scowl made it clear he wasn't interested in hearing about my nights with Valgren.

As an awkward silence threatened, Angus cleared his throat. Cash's bench creaked as he shifted his bulk and Frost, colour-coded for the day, lounged in feminine perfection. Talon was perched on an owl statue whose brass eyes, visible between prehensile toes, looked worried. I know I'd have been concerned if I were in that position – and you never could tell with these statues. Maybe they were bewitched animals or . . . I don't know. In the world of magic, it's difficult to tell if an idea is ridiculous or not.

With a warm squeeze of my shoulder, Valgren rose and strode to one side so everyone could see him. As he outlined our experience in the underworld, I was relieved that he omitted my less-than-professional response to being surrounded by spyders. I pride myself on not being a screamer, but there are limits, and spyders are mine.

"Do you think pig men are connected with these spyders?" asked Dorian.

Valgren shrugged. "Hard to tell. I didn't get a sense of them at the time, but that doesn't mean they aren't involved. They're persistent little swine."

At memories of Napoleon's foul breath, I curled my legs beneath me in an instinctive effort at self-protection. Sin, who'd been asleep on my lap, shot me a glower and snarled a complaint. Irritation in every line of his corpulent body, he made a few circles, found a new position, and settled again. As he started rhythmically extending claws into my leg, I decided I'd had enough so pushed him to the floor where he landed with a thump.

In an attempt to assuage an unfair sense of guilt, I scowled at him. "What's the matter with you? Aren't cats supposed to land on their feet?"

Sin raised his lip in a suspiciously human expression then turned and stalked away, tail straight in the air. Perhaps cat language for, "kiss my . . ."

". . . so, I'd like Raven to come with me."

What? Everyone stared at me. Crap! What had I missed now? I cleared my throat. "Sorry, Dorian. Could you repeat that?"

His half-smile might've carried a smidgeon of impatience. "How far back would you like me to go?"

"Umm, after the 'persistent little swine' would be good."

He crossed his arms. "I'd like you to accompany me on a tour of Altaria. Our overly-developed sense of self-preservation could be helpful."

"*Self-preservation!* What the hell are we looking for?!"

"We know the pig men and Myrador have been in the Caves of Cynbel."

I grimaced at the memory. "No shit!"

"I want to make a full sweep of Altaria to clear out any footholds. I have soldiers looking, but they don't have the same sensitivity you and I do. Even the scrying equipment at the castle isn't foolproof."

I swallowed hard. "How long do you think it'll take?"

He shrugged. "Might be a day; at most a week." His lips quirked. "Do you have someplace else to be?"

Good question. Too bad I didn't have a good answer.

"Umm . . . uh . . ." I adjusted my position. Some might have said I squirmed.

Valgren glanced at Dorian and then at me. "Arwin and I are following up with the spyders, so I'll be gone about a month." He turned to me. "I was going to tell you after the planning session."

I heard myself asking if he could use my help before I realized how ridiculous that was – as if I could do anything he couldn't.

"Where we're going is dangerous. I wouldn't want you with me until your skills are on par with mine," he said. "It's a good time to help King Dorian."

So, Valgren was comfortable with me spending time with Dorian while he was away. Guess I still hadn't wrapped my head around the Gaia attitude. Dorian sent me a questioning glance.

"Umm . . . sure . . . I guess."

"Your excitement is underwhelming," he said with a dry smile. "If it scares you, I can do it alone."

"It's not that . . ." I trailed off.

His lips quirked. "Then what?"

Images of Dorian and me alone caused the initial stages of a panic attack. "Umm . . . yea. I guess that's it. The place scares the crap out of me."

"For good reason."

"I . . . I'll be fine. Of course, I'll come."

Angus cleared his throat. "Cumulos is back te normal, so let us know what ye need."

"I appreciate all you've done for Altaria," said Dorian. "We should be able to deal with it ourselves but, if it gets more than we can handle, I'll call."

I was startled by the sudden growl of a mistimed engine, but it was Cash starting to speak. "I'll come," he rumbled. "Could do with some pork in the cold box."

Now, here's the difference between Cash and me. Although I despised Napoleon, I wasn't about to start eating pig men. Not above *threatening* them, eating was never going to happen. Even the idea was nauseating.

Dorian told Cash he wanted to do some reconnaissance before calling on the huge soldier. The conversation continued for another half-hour, but everything had been pretty much covered by then.

Afterwards, Valgren and I stood on the walkway that surrounded one of the Cumulos Castle towers. The view was stupendous. Songbirds dipped and dove in the flower-scented air as sunbeams refracted into a myriad of rainbows.

"How do you do it?" I asked.

"Do what?" Valgren turned to meet my gaze.

"How do you leave so easily?"

He stroked my cheek. "What makes you think it's easy?"

"Well . . . you're always so calm about everything."

"That doesn't mean I won't miss you. But there's something you don't yet understand about Gaia. As long as you and

I are part of her, we're never separated. We're connected through her."

"Why can't I feel it?"

"You will. It'll take time." A speck appeared in the distance. "Here comes Moonlight." Valgren turned to me, threaded fingers through my hair, and lowered his mouth to mine. As my heart defied the laws of biology and stopped beating, I felt as if I'd been transported to some heavenly dimension.

"Raven?"

"Hmm?"

"Are you okay?"

I opened my eyes to see Valgren's moss-green gaze inches from mine. I swear I'd been turned to rubber.

"Umm . . . yeah . . . Wow! Valgren, how do you do that?"

He smiled and stroked my hair. "*We* do that," he said. Then he stepped back, leaned against the parapet, and hooked his thumbs into his pockets. "You're worried your relationship with King Dorian will compromise what we have."

I looked into the distance. "How can it not?"

"Your heart will make a decision in time, Raven. There's no rush. You cannot determine the depth of your feelings for Dorian if you don't explore them."

I looked back at him. "But doesn't that make me . . .?"

"You're never lessened by real love. What you feel for Dorian isn't lust, Raven. You have deep feelings for the man which you need to investigate. If you don't, you'll always be unsure. Any decision you make will be a guess." He looked away then back at me. "Would it surprise you to know Dorian and I have talked?"

The birds stopped singing and the breeze stilled. At least that's what it felt like. "What? You mean, about me?"

"I felt it was important that he have all the facts and that I understood his feelings towards you. Magic is controlled by feelings. Emotions direct and determine the intensity of energy. I needed to know how he felt – if he was possessive towards you. Those kinds of feelings would impact the clarity of mind you need to do Rider magic."

"And umm . . . how *does* he feel?"

I received an enigmatic smile instead of an answer. "People from the Americas are used to mutual pairing. When children are involved, this is a good idea. Even in Altaria, Dorian will be expected to take a mate to ensure the continuation of the Royal lineage."

I felt a panic-attack in the offing. That these two men were having a casual conversation about my life was disturbing, to say the least. I didn't know whether to be scared or mad. "I don't think I'm in any danger of Dorian asking me to be his queen. I have no royal lineage."

"Actually, you do. I explained it to Dorian so he could include it in his deliberations."

Looked like "mad" was the winner. "What are you talking about, Valgren? You know about my lineage? You'd tell Dorian about it, but you won't tell me? What the hell is that about? Goddamn it, Valgren!"

Unruffled, he continued. "It became important to know, so I asked Gaia. Any decision you make about your future has to be honest. If you knew your background, it would influence your choices. Dorian may ask you to be his queen, but that choice will have consequences that will limit your growth as a Rider for many years." He moved closer until I had to look up. Hands on my shoulders, he said, "There's a part of me that wants to keep you to myself, but I'd never do that to you. If you choose to follow the path of a Rider at this time, know that it will remove Dorian from your life as a mate. You need to understand that."

"Why can't I do both?"

"As a Rider, Gaia becomes such a part of you, she replaces the companionship needs for a mate. You'd then be unlikely to fulfill the emotional requirements of a wife."

"So, when we make love, it would be just the same for you if it was someone else?"

"No, Raven, it wouldn't but, because I'm linked with Gaia, I am complete in myself as you will be in time. For a Rider, relationships are chosen for personal growth and delight in another's company. I'll never *need* you, but I *desire* you.

"A relationship with Dorian would be based to a degree on mutual need. You may find that is enough for you. A great life . . . children." He stroked my cheek. "I am Gaia. Dorian is a king. There's a huge difference between who we are, and this is critical for you to understand. You're not choosing between two men, you're choosing between two lives. One of us knows where you've been; the other knows what you can accomplish.

It's not just about which of us you're more attracted to. This is about your life path. Don't let guilt interfere. Take your time." He gave me a light kiss. "Gaia is timeless."

Then he stepped onto the narrow rampart, flexed his knees, and leaped into space as Moonlight made an aerial turn that brushed his wing feathers against the castle wall. With perfect timing, Valgren landed astride, waved once and, in seconds, they dwindled into a clear sky.

Gaia is timeless. Explore your feelings for Dorian. The world of magic was indeed a strange place.

At that point, I experienced my first real concern about my ability to adapt.

Chapter 21

"I'm not going anywhere near those caves without an army! You didn't say we were going alone!"

"Raven," he sighed, "Scarlet will be there."

"Dorian, have you noticed she's ten inches tall?"

"That means she can get into small spaces and hide almost anywhere, so it'll be easier for her to get close to Napoleon and his cohorts. I don't imagine you want to try stone-walking there again."

My frantic flight through the bowels of the mountain flashed into memory – along with the searing pain of snake-light.

"Not anytime soon."

Dorian stopped pacing across the patterned rug centred in the Odenai castle planning room. "I won't force you, Raven, but you're the only one who's been to Myrador's headquarters in the caves. I have a better chance of finding him if you guide me."

"Why only the three of us? You command an army!"

"This is a reconnaissance mission. We get in, see what's going on, and we get out."

"Can't soldiers do that? They invented the word, for crissake!"

"Few in the military have much in the way of magic. If they did, they wouldn't be soldiers. They don't stand a chance against Myrador, and I won't ask any of my men to do that."

There was that "king" thing again.

"What about the scrying room? There's all kinds of stuff in there. Surely some of it could find Myrador!"

Dorian crossed his arms and rested a hip on a corner of the heavy meeting table. "The only way to know for sure if Myrador is still in the caves is to go there. I won't tolerate someone like that on Altaria, nor will I allow the pig men to stay."

I was running out of arguments – good ones anyway. Dorian knew me well enough to spot a weakness so pressed the advantage.

"How about a couple of hours tomorrow afternoon?"

"Do we have to take Scarlet?"

His gaze became steady and intense. "There's only one reason I'd consider good enough to leave her behind."

I'm embarrassed to admit it took a moment for that to sink in. When it did, I flushed and rolled my eyes. "Okay, she comes."

"It's settled then. Tomorrow after lunch." At my nod, Dorian gave me a wide smile. "It'll be just like old times."

I managed a fake one. "Just like."

***

A distant hawk emitted shrill cries as, lifted by updrafts, it scribed a circular pattern. The sharp scent of pine resin filled the air as treetops scraped my toes. Dorian and I hovered at the mouth of the valley that lead to the Caves of Cynbel where, in my imagination, I saw a dark mist above the black slash in the ground. I squinted. Maybe it wasn't imagination. There was a smudge over the area.

"What are we waiting for?" An irritating voice piped from my left front pocket.

"Easy with the feet, Scarlet," I said. "If you give me a bruise, you'll be flying on your own."

"I'd ride with King Dorian, but he feels it's inappropriate for a king to carry a woman on his person."

"Yea, that's it," I said with a scowl at the king. He seemed busy as he scanned the terrain, but I saw the ends of his lips curl up.

"I think it's inappropriate to sit on another woman's breast, you know," she complained.

"I agree. You should get off."

The ensuing silence confirmed I'd scored a hit. I was enjoying my success when Dorian moved over a cliff edge to float above a narrow canyon. Crap! I did not want to do this!

As little feet pushed into my breast, an annoying voice resumed. "Are you waiting for the mountain to come to you?"

"Scarlet, if you don't shut up, I swear I'll feed you to Sin when we get back."

"He's not fast enough to catch me."

"I'll help him!"

Dorian stopped his broom and turned to face us. "Do you think you two could put a cork in it? We need to focus." He gestured to me. "I need your knowledge of the terrain. I've got a sniffer for the gasses, but you'll know where you dropped out of the sky."

I could've kicked myself. Sucked in by pixie manipulation again! When would I learn? "Sorry, Dorian. I should know by now not to let Scarlet bait me."

"What do you mean, *I* baited *you*?"

"Scarlet," said Dorian, "Altaria can't afford to lose her new king so soon. This isn't about you and Raven, it's about the nation."

Scarlet and I exchanged an uneasy glance. Dorian was right. We must've sounded like a couple of squabbling children. I took a deep breath. "You're right, Dorian. Scarlet, I apologize for my remarks."

Her big green eyes rolled my way as she wrestled with something internal. Finally, she said, "Thank you," and turned her nose away.

I gave my head a shake to release the steam beginning to build and caught Dorian's eye. "I'm ready," I said, unlocking my jaw.

He glanced at Scarlet then back at me as his eyes crinkled with a half-smile. "If we hug the valley wall, the breeze will move the gasses ahead. That should make it possible for us to access the labyrinth without being poisoned. From there, we use the tracking compass to find Myrador."

"You think Napoleon's with him?"

"With the pig's inflated ego, he'll stay close to the man in power."

"I agree," I said. "So, how do we hide from Myrador?"

"My father's mages . . . *my* mages, modified an invisibility spell for us. The problem is we can't use much magic if we want to stay hidden. That's another reason to have Scarlet along. She flies without it."

"What about our brooms?"

"Broom magic is all over the place. They don't identify as belonging to a single person, and it would take enormous manpower to check them all. We should be okay to use them."

I tried to concentrate, but the black gash in the earth made me feel wobbly.

Dorian glanced at a palm-sized device in his hand. "We still have a hundred yards to go."

I inhaled deep, steading breaths, and imagined pure oxygen filling my lungs.

"Hey! You're squishing me!"

"Sorry, Scarlet. I'm attempting not to faint."

"Try not to fall on me if you do."

As blood rushed to my face, I no longer felt dizzy. Guess anger had its uses.

As the jagged black slash expanded, I experienced a familiar sensation. So much for thinking I'd mastered vertigo. Dorian edged further over the abyss then worked his way back and forth searching for an entry point. Realizing I'd look silly if I didn't follow, I moved my broom over the black pit where an ever-fertile imagination produced dozens of clutching hands that reached for my dangling feet.

"You're going to have to get closer than that."

"What?"

Dorian stared up at me from fifty feet below. How had I gotten up there? "Oh. Sorry."

Ten minutes later, Dorian gave a satisfied grunt and pointed to a jagged hole that looked to me like all the rest.

"That looks deep. Let's try it." And he dropped from sight.

As my broom moved in an agitated motion, I realized my fingers were practically leaving imprints in the wood. I sucked in a breath and dropped into the dimness, visions of snake-light lighting my way. *Just keep breathing, Raven. Breathe in; breathe out; breathe in . . .*

My feet touched black sand. Faint light from Dorian's wand illuminated the immediate vicinity, and the overwhelming odour of minerals caused my saliva glands to activate. I swallowed. Perhaps we were in the spa cavern into which I'd crashed but, more likely, there was a chain of them. We moved east until our cavern narrowed.

Dorian extracted a brass compass from a woven bag which hung from his belt. Larger than a regular compass, it had more dials, some of which spun. When my eyes began to cross from staring at it, I gave up. "What does it say?"

Scarlet fluttered from my pocket to perch on Dorian's shoulder. "The compass can be set to find whatever you're looking for." She pointed a tiny finger. "The outer ring is Myrador. See the mage figure?"

Mage figure? I looked closer. Indeed, there was an image of a tiny mage in a hooded robe.

"The next level is Napoleon and his soldiers. See the pig tracks around the ring?"

Hunh. Why hadn't I noticed that? They were clear as day – well, clear enough considering we were in a dark cave. The compass produced a dim glow, just enough to read it.

"Okay," I said. "Same question. What does it mean?"

"If both rings rotate, it means both Myrador and the pig men are here," said Dorian. "You were correct about them being to the east. We're close."

As my personal antennae shot to high alert, I grabbed his arm and squeezed against him. "Kinda *dark* in here, isn't it?"

He slanted a look at me. "Scared, Raven?"

I made an attempt at bravado, but my voice had a definite squeak. "What makes you think that?"

"You're cutting off the blood to my hand."

"Oh. Sorry. I just . . . I'd rather not be close to Myrador."

"Hush!" Dorian laid a hand on mine and lifted his head. "Hear that?"

I froze, but all I could hear was the steady drip of water. "What?"

"That rushing sound."

"What rushing . . ?" As a gigantic grey shadow burst from a narrow tunnel, a scream tore from my throat.

"Bats!" yelled Dorian. He slammed me to the floor and covered my body with his. I glimpsed Scarlet being washed away by thousands of flying mice whose sharp little teeth gleamed in the light of Dorian's wand. Wave-after-wave exited through a fissure in the calcium-encrusted ceiling.

Crushed beneath Dorian, I retained enough sanity to question why a colony of bats would fly midday. The creatures were nocturnal. Before the question was complete though, I knew the answer. Something had alarmed them enough to abandon their safe day-haven which meant – *someone was coming!*

As the roar reduced to an occasional flutter, Dorian lifted his head.

"Scarlet? Scarlet!"

In spite of his weight, I managed to inhale. "She was caught by the bats."

Dorian leaped to his feet. "Scarlet!"

Except for an eerie echo and the occasional straggler, the cavern was silent.

"Scarlet!"

I got to my feet and touched his shoulder. "She's probably not far, Dorian. Without bat radar, it would've been impossible for her to fly with them."

"SCARLET!" The cavern echoed the name with diminishing volume.

I looked in the direction from which the bats had come. "Dorian, we should probably stay quiet. Something scared those bats. Let's make a *quiet* hunt for her."

He covered his eyes in an attempt to compose himself then looked at me. "You're right, of course. I wasn't thinking."

"I understand, Dorian. Scarlet is a living connection to your parents, and she'd give her life for any member of the Royal Family."

His voice was hoarse. "Let's hope she hasn't."

We followed the direction of the fleeing bats, broadening the search as we neared the exit. As I looked for a tiny body in green, I couldn't help but fear we were short on time.

"*Scarlet!*" I hissed in a forced whisper. "*Where are you?*" For the first time ever, I'd have welcomed the sound of her irritating little voice. The abrasive pixie may not be my best friend, but I didn't want her dead. Somehow, she'd gotten under my skin, and my panic was genuine.

I froze as I heard a stone roll down an incline. I turned to Dorian whose stillness confirmed he'd heard it too. "We'd better go, Dorian!"

As he grasped my hand and doused his wand light, utter blackness descended.

"If we move, we might step on Scarlet," I whispered. "Can we use our brooms?"

Two thumps answered my question. Crap! A null-magic field had been activated. How had they known?

With terrifying suddenness, the cavern flooded with light, and pig men poured through a gap in the back wall. Dorian and I took advantage of the brightness to scan the immediate area for Scarlet, but no little body appeared amongst the stones. If we hoped to escape, we needed to move – fast.

We exchanged a look, Dorian's grip tightened, and we sprinted towards a black tunnel in hopes the labyrinth of caves was extensive. As the darkness deepened, Dorian shot a narrow beam from the end of his wand. At least there was enough magic to light the way and keep us from stumbling over rocks and running into walls. I hoped our brooms would rejoin us soon.

It wasn't long before I lost all sense of direction, but the sounds of pursuit dwindled. A half-hour later, Dorian halted behind a pile of boulders and, appreciative of small favours, I used the time to catch my breath.

"Come here," said Dorian, and pulled me into his arms.

I was pondering how to react to this when the glow of his wand flickered and died. Surrounded by absolute blackness, I wrapped my arms around him like a baby monkey, grateful for his presence.

"Hush," he whispered as I started to speak. "Listen!"

Combined with the blackness, the absolute lack of sound was uncanny. I felt the tickle of hair rising along my back and arms, and hoped Dorian hadn't noticed. He might think I was scared.

Minutes stretched. As my breathing returned to normal, I realized Dorian's body felt good. His spicy scent activated all sorts of excellent memories that my body clamoured to repeat. It seemed my hope they'd remain buried had been unrealistic. I felt the fleeting touch of lips on my forehead before he pulled away, my wrist in his grasp.

"Sounds like we lost them," he said in his "friend" voice.

Don't worry; I'm fully aware of how illogical it was to be disappointed. Sometimes I can be so contrary.

"We'll have to risk a light if we don't want to fall down a shaft," he whispered. There was a dim flicker of blue which seemed bright after absolute blackness. "This way," he said, and set off to the right.

Now, I ask you, how could he possibly have known which direction to take? Was this part of his new leadership role? Never appear undecided? Pick a direction – any direction is better than none? Probably. It seemed a good trait to cultivate. It encouraged confidence in his followers which, at the moment, consisted of me – and I needed a confidence boost.

After ten minutes, I felt a tingle along my fingers. I jerked to a stop, pulling from Dorian's grasp.

"What's the matter, Raven?" Dorian looked back, the planes of his face in shadow.

"Did you feel that?"

"What?"

"We've exited the null-magic field. We can call our brooms!"

Dorian felt the air. "You're right." At his esoteric motion, both brooms appeared. Although his leaped into his hand, it took three tries to catch mine. Again, I sensed a certain lack of cooperation. Perhaps I'd offended it somehow. The problem is, how do you have a heart-to-heart with such an item? Mine had never spoken a word nor appeared to want to.

I straddled it, cautiously lifted a few feet then shot after Dorian who'd disappeared into the dimness. My broom, seeming to sense I'd break it into pieces before I'd be left behind, went where I pointed it.

I know I've mentioned this strange broom behaviour before, but giant spyders, evil mages, and smelly pig men had kicked it lower on my to-do list. I gave the item a mental check mark. It was at the top now.

After fifteen minutes, Dorian halted. We were in a cavern with walls covered in moss. Only one kind grew in absolute darkness. Dorian extinguished his light and, in moments, our sight adjusted to the glow.

"Thank heavens for luminosity," I whispered. "It'll make traversing these tunnels easier."

Dorian nodded. "It's the same moss we found in the gnome tunnels."

"I recall giant salamanders lived in those same tunnels," I said with an involuntary shiver.

Dorian glanced at the walls. "We're in solid granite. According to Talon, salamanders can only dig through soil."

I experienced another shiver as I recalled Dorian, Talon, and me hiding while a salamander big enough to swallow me whole had slithered past less than ten feet away.

"We can rest a while," said Dorian. "But we need to get back to finding the mage."

Although I was careful to lean my broom in a v-shaped depression, it slammed to the ground the instant I released it. Dorian's appeared to be attached with Krazy-Glue though he paid little attention to where it was propped. I made an effort to relax my jaw to relieve the pressure on my teeth. I would *not* be intimidated by wood and straw!

As I slid down the wall until my arms rested on upraised knees, Dorian settled next to me. "Let me think," I said.

I'd spied on Myrador and the pig men through the ceiling of a conference room. Maybe I should try the wand-on-the-palm thing I'd learned from Talon. I extended a hand, fingers outstretched, and laid my wand on it. As I concentrated on the feel of the mage, the wand spun slowly until I sensed a faint vibration. When it stopped, I pointed. "We go that way."

Chapter 22

Since we were out of the null-magic field, we changed to stone-walking which made our progress faster. It wasn't long before we stared down into an empty room.

"Are you sure this is it?"

"I'm sure," I growled. "I nearly died here. It's pretty well imprinted into my brain!"

"There's nobody here."

"Maybe they didn't get the memo."

"No need to be grouchy, Raven. I'm just trying to find out what we're up against."

"You're up against a lot!" I hissed in a stage whisper. "This mage has no ethics. Let me repeat – no ethics! He will kill us given the slightest opportunity!"

"I understand, Raven, but that doesn't change my responsibility to Altaria."

More of this king crap! Life had been simpler and a lot more fun when he'd just been my friend. "So, what now, Your Highness?" My question might've carried the slightest flavour of sarcasm though I prefer a higher level of communication as a rule.

"I'll have the army clear these caves, but I can't do that until I've dealt with Myrador. At least we've confirmed the location of his base. Let's see what else we can find."

"It was poking around like this that got me fried last time," I growled. "And I doubt he'll leave himself open again."

"We won't find anything staring at an empty room. Let's keep going."

After another half-hour of moving around the caves and feeling for null-magic zones, we stared into another empty meeting room. I rubbed my shoulder. Although it had healed, the ghostly memory of snake-light lingered.

I tried the wand thing again, and this time it pointed up. "Maybe he's leaving," I whispered with faint hope.

Dorian pointed a thumb upward and, with a distinct lack of enthusiasm at the idea of facing Myrador, I lifted towards the surface. In this area of fewer null-magic fields, it was easier to stay in the rock than to move between the two mediums. As Dorian enthused over the ever-present streams, layers of coal, and pockets of crystals, I realized his apprehension of stone-walking had vanished.

"Look at that!" He pointed to a two-foot seam that gave off a dull gleam.

"What is it?"

"It's a seam of solid gold! Can you remember this spot? Gold is one of the reasons Altaria is such a wealthy nation, and this is a new find." He glanced at me. "I never considered a stone-walker could find gold! How about other precious metals or gems?"

I sent him a narrow-eyed glare. "Don't even think about it, Dorian! I'm not in the mining business! And did you consider maybe you should get Gaia's permission first?"

"How would I go about that?"

"Ask Valgren."

There was silence as he considered the idea but, before he could respond, tree roots appeared. I slowed, put a finger to my lips, and levitated with care, feeling for signs of null-magic. Nothing. Knowing we were beneath thick forest by the network of roots, I hoped the trees would hide us from Myrador. The buzz of my wand indicated he was close.

Taking a deep breath (strange idea considering I was in solid rock), I poked my head through a carpet of fallen leaves. I swiveled to catch a quick three-sixty and swore at the sight of a pair of piggy eyes transfixed by shock and horror. As Dorian's head popped next to mine, the pig man gave an ear-piercing squeal, little eyes rolled back into his head, and he toppled in a dead faint.

Shit! He couldn't have fainted quietly? I levitated the rest of the way and pried cramped fingers from Dorian's wrist. He rubbed at red finger marks as I flexed my hand. Much as I'd have loved for the pig man to be alone, I wasn't surprised to hear the patter of pointed hooves, and the huff and puff of fat pig soldiers hastening our direction.

I turned to Dorian. "Any ideas?"

"Yes . . . run!"

We dove into the forest at an angle in hopes we could get far enough ahead to flee downhill. Since our brooms wouldn't respond to frantic calls, I figured they were affected by one of the null-magic fields in the caverns. They'd show up sooner or later, but later wasn't going to help. If we levitated, we'd be even more visible, so the only option was to out-run our pursuers.

I hadn't known Dorian could sprint so fast. His long legs flew over deadfalls and rocks like a human gazelle. As I huffed along behind, it occurred to me I'd probably been a porcupine in a past life – slow and touchy. As the distance between us grew, I gritted my teeth and plowed on. An old joke about "*not needing to outrun the bear; you just needed to outrun your companions*" came to mind. Puff! Puff!

Mental note: Never challenge Dorian to a foot-race.

Second mental note: Had he remembered the bear joke too and realized he had nothing to fear?

Now this is a prime example of my lack of ability to focus. Here I was running for my life, and my thoughts jumped around like jackrabbits on speed (or the current equivalency; I don't keep up with the drug scene).

We encountered a steep section down which Dorian already flew (metaphorically speaking). My legs were rubbery and, as I braced to skid down an irregular spot, my knee buckled. I was instantly airborne which was, unfortunately, a temporary state of affairs. A good deal further along, I landed with a thump and a grunt, bounced, sailed through the air again, bounced some more, and passed Dorian at shoulder height. The next time my bruised body connected with the ground, I tumbled and slid along a carpet of slick grass. An eternity later, I slammed against something immovable. Fortunately, it was covered in soft moss. Unfortunately, it was a tree.

Have you ever had the wind knocked out of you? Awful sensation. You swear you'll never breathe again. It's happened to me more than once. As I lay there, mouth opening and closing like a stranded fish, I saw Dorian skidding and sliding towards me.

"Raven! Raven! Are you alright?"

Then he was hovering over me, afraid to touch anything in case every bone in my body was broken.

"Raven! Say something!"

At that point, he was fortunate I couldn't say anything.

"Raven, you're not breathing!"

Like I didn't know that! Idiot!

"What . . . what's wrong? Why aren't you breathing?"

I continued a panicky effort to suck air into flattened lungs.

"Did . . . did you get the wind knocked out of you?"

Come on, Dorian! Thought you were brighter than this! Figure it out before I die!

"Raven, you need to breathe!"

No shit!

"What if . . . maybe I can do it for you."

Just do something!

He covered my mouth with his, pinched my nostrils and blew gently. Nothing happened. He blew harder. I jerked my head to the side and nearly exploded with the inhalation, sucking in great gulps of pure, fresh, wonderful air. I rolled to the side and enjoyed the sensation of using my lungs. In fact, it felt so good, it took a full minute to realize every part of my body screamed with pain.

Didn't I slide down a mountain on the pig planet not so long ago? Wasn't once enough? Maybe not so unbelievable. I spent time in alpine terrain and was often pursued by something awful, so chances were good I'd come to grief on a mountain. At least I hadn't dropped over a cliff this time. My levitation skills weren't bad now as long as I had time to focus, but falling down a mountain wasn't conducive to concentration. Much as I wanted to curse it (and I did), the tree had done me a favour by halting a headlong plunge.

Dorian began a gentle exploration of my limbs, asking where it hurt. I scowled at the ridiculous question. I hurt everywhere! I pushed him away and eased to hands and knees. After taking inventory, I was surprised to find all my parts worked. Who'd have thought? A story for those imaginary grandchildren.

"Dorian, are we far enough away to get our brooms?"

He closed his eyes and, seconds later, they materialized. As I may have mentioned, brooms can be delayed but never prevented from reuniting with their owners. As I reached for mine, a shrub next to me exploded.

"Don't scream, Raven! It'll help them find us! Let's go!"

I wanted to explain how I wasn't a screamer but couldn't summon the effort. I lunged for my broom, wrestled it to the ground, and managed to mount. More explosions scattered leaves and branches.

Dorian was bursting with urgency. "Now! Now! Now!"

I growled at my broom, gave it a signal, and shot after him. Three birds the size of pterodactyls circled above. Explosions erupted around us but we managed to avoid most of them. Then something painful slammed into my back, my broom gave a violent lurch, and I plummeted. The concussion of the attack made it difficult to think let alone manage a levitation spell. In a lightning-fast move, Dorian grabbed me around the waist and hoisted me in front of him.

"We'll never outrun Myrador's spy birds," he said, voice tight. "And that was too close! If memory serves, there's a shepherd's cottage in the forest across that valley. I'll cloak it, and an invisibility spell over us should confuse the birds long enough for us to get inside. You need to rest, and we're easy targets like this."

"I don't need to rest," I declared. "I'm fine!"

As we raced at breakneck speed over the tips of the forest, I had the oddest sensation that the trees were spinning . . .

Chapter 23

The aroma of frying fish brought me back. I tugged an old patchwork quilt to my chin, rolled over, and groaned at the places on my body that complained. Before I could drift back to sleep, my stomach again caught the whiff of food and, like it had a nose of its own, began to growl. I peeked across the room. An iron frying pan was balanced on a trio of glowing rocks set into a fireplace.

Dorian gave me a quick smile then returned to the fillets. "Good morning. Thought the smell of breakfast would bring you around."

I licked dry lips. "It's morning?" I croaked, trying to rub the blur from my sight.

"The sun will be up soon. After that nasty fall, I was worried I'd need a healer from Odenai."

"I feel like I've been in a car crash!" I moaned.

Speaking of feeling . . . rough fabric against skin. What the . . . I glanced beneath the covers. Naked . . . I didn't remember . . . A rising panic threatened my self-control.

"Where are my clothes? We didn't . . ?"

He jerked a thumb at a row of pegs draped with clothing. "You skidded through a lot of stuff, some of it from a bear that loved berries. I preferred the fuss of you waking up naked to the meltdown you'd have if you woke up covered in that amount of excrement, so I washed them."

"Really . . ?"

His eyes crinkled at the corners. "I don't have to resort to trickery to get your clothes off, Raven. Besides, there may not be enough soap to clean that much scat from the bedding."

My cheeks burned. "I wasn't suggesting . . . I didn't think . . . *(yes, I did)* . . . never mind." Sigh.

I wrapped myself in a sheet, shuffled to the fireplace, and settled onto a creaky wooden chair. I noticed Dorian edge away.

I narrowed my eyes at him. "What?"

He gestured towards my tangled locks. "I washed your clothes, not your hair."

There was a beat of silence as I rolled my eyes towards my leaf-and-twig-littered mane. Now that I was focused, I discerned a distinct odour.

He pointed. "I filled a bucket with warm water and soap."

I managed to find my voice through the horror. "But I can't *touch* it!" I wailed. "How am I supposed to get it out?!"

His expression turned smug. "I could do it in exchange for amnesty. No repercussions for removing your clothes. Under the circumstances, you'll agree I had no choice."

The thought of Dorian performing such an intimate act while I was unconscious had me in an instant sweat.

He canted a look towards me. "If you get much redder, you're going to pop a blood vessel, Raven. While you think about it," he added, sliding fish fillets onto two wooden plates, "let's eat." He popped a piece of fish into his mouth and chewed. "This is incredible," he said and pointed to the other plate. "Would you like some?"

If I moved, my soiled hair would touch my face. "How am I supposed to eat with this crap in my hair?" I hated the whine in my voice.

Dorian took another bite and looked thoughtful. "I'm sure you'll think of something." He inclined his head towards the second plate. "Your fish is getting cold."

My stomach, not as fastidious as the rest of me, indeed, clamoured for attention, but I couldn't stand this much longer. I'd be shaving my head in the next few seconds if my hair wasn't cleaned – sterilized! Were bald women still feminine?

For some bizarre reason, Dorian's lips curved into a smile. "I'm smelling smoke, Raven. You'd better make a decision before you short-circuit." He propped his feet on a low wooden table, popped another piece of fish into his mouth, and chewed happily.

I was breathing through my mouth in the insane hope the smell would diminish. Why did that old myth continue to circulate even though it was demonstrably false? Although I searched for an alternative, it was clear there was but one option.

"Okay," I muttered.

"What's that?" He cupped a hand behind his ear.

"I said, okay!" I growled. "You have a deal! No repercussions."

"Ever?"

"What's the matter, don't you trust me?"

"I like to have things clear."

"They're clear, alright?" The knowledge that bear doo-doo was soaking into my hair was making me crazy.

"You don't want to eat while the fish is hot?"

The daggers from my eyes seemed to be answer enough.

"Alright then. We'll save it for later."

He popped a final morsel into his mouth and slid the plate onto a nearby shelf. With a swift movement, he grasped the bucket and clunked it onto a low table.

"Stand up, rest your hands on the table, and dip your head in the bucket."

A horrific thought. "I'm not putting my face in with . . . bear shit!"

"You've got the correct noun but, like it or not, your face is going to get wet." With a swift motion, he stripped off his shirt.

I clutched the sheet. "What're you doing?"

He looked at me as if the question had been insane. "I don't want to get my shirt wet."

Trying hard not to peek as Dorian is a magnificent specimen of manhood, I lowered my head while he gathered ebony locks into a pile. I glimpsed dark stains on emerald. Ugh!

Three scrubbings later, the soapy pail had been exchanged for warm rinse water. Now the icky stuff was gone, I began to enjoy the gentle ministration of Dorian's fingers. Ripples of sensation coursed over my scalp and down my spine to a target deep inside. If I wasn't careful, such small beginnings could morph into a perfect tsunami of passion. As you know, I'd been caught up in that fantastic storm a couple of times already.

Just a few more minutes. I could do it. Sure, I could.

A tingling sensation ran over my scalp as he sluiced warm water through my hair. His muscular chest was inches away. How could so much power be so gentle? The disobedient part of me provided clear memories of being held in those arms high in a distant forest. Those same gentle fingers traced the contours of my body . . .

Deep breaths, Raven! Deep breaths! Think about something else. Christ! When did I get so weak?

Dorian's voice had taken on a soft tone that made my knees wobble. "Is that better?" His touch had become a sensuous, gentle massage. More warm water trickled, creating an involuntary response that exploded within.

"Umm . . . I think . . . I think . . ."

He made a low sound in his throat, lips close to my ear. "There's something else I can help you with," he whispered.

Breathe, Raven! Breathe!

"Umm . . . what?" The thin sheet I wore suddenly felt transparent.

Still whispering, he said, "Some of the bear scat is on your skin."

I froze. I should get the "stupid" award of the year! I was covered in bear shit and hadn't even realized it!

"Raven? Are you alright? You're not moving, Raven. Say something."

"I think I'm going to be sick."

"Not exactly what I had in mind. How about this instead?" He squeezed excess water from my hair and pulled me erect, hands on my shoulders. He lifted my chin with one hand so I looked into his eyes. With the other, he began a gentle, circular motion with a soapy cloth along my shoulders and chest.

I couldn't move, mesmerized by deep chocolate eyes and the rhythmic strokes. It took three tries to find my voice.

"I think we should . . . I think we should . . ." I faltered, desperate to regain control of the situation, to escape his magnetic pull. I wasn't ready for this regardless of what Valgren had told me.

As Dorian leaned in to kiss me, he tugged at the knot between my breasts, and the sheet pooled at my feet. "I think we should too," he whispered against my lips.

***

I awoke to a warm body beside me, the soothing sound of gentle breathing next to my ear. The light scent of cinnamon musk permeated the bed.

Son of a . . !

I opened my eyes without moving, loathe to enter into a morality discussion with either Dorian or myself. I could fall into a bottomless pit of pointless introspection that I knew from past experience went nowhere. Despite Valgren's assurance I needed to clear my mind about Dorian, I still found it difficult to transgress childhood indoctrination.

I believe I've mentioned before that I don't engage in introspection because, in my experience, it's never terribly helpful. It just makes me feel bad about myself, and nobody in her right mind wants that, right?

Wait a minute . . . I blinked. Maybe I'd hit that tree harder than I'd thought. Nasty green eyes glared at me in the late morning light. Red brows met over a tiny nose. As the fuzzy image solidified, I perceived a cap of flaming red hair, two tiny arms akimbo, and a foot tapping the bed in staccato rhythm. There were scrapes along her cheek, chemical stains in her hair, and her clothing was torn and dirty.

I was relieved for a full second. Plenty long enough. Determined not to get into an argument, I gave her a smug smile, turned my back, and snuggled against Dorian's chest. Nothing I could say would help the situation anyway. I figured this was one of those Royal responsibilities Dorian could handle. Dorian made a soft sound, stroked my back, and pulled me against his warmth. His hands had begun to explore when I stopped him. At his questioning glance, I motioned with my head.

I felt his start of surprise. "Scarlet! You're okay!"

"No thanks to you two!" she spat. "Did you *see* how many bloody bats shot out of that cave?!"

"Yes, Scarlet. We were there." He made a hand motion and the room brightened.

Scarlet fluttered to stand on my hip, little body aquiver. "Then, why in hell did you leave me there?!"

Dorian knuckled his eyes in an effort to fully awaken. "We tried, Scarlet, believe me. Raven was nearly killed because we waited too long trying to find you. I'd planned to go back this morning after . . ."

"Yes, Dorian, after what?!" Her furious green gaze flicked to me so I closed my eyes. I wasn't excusing my sex life to a ten-inch person I could squash like a bug. She fluttered a few inches higher. Maybe she felt it gave her an advantage.

I could feel Dorian tighten. His voice took on an edge I'd learned to recognize and respect. "Raven nearly died trying to help Altaria yesterday." To my shock, he flipped the covers off of me. "Perhaps," he said with a hard look, "you'd like to count her bruises."

Bruises? I had bruises? That's why I ached so much. I'd thought maybe . . . well . . . never mind. I should've known Dorian would never hurt me. Hmm . . . now, that bit of trust had come right out of left field without any warning whatsoever. Kind of like an ambush. Had Dorian been weaseling his way beneath my anti-trust walls?

From the look on Scarlet's face, I surmised the sight of my naked body wasn't good. She turned to Dorian. "If I didn't know better, I'd say you'd given her a good beating!"

"Hey!" I snarled. "There's no such thing as a good beating! What is *wrong* with you?"

"Well, look at yourself!"

I buried my face in Dorian's chest. "I'm afraid to. I remember smashing into a tree and being knocked senseless. It's a wonder it didn't break every bone in my body."

She looked pensive. "You were really trying to help Altaria?"

"Did you think I came along for the battering?" Despite my determination not to let her get to me, my blood pressure was rising.

Dorian replaced the blanket. "Raven should rest. Now that you're here, there's no rush."

With a lightning change of subject, Scarlet glanced towards the dark fireplace. "I smell fried fish. Got any left?"

"Help yourself," said Dorian.

"It's cold in here. I could use some body heat."

Dorian muttered a spell. "There are heated rocks in the bed in the other room."

"But I'll be all alone."

He covered me with his upper body, weight on his elbows, an intimate smile on his face. "And so, will we."

I inhaled the scent of cinnamon musk. If I was bound for hell, the trip was damn well going to be worth it! Besides, those bruises needed to be stretched a little . . . you know . . . to help them heal . . .

Chapter 24

Angus paced the polished stone of Dorian's throne room as Talon floated above a planning table. I wondered if his legs would be less spindly if he spent more time walking like the rest of us – not that I planned to suggest it.

"So, Myrador is still up te something. At least we know where he is. The pigs would nae be there if Myrador wasn't close. De ye think maybe tis time te toss him into the stream along with his brother? I can lend ye Cash and a good number o' soldiers, plus ye have an army o' your own, lad. Bluescale's still in the area. Seems like as good a time as any te rid ourselves o' a giant headache before his next attack."

Dorian lounged on his throne, an ankle balanced on his knee. I doubted most kings were as casual. He wore a blue velvet cape, and the white streaks in his hair reflected soft candlelight. I'd been running my fingers through those streaks as he nuzzled a slow trail down my body a few hours previously . . .

"I agree," said Dorian. "It's time to get rid of Myrador. As long as he's around, no one's safe."

Angus took a chair opposite me. "De ye think ye could talk with the dragon, Raven? We could use his help. . . . Raven?"

"Oh! . . . Sorry! I was . . ." I saw the slight curve of Dorian's lips and could've kicked myself. "Never mind. What were you saying?"

I promised Angus I'd contact Bluescale. I expected the dragon would consider it double-the-fun to have both dark mages to entertain him in his stream.

The door opened, and three of Dorian's mages entered. As usual, they wore dark robes. I'd gotten to know Morgan, Dorian's aunt, but had not spent time with Shain and Wynn. I would've been hard-pressed to guess any of their ages – somewhere between thirty and . . . a millennium or two. For the first time, I wondered if I also would acquire an extended life span. What would that mean? I could see how relationships with mortals would become difficult as human beings have such short lives. Who wanted to be in a constant state of grief? Perspective was everything. Perhaps Dorian too . . .

". . . if ye could call Bluescale now, Raven?" Angus watched me with raised red brows, no doubt wondering why, yet again, I wasn't paying attention.

"Sorry again! I was . . . I'll call him now." I saw Dorian suppress a smile and give an infinitesimal head shake. Wait until the next time I got him alone . . . wait a minute! Where was I going with this? It was supposed to be a one-night thing – circumstances and all that. Sigh.

"Bluescale, where are you?"

Silence.

"Bluescale! I know you can hear me!"

Silence.

"BLUESCALE!"

"Jeez! You nearly blew my head apart! Could you turn it down? I was taking a nap!"

"Sorry. I don't know how loud I need to be."

"Well, now you do! No bellowing!"

My desire to apologize flew out the window along with my patience. *"When you've finished with the attitude, can we get down to business?"*

"What business?"

"We're collaborating to get Myrador into the stream with Mydryth. Then you'll have two playthings." I couldn't help but smile as I imagined his grin.

Dorian watched me. "I take it you've got him on the line, so-to-speak?"

I nodded. "He'll be in the courtyard in ten minutes."

There was a flash of red as Scarlet fluttered into the room. Her cheeks had healed, and she sported one of the outfits I'd bought for her in Denver – form-fitting jeans and a white sweater. Funny, she didn't look like she had the personality of a wolverine. She settled on the back of the throne to survey the room as if she was royalty.

Frost flowed into the room trailing yards of glittering fabric followed by Cash loaded with weapons. An unexpected shiver rippled through me at the realization the most powerful mages in both Altaria and Cumulos were in the same room. The adage about eggs all in one basket shot to mind. I was about to point it out when I noticed a disturbance in the air much like the surface of still water after a stone has been dropped into it – except the motion was vertical and shot from one side of the room to the other in a matter of seconds.

I shook my head, wondering if I'd imagined it as the others continued to converse. My fingers of their own volition tapped a pattern on my chair arm, unease snaked along my spine, and goose bumps lifted the hair on the back of my neck.

Dorian noticed my shiver. "What's the matter, Raven?"

I hugged myself. "Did anyone else see that?"

"See what?"

"Waves of . . . *something* went through the room. Like ripples on a lake." As the others shook their heads, I added, "It reminded me of being scanned in a sci-fi movie."

Dorian shot a glance at Talon who pursed thin lips which made him look like a puzzled purple rabbit. He closed his eyes and executed esoteric hand motions. Black toes twitched a few times then he lifted thin shoulders. "I detect nothing." He cast me a dismissive glance. "She's not very good at magic. Most likely, she's wrong. I wouldn't worry."

I leaped to my feet. "Don't make me sorry I saved your ass!"

Big mauve eyes rolled my way. "I've been sorry for quite some time."

"Well . . . well . . . I'm not wrong!" I turned to Dorian. "Something happened, Dorian! You need to trust me on this!"

As the ends of his lips curved upward, I was aware of the incongruity of such a request coming from me. Miss "I-don't-trust-anybody" asking him to trust her. Worse yet, he knew I knew. Damn!

He scanned the others. "Anybody else see anything?"

Nothing.

His pensive gaze returned to me. "I'm going to go with Raven on this. I want every Altarian mage and apprentice looking for the disturbance." His mages tipped their heads. "Until this matter is investigated, I'm postponing the issue of Myrador's entrapment."

Angus watched me, deep in thought. "Raven's abilities have always been unusual, so I'm inclined te agree with ye, Dorian. We may ignore this at our peril."

The meeting adjourned, and I was almost at the front doors when I heard bellowed curses and the screams of terrified horses. Oops . . . Should've warned the cavalry about the dragon's arrival. They were gonna be mad. As the sound of stampeding hooves faded into the distance, I trotted down the outside staircase.

"Hi, Bluescale. I see you're making friends."

The dragon looked at the empty courtyard. "I don't understand. It was full a minute ago."

His front end was half-way up the stairs. He swung his huge head around to me, an anticipatory grin exposing enormous canines. "So, we're hunting Myrador at last?"

"Hate to disappoint you, old buddy, but plans have changed. Myrador's been put on the back burner."

His expression froze. "But . . . you said just minutes ago . . ."

"Something came up."

"In *ten minutes?*"

"Bluescale, did you notice anything unusual when you were flying here? Something strange with the air?"

He stared at me in silence.

"Well?"

"I don't know how to answer that, Raven," he said. "How can air be strange? It's just air."

"How about ripples in the air?"

He took a step back, worried that whatever I had might be catching. "Of course, Raven. It's called *wind.*" His lids half-lowered and his head cocked. "Are you alright?"

"Of course, I'm alright!" I stomped back up the stairs. "Everybody else is crazy!"

He called after me, "You know what it means when you think it's everybody else!"

"Shut up, Bluescale! I'm going to figure this out with or without help!"

He yelled to make sure I heard as I entered the castle, "Okay, then. I'll just be . . . you know . . . out here . . . waaaaiting! I'm sure sooner or later you'll need me to fix this . . . *air* thing. Maybe you could send somebody to explaaaain it!"

I slammed the great doors behind me. Why couldn't people just believe me? Why did I always have to prove stuff? As I stomped down the great hall, it started to rain. Huh? I looked up. My fury had produced a personal rain cloud that burst and soaked me to the skin. I growled and kept going. Sometimes this magic stuff ticked me off. Couldn't even enjoy a good temper tantrum. I lost count of the stairs it took to get to the viewing room, but each acquired a puddle as I squished past.

Morgan, quill in hand, was writing in a book when I entered. She glanced at me with a raised brow.

"Don't ask!" I growled as I grabbed my hair and wrung water into a basin. Morgan smiled, made a hand motion, and the cloud disappeared. Now, I felt stupid. Why couldn't I have done that?

"Relax, Raven. We're all working on this. We'll figure it out."

"You believe me?"

"Of course. It seems a silly sort of thing to make up. Because we haven't experienced it before doesn't mean it's impossible. New things happen all the time. That's how Gaia works."

"I doubt it was Gaia." I knew I sounded grumpy.

"I doubt it too, but it's within Gaia's rules or it wouldn't happen."

"Gaia has rules?"

"You might recognize them as laws of nature."

"Oh."

"Gaia is complex, and unravelling her mysteries makes life exciting. She can be harsh as well as gentle and loving."

"How long have you been working on all this?"

"Two-and-a-half millennia." She smiled. "Give or take. After that much time, years lose significance."

I cleared my throat, nervous about the answer to my question. "Will I have a mortal life span?"

"That's up to you. It's possible to attain immortality. If your path makes it necessary, it will happen. Longevity though, isn't the point as immortal people can be killed. Learning to rebuild your body after it's been damaged is far more important as it enables eternal life."

"How do I do that?"

She pressed a gentle hand on my arm. "It'll come, Raven. You're following your path. Trust that nothing has been left out."

There was that trust thing again. I might as well admit it. "Trust is not easy for me."

"That's to be expected considering your upbringing. It will come as you gain confidence in your abilities."

I gave a bark of laughter. "Right! My abilities are a joke!"

"Don't sell yourself short, Raven. It's obvious your birth was no accident, and your skills are . . . unusual. You were the one to perceive the incursion this morning."

"If that's what it was. Maybe it was just a ripple of magic and didn't mean anything."

"The movement of magic always means something." She gestured to a table covered in mysterious objects. "Let's see what we can find out. Shain and Wynn are scouring Odenai, and we've dispatched a dozen cathasach birds to look for disturbances throughout Altaria. You and I will search from here. It's time you learned what some of these devices are for anyway."

Chapter 25

From one of the towers of Odenai Castle, I watched scattered cloud shadows slip over the city. The turquoise sea sparkled with reflected sunlight. A perfect day – and perfect days make me nervous. They're disasters in pretty clothes.

It didn't take long. As I felt his approach, I cast a furtive glance for my broom which I'd propped in a corner. Before I could grab it, it shot to Dorian's outstretched hand.

"You're not going anywhere, Raven."

"What the . . ? How did you do that? My broom doesn't even do that for me!"

"Maybe you should be nicer to it."

"I am nice to it! I mean . . . what are you talking about? It's a *broom* for heaven's sake!"

"See what I mean? You treat it like it's an object. In fact, it's magic and, like all magical items, it possesses a degree of sentience."

"Are you telling me I've been hurting its feelings?"

"A dash of respect wouldn't hurt. After all, your life depends on it keeping you in the air."

Hmm. True. "So, how do you respect a broom?"

"I didn't come here to talk about your broom, Raven."

"You brought it up."

"Only to keep you from bolting."

"What makes you think I'd bolt?"

"Experience."

I crossed my arms and felt my metaphorical mule ears lay flat.

"You see? You're already obstinate."

"People often mistake strength for obstinacy."

"Let's agree you have a generous helping of both."

Most likely he was right about that. I waited.

As I'd been watching the cloud shadows, I'd been contemplating my love life which had suffered a violent upheaval considering recent events with Dorian. The first night I'd spent with him, we'd both been loaded on pot, so that hadn't been my fault. The second time, we were in a romantic, distant land, trying to process what had happened the first time. But the thing in the shepherd's cottage had me spooked. There'd been no excuse for that other than . . . sigh. He was just so damn gorgeous and . . .

It would've been far simpler if Valgren had insisted I kept my distance from Dorian, but it wasn't Valgren who was the issue here. It was me.

Dorian's reticence about a relationship with me had vanished with his ascension to the throne, and he didn't seem the least bit worried about poaching on Valgren's . . . Valgren's what? Property? Even Valgren didn't consider me his property. Was I the only one who had a problem with this?

I'd reached this point in my thoughts when Dorian blocked my escape route by resting his elbows on the ramparts next to me. He set my broom against the wall behind him. "Let's talk."

I could feel the muscles in my jaw tighten. "Whatever happed to Mr. Tall, Dark and *Silent*?"

"I don't need to hide any more. You're in no more danger here than the rest of us." He gave me a sideways glance. "I won't pursue you, Raven, if that's what you really want, but don't expect me to back off when all your signals are green. Considering your response to me, I have to wonder about your commitment to Valgren. There wasn't a whiff of pot smoke anywhere near that cabin nor in the village of the forest-dwellers."

I could feel chips coming off my teeth. "Did you think I was up here for the view?"

He scanned the city. "It's a pretty great view."

A heavy silence developed. A robin alighted on the wall next to me, black, inquisitive eyes examining us as it strutted, proud of its russet breast. As I watched, its tiny store of courage fled, and it soared into the morning sky with a flutter of wings and a gift of clear, musical notes. The world continued to turn.

I felt something wet and realized silent tears ran down my cheeks. I wiped them away with a quick motion.

Dorian expelled a breath. "I don't want to add to your confusion, Raven," he said in a softer tone, "but you were right about me getting pressured to take a queen. Altaria would be stabilized with a monarch pair." His lips quirked. "I didn't realize there were so many eligible young women in Altaria, but most of them have been paraded before me over the past month. I feel like a bull at a cattle sale."

I continued to stare into the distance.

Forearms over the wall, Dorian threaded his fingers, wrists loose. "I'm not trying to pressure you, Raven, but you need to understand I must consider Altaria in *all* my decisions. No one will force me, but pressure will increase as time goes on. I want to be honest about that."

I managed to find my voice though it wavered. "Don't try to get me into a competition, Dorian. I'm not interested in political games. If that's how those kinds of decisions are made, please pick someone else." I kept my gaze averted.

He turned me to face him, wiped my tears away with his thumbs, and pulled me close. "I know you don't play games," he whispered into my hair. "It's one of the things I love about you. And I understand you're honestly confused." He kissed me on the forehead and stepped back. "Just so you know, I will not allow politicians to pick my queen. I have meetings to attend this morning, but I'll be around. Enjoy the day."

In seconds, his footsteps faded on the stairs. I sniffed and scrubbed at my face, embarrassed Dorian had witnessed my tears. I was jerked from my self-absorption when, out of the blue, my broom toppled to the flagstones with a loud clatter. "Traitor!" I snapped, squinty-eyed, and changing gears into anger. "You don't fool me with that feigned innocence crap!"

No response. Big surprise. But its passive-aggressive actions were on the increase. I'd better deal with it soon.

A distant speck expanded to become Bluescale, the slow beat of huge wings belying his speed. I knew sensitive dragon-sight would've already spotted me and, if anyone could provide a distraction from my problems, it would be Bluescale. He grew until, with a blast of wind, he squeezed onto the walkway and gave a sigh of satisfaction. "They have the best trout here!" A belch was followed by a puff of smoke.

I wrinkled my nose and waved a hand. "Couldn't you have done that on the way? You smell like smoked fish!"

"I could catch you one." He looked eager.

"Thanks. I've eaten."

After I described the mysterious magical ripples again, he agreed it would be fun to look for them. Since there was no immediate danger at the moment, boredom had set in.

I climbed up a massive front leg, squeezed between his backplates, and tried to suppress a scream as he leaped into space. As membranous wings shot out to catch rising air currents, we lifted like a feather, and I was reminded that Bluescale's enormous size belied his weight. His body had two huge cavities for storing chemicals and one for mixing them. When mixed, the chemicals were incendiary, hence his ability to spew fire. Hollow bird-like bones added to his light weight. I'm not that far off when I call him a big bag of wind.

A warm breeze lifted my hair, and scattered clouds created scattered shadows that slipped along the ground. The sky was a deep, almost artificial blue, the distant ocean calm and serene.

Oh, yes – another perfect day. I had a dragon with me this time, though. That should help, right?

As we flew through magical perfection towards the disaster that most assuredly awaited me, I'd have turned tail and run if I could've come up with a reason that didn't sound insane. We'd followed the coast to a range of mountains and were on the return trip to Odenai when I perceived a ripple in the air below. I squinted and adjusted focus to recapture the fleeting impression.

"Did you see that, Bluescale?"

He turned his head so one green eye peered over a massive shoulder. "See what?"

Guess not. "Loop back to that rocky ridge."

Bluescale dropped a wing to make a smooth circle.

"What are we looking for?

"Ripples in the air."

"Still?"

"Still."

"Not wind?"

"More like vertical heat waves. They're fast and easy to miss. Dragon sight is better than mine, so I'd appreciate your help."

Like many males, a stroke to Bluescale's ego did wonders. He acquired a smug expression and began scanning the area, determined to confirm his superior skills. I was fine with that so long as I found what I was looking for.

We made two full circles and started on a third. I decided I could think about the situation with Dorian and watch for magic ripples at the same time. He'd come to me to talk, and I'd dismissed him. Although my cowardly instincts told me to stay away, I'd been trying to strengthen my character by facing challenges. Perhaps I'd start with that one. Go to Dorian this evening and have an adult conversation. There may be a solution that had so far eluded us.

An undulating movement caught my eye. "Did you see that, Bluescale?"

"What?"

So much for superior dragon vision. We made a tight turn as I searched for an almost invisible fluctuation.

I was wedged between Bluescale's backplates watching below when, without warning, something knocked me from his back. Too startled to scream, I plummeted headfirst until, out of nowhere, my broom thrust itself into my hand. Not inclined at that precise moment to ask questions, I righted myself and straddled the thing which, as soon as I was balanced, shot off at tremendous speed. Bluescale dove after me. As I slit my eyes against the wind and held on for dear life, I wondered how many people had been abducted by their own brooms.

It was soon clear where we were headed – Odenai Castle. Had Dorian cast a spell on my broom to bring me back? If that was the case, he'd get a piece of my mind!

We shot over the castle walls, and I was unceremoniously deposited on the courtyard stairway as my traitorous broom clattered to the ground. Bluescale landed seconds later to the accompaniment of stampeding horses and loud curses. I'd have to ask him to land on top of the castle in future because, if this continued, the soldiers would refuse to guard the castle, and horses would balk at entering the courtyard.

Not knowing how to react to the incident, I waited for something to happen. The situation made no sense. Who kidnaps a victim just to take her home? Home? More confusion. Not going there.

Dorian strode from the castle, short-sword strapped to a carved leather belt, long legs encased in high boots. When he saw us, he halted. "What are you two doing out here?"

Both fists popped onto my hips in a horrifying imitation of Scarlet. "As if you didn't know, Dorian!"

His expression of fake innocence was superb.

"Raven, what the hell are you talking about?"

I resisted the urge to stamp my foot. "What kind of spell did you use on my broom?"

"I called it to me this morning. You were there." He stepped closer. "What's going on? Why do you look like you've been in a wind tunnel?"

My hands flew to my hair. Ugh! A rat's nest! It would take hours to brush. Where was Valgren when I needed him? One touch and it would all be perfect. It was shocking to think I might want to take advantage of the man – turn him into my personal hairdresser. Fortunately, I knew for a fact he'd never let that happen, and I wouldn't want it to.

"Never mind my hair!" I snapped, tucking it into my collar. "Why did my broom abduct me?"

Dorian's attention moved to the broom which lay on the stones. "Kind of disrespectful to leave it on the ground, Raven."

I huffed, stalked over, and picked it up. "It dropped *itself* on the ground! Now, explain please!"

Dorian hooked his thumbs into his pockets, stared first at my broom and then at me. "I told you, Raven, I don't know what you're talking about. My mages and I spent the morning trying to figure out what you saw. Besides the fact there's been no time to come up with practical jokes, I know how much you hate them. Don't assume my new position has made me stupid."

Hmm. He seemed almost . . . *sincere*.

"Then what happened? I was flying with Bluescale when it slammed me off his back and brought me here. Why would it do that?"

At Dorian's glance, Bluescale nodded. "Nearly knocked her senseless."

Dorian frowned. "I'll have Wynn and Shain take a look at it. Maybe it's faulty."

In my opinion, there'd always been something evasive about it. "Good idea. An examination is long overdue."

"You think it came from your father, right?"

"I've always believed my father left it for me but, honestly, I don't know. It just showed up one morning."

His frown deepened. "Come to think of it, I don't know who gave me mine. Same thing. It just showed up. I've always assumed it'd been arranged by my mother, and I've never had issues with it."

We stared at each other and then at the object. It looked like an ordinary magic broom (if there's such a thing).

Bluescale's light nudge almost knocked me to my knees. "I'm going deep-sea fishing. Worked up an appetite today. Want anything?"

The possibilities made me shudder. "I'm okay. See you later."

There was a blast of wind as gigantic wings gave a formidable downward thrust and, in seconds, he was a shrinking speck in the distance.

I dug dirt from my eyes that'd been embedded by the mini tornado caused by Bluescale's departure. Of course, in seconds, tears streamed down my face. I took Dorian's proffered handkerchief, mumbled thanks, and blew my nose. As I swiped at my tears, I glimpsed Dorian shake his head.

"What?" I snapped.

"I don't know how it happens."

"How what happens?"

Then I noticed that although he stood right next to me, he didn't have a hair out of place. I didn't want to know what I looked like now that I had dirt combined with tears combined with wind. Maybe I should be thankful mirrors were scarce in the magical realm.

"I'll see someone brings extra towels to your room," he said. "My mages will examine your broom, and we'll talk after lunch."

I sniffed, rubbed my nose, and peered up at him. "You really didn't do it?"

"No, Raven, I didn't."

That was disappointing. Would've been simpler if it'd been him. I'd fuss and fume for a bit, and it would be over. Instead, my problems had expanded.

Chapter 26

The oak door swung open on silent hinges. The workshop was long and narrow with high windows pierced by afternoon shafts of sunlight. My conveyance floated over a table flanked by Dorian and Wynn.

"Hi," I said. "How's it going?"

"Not sure yet." Wynn had a voice like a smoker though I doubt he'd had a cigarette in his life. He had thin features, piercing hawk eyes over an impressive set of cheekbones, and a surprisingly warm smile. I didn't know whether to be afraid of him or to ask for a hug. I settled for a handshake.

The broom made slow rotations as Dorian stared at it, hands stuffed in his pockets. "We've looked for everything we can think of but can't find an abnormality."

I moved closer and the broom shied away. I flicked a look at the others. "Did you see that?"

Thick lines appeared between Wynn's brows. "I did indeed. Now, why would that happen? It *is* your broom, isn't it?"

Dorian and I locked gazes then explained how neither of us remembered how we'd gotten them. How did everyone else get theirs? Was it like finding a wand at the library?

Wynn leaned against the table and folded his arms. "Magical people get their first brooms when they're five – old enough to be able to hold on. Since each broom has different characteristics, parents are careful to shop around. They want the child's first flying experience to be a positive one. Aggressive children shouldn't be matched with timid brooms and vice versa."

I felt my brows climb. "Brooms have personalities? Are you kidding me?"

Wynn canted his eyes to the floating broom. "You said this broom avoids you."

"It seems to. Maybe I'm imagining it."

"Probably not if you haven't had an official introduction."

"Introduction?"

"It's a ritual performed whenever someone gets a new broom. Fuses their personalities so there aren't any communications issues."

"Are you serious?" If someone had taken a picture of me at this point, I'd have made the cover of *Incredulous Magazine*.

His brows rose. "This is something everyone knows, Ms. White Raven."

Dorian and I exchanged a look. Yet another gap in our education. "Why haven't I had issues?" asked Dorian.

"As a prince, your broom would've been selected and bonded to you when you were born."

I turned to Wynn. "How do I find out who gave it to me?"

"Ask it."

"I don't normally have conversations with cleaning utensils, so how would I go about that?"

He made a gesture which was followed by a flash of blue light that enveloped the floating broom. Mumbled incantations produced sparkles within the glow. Wynn spoke in (to me) an unknown language. The broom spun and bobbed as if excited. After a few minutes of whatever that was, Wynn turned to me.

"You are correct. It was a gift from your father. He brought it one night when you were asleep and wove a dream-spell with a memory lock. You'd know how to use it but wouldn't remember his visit."

So, I'd been right about it being a gift from my father but . . . he'd stood in my room? Watched me sleep?

Wynn turned back to the broom. "It claims you neglected to give it a name."

I jerked my thoughts back. "It's not a common practice to name household supplies in Denver."

"It's not an inanimate object, Raven. Part of the ritual involves your broom's acceptance of a name which results in a permanent connection between the two of you."

I stared at him. "How could I possibly have known that?"

"Your father probably hoped you'd figure it out. There's only so much information he could impart in a dream-spell if he was to remain anonymous."

A growl worked its way through my back teeth. "I'm his *daughter* for chrissake! He sired me for a reason! What's the big mystery? Why the hell couldn't he have introduced himself? Say 'Hi! I'm the guy who knocked up your mother then disappeared, the guy who let you grow up with a big, fat stupid person as a father! How are you today?!'"

"That's not my secret to divulge. I can however, perform a naming ceremony for you."

Hope sprang to my breast. "You know who my father is?"

"I can't discuss that. Would you like to proceed with the naming?"

I could see by his implacable expression I'd get no further.

Here's the thing about me. I don't like secrets, perhaps because I've had to keep so many. I swore then and there I'd get my father's identity out of either Wynn or Valgren. I was fed up with this cat-and-mouse game. One of these days I was going to find my real father, and he'd have to deal with it!

Meanwhile . . . "What about Dorian's? Does his broom have a name?"

"If you focus on your broom," he said to Dorian, "its name will come to you. Helena had already done the pairing, but threw a forget spell around it until you were adult enough to handle the responsibility. Children have a tendency to take foolish chances."

I thought of Reg and saw Wynn's point although I doubt Dorian was ever that dumb or that obnoxious. He'd have been the kid watching from the shadows. I'd never thought much about how lonely and lost he must've felt after Helena's death. He'd been a child alone in a hostile world. At least I'd had my family such as it was.

"Well, Raven? Shall we proceed?"

"Hmm? Oh, yes. My broom. Do you really think this'll help? It doesn't seem to like me." I eyed it with misgiving.

"That's because you insult it on a daily basis by not giving it a name."

Great. A hyper-sensitive broom. I exhaled a puff of air. "So, what kind of name does it want?"

"You have to come up with one."

"It's never liked anything I've done so far. Probably wouldn't be happy with whatever name I chose either."

"The name has to be appropriate."

"Appropriate to what?"

"What does your broom mean to you?"

I was flummoxed by the question. "Umm . . . transportation?"

"Your broom is a companion of sorts, like a favourite horse. It's more of a partnership."

I stared at it floating before me. A horse I could understand. Maybe I'd been right to put saddle parts on it. Then again, with its *sensitive feelings*, maybe I'd embarrassed it. Sigh. "Do I have to come up with something right now?"

"Sooner is better if you want a good working relationship."

"Okay . . . okay." I gave a dismissive wave. "I'll think of something. Different question here. Why did it knock me off Bluescale and return me to the castle?"

Wynn made some hand motions, I heard a few mumbles, and the sparkles around the broom became agitated. It was the strangest conversation I'd ever witnessed.

Wynn turned back to me. "She says she saved your life."

"Huh? I was riding a *dragon* at the time! What danger could I have possibly been in?"

"You were about to be sucked into a vortex caused by a confluence of the magic ripples you saw this morning. By the time you felt the force, it would've been too late for both of you."

I grabbed the table as a wave of dizziness swept through me. "What . . . what would've happened?"

"The vortex would've pulled you into a one-way trip to another world. You might call it a different dimension."

"How did the broom know?"

"She can sense danger to you and, even though you haven't named her, she feels the responsibility given by your father."

It. A broom. An object. That's how I saw it. "It's a she?"

"She has female energy, yes."

"I didn't know . . ."

As he smiled, I felt a rush of warmth and wondered how much magic was in that smile. It made me want to trust him – offer him my first-born.

"I'll . . . think about it and get back to you." I looked at the broom again. Is it . . . she . . . going to cooperate in the meantime?"

"That depends on how you treat her."

"Tell her I'll . . . give her a name as soon as I come up with something meaningful." The odd conversation gave me a surreal sensation.

Wynn sent me that melting smile again. "She'll cooperate for now."

"Uh . . . tell her thanks."

***

Bluescale would stay near the castle while Wynn and Shain worked on a spell to make the ripples, especially the vortices, visible. Dorian's fourth mage, on an extended trade mission, was unavailable. My self-imposed task was to review lists of magical names in hopes one would leap out at me as being acceptable to my broom. I have to say, this felt odd. What next? Birthday parties for the dustpan?

I was ensconced in the Odenai Castle library mumbling names aloud when Dorian slipped into a chair next to me and propped an ankle over a corner of the table.

I sat back to rub my eyes. "This is hopeless. How am I supposed to pick a name?"

"Did you have a favourite friend or pet when you were a kid?"

"I had lots of pets."

"Which one gave you the warmest fuzzy feelings?"

"Umm . . . a calico cat named Gladys. She'd follow me around and not judge when I tried to do magic. She slept on my bed and listened to my troubles."

"Does the name give you a good feeling?"

I thought about that. "The cat does, so I suppose that includes her name."

"Try that one. It doesn't have to be a magical name, just something your broom will accept."

"It . . . she's never met my cat."

"But you have, so the name will translate into warmth and caring. Thoughts about the original Gladys will open your heart, and your broom will know that."

I tipped my head back to look down my nose at him. "When did you get so wise?"

He grinned. "Pretending to be wise is part of the job description."

"I guess this magic ripple issue is just business as usual, isn't it? Things like this will happen all the time."

"I imagine. It's a good thing I've also inherited mages." He paused. "It takes some getting used to, stepping into my father's shoes. My mother could only tell me what a twelve-year-old could understand, so the mages are supplementing my family education. A lot of it hasn't been pretty. Any kids of mine will get a ton of oversight from me."

I felt a twinge in the neighbourhood of my heart. Dorian had indeed become a man when he could speak so calmly about a family. I guess, for him, it was expected whereas I still had reservations about getting a goldfish. Perhaps my maturity level lagged behind his. Besides – there was Valgren.

Dorian glanced up from beneath lowered lids. "So, how's Valgren these days?"

I swear the man can read my mind. I twitched my shoulders. "On an errand for Gaia. He'll be gone another couple of weeks."

He gave me a searching look then abruptly rose. As he strode to the door, he tossed back over his shoulder, "Got to get back to work. Good luck with the broom."

I grumbled and went back to looking for a better name than Gladys. I'd loved the cat but wasn't crazy about the name. She'd had it when I got her and, even though I'd tried to give her a new one, it had stuck like a burr.

* * *

Wynn stood nearby as my broom hovered over the workshop table. I eyed it with suspicion. "You think this'll work?"

"I'm certain it won't work if the ritual isn't completed."

Okay, then. "What do I do?"

What followed was a confusion of, "Say this; do that." Although I followed instructions, the broom seemed unchanged. After a time, I asked if we were wasting our time. Wynn said the ritual was more complicated because we hadn't been properly bonded in the beginning. I was to be patient.

Not one of my strong points as you know. I was shifting my weight from foot-to-foot when Wynn's mumbo-jumbo stopped, and he seemed to expect something from me.

I hadn't understood a word for the past ten minutes. "What?"

"This is where you pronounce the name you want to give your broom."

"Oh. Uh . . ." I cleared my throat. "Gladys." As I envisioned cuddling my friend of long ago, an unbidden emotion filled my chest. I did miss her. She'd been my one real friend and witness to my magical failures and successes. I could probably even conjure up a tear or two.

"No need to overdo it, Raven," said Wynn with a sardonic smile. "That'll be enough."

Right.

As Wynn made a casting motion, a sparkly blue cloud surrounded the broom. "If she accepts the name, the cloud will encompass you."

The communal tick of pendulums swinging in sync filled the stillness. A water-clock trickled. Was I about to be rejected by a cleaning utensil? How embarrassing would that be? I glanced at Wynn, but he made a downward motion with his hand, miming I was to remain still.

I was feeling stupid when the sparkling cloud made a sudden expansion to encompass me. It was the strangest sensation. It felt like an intelligence knocked at the door of my soul. I glanced at Wynn for direction, but he turned away with what looked like a roll of his eyes.

I opened myself to the visitor which felt like a gentle presence. Aww . . . It reminded me of my cat. I felt mushy. The crazy idea of whether cats could reincarnate as brooms flashed onto my mental screen – but not for long. Magic could only stretch so far.

As the presence filled me, I realized it was indeed feminine. Very feminine. Darn! I'd been hoping for something braver. And I got along better with men. Hurdle number one was over though. She'd accepted me as her partner. I wondered if I'd have to ask permission every time I wanted a ride.

I was shocked to feel a response. It wasn't in words, but the understanding was clear. I was in charge . . . unless she over-rode me. Hmm. We could communicate at any time, but she wouldn't be a constant presence in my head. This sounded good. I got the sense of being thanked for her new name. She liked it. Seemed it made her think of kittens.

When the introduction was over, Gladys moved within easy reach. I closed my fingers around the handle and it (*she*) hovered in place. It'd have to remember the gender thing if I didn't want to insult my new best friend.

Wynn smiled which drew warm, fuzzy feelings from me. *Don't even go there! He had some kind of spell on his smile!*

Shaking off my response, I thanked him, straddled Gladys, made a circuit of the room, and shot out an open window. This was more like it! She responded to my slightest movement. As we performed rolls, loops, and ducked through the clouds, I realized how tense I'd been not being able to trust my broom.

I patted her bristles. "Thanks, Gladys. Sorry for the delayed intro."

Chapter 27

"Could we use the vortex against Myrador and the piglets?" I asked. "I'd like to send them all to another world."

I was sprawled on an overstuffed chair enjoying the flickers of hundreds of rainbows. Although Odenai Castle was built of stone, cut crystals floated in sunbeams to create a colourful kaleidoscope.

We'd chosen a comfortable common room at the base of one of the towers in which to brainstorm. Angus, Frost, and Talon had joined us leaving Cash in charge of Cumulos. No one doubted the cloud castle's safety with him in charge. Dorian, much to Frost's disappointment, was reclined with his feet up on a comfortable couch. As she took the nearest chair, I gave him a surreptitious glance. A faint curve of his lips assured me he was quite aware of the witch of Cumulos. I wondered if he'd ever . . .

I gave myself a mental head-slap. Don't even go there! As long as I was unwilling to give up Valgren, I'd decided Dorian should remain out-of-bounds, and I'd do my best to keep it that way.

Soft footfalls preceded the arrival of Dorian's mages. I wondered if they became so silent because of their lives of constant study. As Dorian dropped his feet to the floor so Morgan could sit beside him, I shot a glance at Frost whose scrutiny acquired a most unpleasant gleam. At that point, I realized she hadn't spent time with Dorian's new mages.

"By the way, Frost," I said, hoping to avert disaster, "Did you know Morgan is Dorian's cousin?"

She took a closer look at Morgan. "Of course. The white streak. I hadn't realized."

Morgan made a dismissive gesture. "I don't trade on the family name. I'm a mage, pure and simple." She put her hand on Dorian's. "And I'm so grateful Dorian has returned. I'm next in line for the throne and, frankly, I don't want it. I love being a mage."

"Then you must've been one of Gargeran's targets as well," I said.

"I can protect myself from Gargeran, and I'd have challenged him if he'd found Dorian while he was with the mortals." She squeezed his hand. "Dorian was the one born to rule."

After his handling of the Altarian citizens and witnessing the country's rapid recovery from Gargeran's occupation, I'd already come to that conclusion. Dorian was where he belonged. What about me? Where did I belong? It was the perennial question to which I never had an answer. And, once again, I parked it on a dusty mental shelf to be reviewed at a future date.

Frost's jealousy averted, I focused on the issue. "Can Myrador see the vortices where the magic ripples intersect? Could he be involved in creating them?"

"Good questions, lass," said Angus from across a low table, "but we don't think Myrador is the cause o' the magic ripples. They seem te be a bleed-through from another world. Might be nobody here's responsible at all."

"Can we close the opening?" I asked.

"It can be done, lass, but this might be an opportunity like ye said, o' removing Myrador and the piggies permanently."

"I'd feel bad to dump them on somebody else."

"We live in a universe o' infinite worlds, so there's no way te tell. Also, we could be the recipient o' evil from somewhere else. The spyders, for example, come from another world."

"Everyone dumps their garbage on everyone else? Humans have been doing it for years and, believe me, it doesn't work. There must be a better way."

"We're open te suggestions."

All eyes turned to me. Rats! How had I gotten myself in this position? Instead of making the problem better, I'd made it worse, at least for me. Now it seemed I was to solve it. I chewed my lip as a partial idea lit my brain. "Do we know if the ripples go through the ground as well as the air?"

"They're aerial," said Wynn. "Curtains of magic touch the ground but move sideways. They shift a lot like Aurora Borealis – the Northern Lights, only the ripples are invisible."

"Then I can stone-walk below them?"

He nodded, a frown between his brows as he tried to get my train of thought.

"Can we predict the formation of a vortex?"

"They form where the curtains intersect so, yes," said Angus, "we should be able te figure it out once we can see the curtains. Why?"

"What if we used a conjunction of the curtains to hold open a portal to the other world, and what if Myrador and his pigs could be coerced into being there?"

"How de ye suggest we get him there, lass?"

After a beat of silence, Dorian leaped to his feet. "Don't even think about it! You're not using yourself as bait! As king, I forbid it!"

My spine stiffened. "I'm not a citizen of Altaria, Dorian! Which means you can't tell me what to do!"

"Then I'll chain you in the cellars! We'll find another way!"

"Valgren is the only other stone-walker, and he's away for another couple of weeks."

"What about that other Rider you told us about? What's his name? Arwin? Where's he?"

"Haven't a clue. I only met him once." *And since I didn't want everyone knowing about that embarrassing encounter, I wouldn't be looking him up anytime soon.*

"Myrador already hospitalized you with snake-light! Another second, and you wouldn't be here at all. I won't allow it!"

Dorian can be mule-headed.

"I'm not going to be stupid about it, Dorian!" I gestured towards the others. "And I won't be alone. With all the magic in this room, we should be able to come up with something. We need Myrador out of our hair before he causes real damage, and Altaria will never be safe so long as he and the piglets are plotting who-knows-what. I'm the best choice for bait. His hatred of me might make him careless."

"Or more determined," growled Dorian, less than convinced by the validity of my rock-solid logic.

"I'm magic too, you know!" I jumped to my feet. "I'm not helpless!"

He rolled his eyes. "No insult intended, Raven, but you just learned the protocol for riding your broom this morning."

I spluttered. "Well . . . you didn't know either! And I'm not dumb enough to pit myself against Myrador without help!"

He thinned his lips. "You see, that's exactly what I think you'd do."

The whirr of tiny wings and an annoying little voice interrupted a conversation that threatened to become heated. I huffed out a breath and groaned without turning around.

"What'd I miss?" Scarlet buzzed to Angus' shoulder, made herself comfortable, crossed her little ankles, and basked in the shared glory of authority.

"We'll continue this later," I said, flopping back into the chair, fingers drumming against the arm.

"Nice to see you back, Scarlet," said Dorian. "How's the family?"

Scarlet made a dismissive gesture. "Relatives are overrated. It'll be another thirty years before I make that trip." She shot a look at everyone. "What's going on?"

Dorian brought her up to speed.

"Hunh," she said. "I've never heard of such a thing."

"You mean magic waves?" I asked.

"Those too. Mostly I'm surprised a broom would bother to rescue an impaired rider."

A vein in my forehead throbbed.

"The broom was programmed by her father," said Angus.

Big green eyes blinked at me. "I thought she didn't have a father."

A growl pressured to burst from my throat. "Of course, I have a father! I just don't know who he is!"

"Is there a difference?"

"I think we're getting off topic here," interrupted Dorian, no doubt worried about being scalded by the steam that shot from my ears. "Any other suggestions about the magic ripples?" He swiveled his head to glare at me, "that does *not* involve Raven as bait for a homicidal maniac?"

To tell the truth, I was on his side. I didn't want to be bait either, but nobody had a better idea. In the end, my plan was selected because I could stone-walk beneath the invisible waves to find Myrador and his henchmen. Dorian insisted on coming along, of course. The simple fact was, though Dorian may not be able to control me, he controlled nearly everybody else.

Part of the plan involved Bluescale so, after the meeting broke up, I wandered to the courtyard. Bluescale may be goofy, but he was a gutsy bag of wind, so I'd little doubt he'd be excited to participate. About to call him, I noticed half-a-dozen saddled horses tied to hitching rails. They looked comfortable dozing in the afternoon sun and, if I didn't want to be the cause of an uproar, I'd best meet the dragon outside the castle walls.

I called Gladys whose prompt response made my jaw drop. Amazing how a small thing like a name could make such a difference! We soared over the walls towards a nearby stream where Bluescale liked to hang out.

I followed the stream until I noticed a hump of reflective blue-green. Waking a snoozing dragon can be risky, so I made a looping turn to settle onto the grass at a distance that would ensure he wouldn't mistake me for a snack before he was fully awake. Light snores drifted from a half-opened jaw, and a gigantic pink tongue lolled onto a boulder. As he didn't respond when I called him, I resorted to tossing pebbles at his nose.

That worked better – almost too well, in fact. He gave a snort, and a burst of black smoke shot from his nostrils, a roar from his throat, and a snarl showed many pointed teeth as his snake-like head searched for the attacker.

"Stop! Bluescale! Stop!" I screeched. "It's me, Raven! Relax!" I nearly got grass stains on my face as Gladys whipped us behind a sturdy oak.

"Talk about waking up cranky," I griped from behind the tree. "Take a pill!"

"Oh. It's you," he said as a final puff of smoke drifted away on the breeze. "Not a good idea to surprise me."

"No shit! Next time I'll use a water gun."

"Next time use telepathy."

"You couldn't hear me over your snoring." This was getting nowhere. "Moving on . . . I'm here to ask for help."

Big eyes widened. "Again?"

You see, this is why I hate asking Bluescale for help. He always makes me feel so incompetent. I gave an impatient huff. "This is for Dorian and Altaria."

"Well, then that's different."

"What do you mean, 'that's different'? What's different about it?"

"King and country and all that."

"You don't give a damn about king *or* country, Bluescale! You're a dragon for Pete's sake!"

"So . . . what is it you need?" he asked, ignoring my point.

"*King* Dorian has asked for your assistance in shoving Myrador and as many of his pig cohorts as possible into one of the vortices." I outlined the details.

When I was finished, he lifted a claw and said, "One question."

"What?"

"Why do I have to take the pixie?"

"We all make sacrifices, Bluescale. Besides, I'm usually the one stuck with her."

"And I'm good with that," he said.

"No doubt."

I left him with a reminder to collect Scarlet at the castle before sunrise. He was still grumbling as I sped away.

Chapter 28

Early dawn promised another nice day. I rubbed my shoulder, viewed scattered pink clouds, and recalled my previous narrow escape from Myrador. Dorian was going to be mad as hell, but there was no way I was taking him with me. Getting close enough to Myrador to provide irresistible bait would take everything I had, and I might hesitate to take a chance if I was responsible for Dorian's safety. Worse yet, I might make a mistake that would get us caught.

I yawned my way onto a wide balcony that overlooked the city, rested my elbows on cool stone, and waited for the others. Gladys floated to my left as I gazed at the beautiful view. Why was there always someone who felt the need to destroy?

I sent a mental prompt to the dragon. *"Are you ready, Bluescale?"*

"Ready!"

"Scarlet with you?"

"So far."

"What do you mean, so far?"

"Do you realize she never stops talking? I don't know if I can stand it, Raven! Dragons have sensitive hearing, you know."

I wondered if the competition was too much for him. *"If I can stand it, so can you. We need her pixie dust . . . What did you say?"*

"Never mind. I was trying to get a word in edgewise, but she just keeps yammering on. Think I'll stuff dandelion leaves in my ears."

"Before you do that, do you remember our plan? Yours and mine?"

"Not sure . . ."

"Bluescale!"

In the midst of a rolling chuckle he said, "Don't get excited, Raven! I'll be there. Cheez!"

"I'm depending on you to keep Dorian safe."

"The pixie's harping in my other ear. Says my backplates aren't soft enough. I've gotta shut one of you off. Give me a shout when it's time."

And the connection went dead. It was like having someone hang up on you. Perhaps it goes without saying: I wasn't filled with confidence when it came to those two.

***

Angus had confirmed Myrador was still in the Caves of Cynbel but hadn't probed further for fear of alerting the dark mage. Shain, Wynn and Morgan, along with a contingent of soldiers, would guard Odenai Castle against a surprise attack. If Myrador got a foothold there, it would be impossible to evict him, especially with the magical tools in the lab. Cash and his soldiers guarded Cumulos.

That left Dorian, Angus, Talon, Frost and me along with Bluescale and Scarlet. I hoped it would be enough because I was tired of worrying about this twit lurking in the shadows. Dorian's mages had confirmed Scarlet's pixie dust would make the magic ripples visible, and we hoped the vortex would hold long enough to send Myrador and his hench pigs through it.

I turned as Dorian stepped onto the rampart. He looked . . . incredible.

He slanted a look at me. "What?"

"Nothing. Just . . . nervous."

A grimace crossed his face. "We all are. There's a lot riding on this, and it could go either way. Altaria just got rid of one despot, she doesn't need another."

It was interesting to see how he'd incorporated his responsibilities to Altaria, thinking of the country as a *she* that needed protecting. I'd like to have been offended by that but, after all, he'd rescued me a time or two. He had a knack for making people feel safe and somehow, I was drawn to that. Was that all it was? I checked out the strength of his shoulders and the fit of his trousers. *Nope. Safety was not at the top of my list.*

"We should go down to the courtyard," said Dorian. "Angus will be here soon."

I nodded and reached for Gladys.

Angus arrived attired in what I thought of as his mage apparel – dark green bonnet, matching tartan over one shoulder, and kilt enhanced with a rabbit-fur sporran. A carved silver pendant hung on a heavy chain around his neck, and his ancient broom hovered nearby.

"We need a second stone-walker," complained Talon as he floated into view, legs twisted as usual. "A great deal is going to rest on someone with miniscule experience in magical conflict."

"The greatest risk is te her, nae te us," said Angus. "We should be grateful she's willing te put her life on the line te assist Altaria, not complain about her inexperience, a condition she's worked hard te alleviate since I've known her." He turned a hard gaze on Talon, something I'd never seen him do. "We need te trust each other and work together. If ye cannae do that, perhaps ye should return te Cumulos where I'm sure Cash would be grateful for your help."

Talon seemed as surprised as the rest of us at Angus' retort. He nodded in acquiescence. "I will remain. My intent was simply to point out a weakness in our plan."

"We're all aware o' the risk, none more than Raven."

Frost, in figure-hugging black silk, inserted herself between Dorian and me. "I'll remain close to His Highness to ensure his safety."

Dorian glanced at her. "I'll be underground with Raven, so that won't be necessary, but I appreciate your concern."

As Frost slid me a look, I shook my head a tiny fraction. Her lips curled in satisfaction as she turned back to Dorian. "I'll be ready . . . just in case." Dorian glanced at me in time to catch an eye-roll that nearly dislocated my eyeballs. His smile was smug.

Angus glanced towards the east. "The sun will be up soon. Tis time te go, Your Highness."

Dorian nodded and mounted his broom. I grabbed Gladys who floated nearby, and we were off. I stuffed the thought into a deep dark recess in my mind that I might not return. Doubts were dangerous. Talon was right. I had little experience, but I'd put up a damn good fight.

* * *

We hovered not far from the caves of Cynbel, the topmost branches of a stately pine brushing my toes. My heartrate soared as memories of falling into the abyss clamoured for attention.

"This is a good place to start," said Dorian. "We can stone-walk into the tunnels from here." We drifted lower and, as our feet touched a carpet of meadow flowers, he glanced at me. "Where's Bluescale?"

"He and Scarlet are waiting for my signal."

"Want to let them know we're here?"

"Bluescale! You listening?" Nothing. *"Bluescale! Where's that wonderful dragon hearing you brag about? BLUESCALE!"*

"Geez, Raven! You nearly blew my skull apart!"

"You weren't answering."

"I couldn't hear you over Little Red's complaining! I have a headache already!"

"Don't let her get to you, and the headache will go away."

"Easy for you to say. She's not perched on your head!"

I heaved a sigh. *"Could we focus, please? Scarlet's not that bad."*

What had I just said?! I must've misheard. I pressed a mental "replay" button. Nope. That's what I'd said. In spite of everything, she'd grown on me. Like a fungus – a little at a time. Since it might take centuries to actually like her, I was in no immediate danger.

I focused again on Bluescale. *"Remember what we talked about? Now would be a good time."*

As I watched Dorian in silence for a few moments, he glanced down at me. "What?"

"I'm going to apologize for this in advance since there's a chance I might not be able to later. I'm sorry, Dorian. This is for your own good."

Puzzlement then suspicion crossed his face. "Raven, what have you done . . ?"

There was a blue-green flash and a terrific rush of wind. Powerful claws wrapped around Dorian, and he was swept into the blue.

I spun to Angus. "I'm going after Myrador alone. Keep the pigs as distracted as you can."

Before he could say a word, I sank into the coolness of mountain stone. Tree roots dwindled until there was only stone and flowing water. Myrador was east. I took my time to ensure the others had ample opportunity to set up their distractions and hoped the invisibility talisman around my neck would hide me from the pig men. I wasn't so confident it would work with Myrador.

I wished Valgren was with me, but he was out of touch for a few more days. This would've been easy for him. In fact, he wouldn't be any happier than Dorian was that I'd done this on my own, but the opportunity was now, not next week. We had no idea how long the energy curtains would last.

After a time, my wand vibrated a warning that a null-magic field was near. If I stumbled into one while stone-walking, it would be the last thing I ever did. I sent a mental thanks to Angus for augmenting my wand.

After my last visit, Myrador would've ensured the planning room was enfolded in a null-magic field large enough to prevent eavesdropping. Scraps of maps in Odenai showed the locations of tunnels were incomplete to say the least, and Myrador was capable of melting new ones. Which meant, of course, that I'd have to guess a lot.

I looked at my wrist to check the time – and wondered how long I was going to keep doing that. A bare wrist met my gaze, of course. Electronics didn't work on Altaria, and I'd lost my wind-up watch. Most irritating. Sometimes I missed my conveniences: electric stoves, microwaves, television, music, but I supposed the trade-off for magic was worth it. Well, maybe not at the moment since I was sneaking up on a truly powerful bad guy who wanted to kill me.

I tapped my fingers on my leg. How long had it been? Maybe Bluescale would know. *"Bluescale? Bluescale! You there?"*

"Raven, I suspect humans are evolving into dragons. I do believe Dorian has smoke coming from his ears. Wrong orifice, but maybe he'll learn."

"Don't tell him you're talking to me!"

"Why not?"

"Do you think he has anything good to say to me?"

There was a pause. "Probably not at this point. He's been creating new curses for you since I picked him up."

No doubt. *"Are the others ready?"*

"Just about. We've spotted three magic ripples in the area. Talon, Angus, and Frost are pushing them towards a volcano that Angus says is ready for a minor eruption. They'll manoeuvre the curtains into a triangular shape that should provide walls strong enough to direct the lot of them into the other world."

"How long will it take to get the curtains in place?"

"About an hour. I'll let you know when they're set up."

Time to get into the tunnel network. I skirted a null-magic field until a wide tunnel lit by the ever-popular glow-globes appeared. A main thoroughfare. I was thrilled to feel the faint tingle of magic as I stepped into it.

I wondered what Myrador did down there. What was his motivation for taking over the world anyway? Didn't he have anything better to do? I could suggest a dozen hobbies.

I turned left along a tunnel that sloped upwards at a shallow angle. At least I was going towards Myrador's headquarters. As there wasn't a null-magic field in the tunnel itself, I felt a renewal of hope. I suspected the prospect of manual labour was anathema to the pigs, so they'd be unwilling to haul stuff by hand. I was also pretty sure that even if Myrador gave instructions for null-magic fields to surround the main area, they'd omit them in some tunnels and ensure they forgot to tell him.

I scuttled along irregular rock walls, ducking from one outcropping to another. The renewed feel of null-magic rippled through my back as I pressed against stone. Yep. That's exactly what they'd done. The null-magic areas were sporadic. Myrador would be pissed if he knew.

I figured I'd keep moving towards Myrador's headquarters and hope the pigs were busy elsewhere. There were a lot of tunnels to guard. At the sound of a rolling pebble, I slunk into the shadows of a passage that joined the main tunnel at an angle. It hadn't been important enough to warrant globe-lights. Wand in hand, I took deep breaths to regulate my breathing and moved away from the null-magic spell in the wall. Another pebble rolled followed by the regular tramp of feet.

I was startled by the screech of a woman. "I don't want to hear any more excuses, pig! Someone is causing this rain of pebbles. It doesn't happen by itself!" Hmm. The voice sounded familiar.

There was a whining response. "But they come out of thin air! How can we catch who's responsible?"

"By using your miniscule brain, you idiot!"

It was clear Angus' initial move was underway – the plan to confuse and annoy the pig men. They'd search in vain for the cause of a hail of small stones throughout the tunnel system.

As they approached, I moved deeper into the shadows. A dozen pig soldiers marched past led by a woman dressed in something form-fitting and dark blue. *Nightshade!* So, this is where that tramp had gotten to!

She'd used Dorian not long ago to get the layout of Cumulos, and Angus and company had barely succeeded in overcoming the attack that followed. Dorian had been less than pleased at being used in such a way, and I wouldn't want to be Nightshade when he caught up with her. He'd strip her magical abilities with relish and exile her to the human world without a lick of remorse. Come to think of it, the volcano might be a better choice for her.

Nightshade's presence meant an adjustment of plans. I'd have to elude her while looking for Myrador. As if I didn't have enough to deal with already. Damn!

Should I find out what she was up to? I activated the invisibility amulet as my feet made the decision to sneak along behind. I had a score to settle with her, and the pigs made enough racket to cover any noise I might make.

It was impossible to tell one pig man from another, so I'd no idea if the officer running to keep up with Nightshade was Napoleon or his clone. In fact, the only way I could identify Napoleon was by his baby-poo sash and epaulets and, if I got close enough, he had a pale grey streak along one side of his snout. Since the pigs' high-pitched squeals were hard on my ears, and I was some distance away, they must've been driving Nightshade crazy.

"Could you just *shut up*?!" she screamed. "Stop talking!" As her companion stuttered to silence, I heard her snarl, "What Myrador sees in you idiots is beyond my comprehension! All I'm doing is sealing a tunnel. This is not rocket science!" The pigs looked at one another without comprehension. Guess they'd never heard of rocket science. "I don't need you incompetent imbeciles as guards! Myrador's paranoia about an attack is ridiculous! The new king of Altaria is nearly as incompetent as you lot!"

I was almost sorry for the pigs. The woman had a rampant case of megalomania I'd be happy to cure. I wasn't crazy about following the waggling fat butts in front of me since, in my opinion, their tunics covered the wrong halves of their bodies, but each to his own. I scuttled along in their wake, wondering how far they planned to go.

Ten minutes later, our entourage approached a thick stone disk designed to seal the tunnel. As Nightshade waved her wand, the stone rolled slowly into place. I was about to return the way I'd come when the witch turned and seemed to look directly at me.

Startled, I backed up – right into a wall. There was a *zzzzt* as I touched the edge of a null-magic field. I felt the invisibility shield flash and falter. Damn!

Nightshade's eyes widened. "You!" she screamed, and hurled a bolt of energy.

Not waiting around to be roasted, I sprinted back along the tunnel, the sound of pig hooves thundering behind.

Chapter 29

This wasn't going quite as planned. I scurried about looking for a hiding spot, the Wicked Witch of the West on my ass, and the walls lined with null-magic fields. If inclined to be self-critical, I might've suspected I'd stumbled into a trap.

My thighs burned before I remembered the spell to lessen my weight. I mumbled the incantation, grateful when the pressure eased. The problem was, Nightshade would've been using it all along, most likely the reason the gap between us had narrowed. I ducked an incoming blast.

An open area intersected by four tunnels appeared – a major juncture. Which way? Bigger tunnels were less likely to be dead ends, and the widest continued straight ahead. Maybe it would lead to Myrador. Wouldn't it be wonderful to trap both the Dark Mage and Nightshade in the vortex? I'd dance for a week if I could pull that one off. I charged across the open area into the tunnel straight ahead.

I must've had an insane streak of optimism to think I could snare Myrador while jumping like a jack-rabbit ahead of Nightshade. As rock shards exploded next to my face, I shrieked and grabbed for the invisibility amulet around my neck. There was a ripple and . . . the pigs skidded to a halt. They stared at one another, at Nightshade, and shuffled in confusion. Nightshade's beautiful face twisted into something less attractive.

"Don't think an invisibility spell will save you!" she shrieked. "Your powers are infinitesimal compared to mine!" I stifled another scream as shrapnel spit from the wall. As I charged down the tunnel, it didn't occur to me that I was leaving footprints in the dust. Invisibility can only do so much.

Think, think, think! My broom! Gladys could fly as long as the tunnels remained free of null-magic fields. I prayed the pig men were as lazy as I suspected. I dove around a bend in the main tunnel, materialized Gladys, and bailed on. The walls flashed past like images in a video game. The difference was if I hit anything, it was game-over . . . no re-set.

A glance over my shoulder revealed the pig men puffing and struggling to keep up with Nightshade. She, on the other hand, was doing splendidly. She'd also materialized a broom and, by the looks of things, knew how to use it. If she hadn't been trying to kill me, I'd have asked her for lessons.

She spoke into her wrist. Probably a report to Myrador. Was I being pushed where they wanted me to go? Probably would be soon if I didn't take charge of the situation. And, yes, I realize how ridiculous that sounded. But when you're in a no-win situation, it's helpful to make yourself believe you've got a chance, even if all it does is lower stress levels.

As Nightshade closed the distance between us, another juncture appeared with five exits. Before I could make a decision, there was a brilliant flash, and red curtains of light closed off the exits one after the other. It was doubtful Nightshade had the extra concentration to do it which meant . . . Myrador.

I pushed Gladys towards the nearest open exit and shot into darkness. "Gladys, can you see in the dark?"

"Perhaps you've noticed brooms don't have eyes? Lack of light is not relevant."

Apparently, Gladys could talk inside my head. "So, how do you . . . never mind."

"We seem to be in a hurry. Do you have a destination in mind?"

As a bolt of lightning blasted a chunk of rock from the wall beside us, we ducked away from flying debris.

"The witch behind us is trying to kill me! I need to get her and the pigs over the mountain crater which means I need to keep them following but not catching up!"

Gladys bucked. I heard a sharp screech, caught the whiff of burning straw, and the walls became a blur. Since I couldn't begin to steer through the dark tunnel at this rate, I decided to hang on and trust Gladys. When a faint glow appeared, I realized that part of the labyrinth was old enough to be filled with the luminescent plants we'd found in the gnome tunnels. Thank heavens for small favours. I could see again.

As the tunnel morphed into a cylindrical lava tube that looped like a snake tied in a knot, I glanced over my shoulder to see how Nightshade was doing. She'd lost some ground after Gladys had found another gear and looked to be struggling to keep up. The pig men had been left behind. Go, Gladys! Maybe there were advantages to having a timid broom after all.

I was unnerved that Myrador hadn't put in an appearance. Not that I wanted him added to the pack but, if he wasn't there, he was somewhere else. Setting a trap? As I skimmed a sharp corner, I perceived a gaping hole in the floor ahead. Nightshade wasn't in sight. I shot over the edge then dropped into it to hover below the lip. The shaft was about twenty feet deep and, if the witch saw me, I had nowhere to go. The walls were still filled with null-magic.

A few short seconds later, there was a swish of air, and Nightshade shot past, leaned forward, focused ahead.

A sly smile pasted itself on my face. "Gladys, let's see how fast you can fly!" I blasted after Nightshade.

In the convoluted tunnel, I needed to concentrate to keep from falling off as Gladys ducked and dove. *Keep it simple. Catch the witch. Make her unconscious (I couldn't kill people). Get away. Details to follow.*

A sponge-like material stretched across the tunnel ahead. Splotches of pale grey stuff started to decorate the walls and got progressively thicker. It made me think of travelling through the nose of a giant with a cold. Ick! Nightshade slowed to navigate, probably thinking I was hidden in the gloop.

I remembered old cowboy movies where good guys were honour-bound not to shoot an enemy in the back. I thought about that for a beat. "Welcome to the 21st century, bitch!" I hurled an energy bolt with all my strength.

Through sheer dumb luck, it hit smack between her shoulder blades. I squashed a twinge of remorse as she tumbled to the floor and skidded through the goo. Eeuw! As I shot past, a string of unladylike language followed me.

I wanted to get back into the mountain but, to do that, I had to find a gap in the null-magic spells. When I found a clean piece of wall, I dismounted to give it a light touch. No doubt Gladys could be harmed if the field flowed through me to her. *Zzzzzt!* Ouch! I moved further along the tunnel. Still no luck. Surely the entire system wasn't encircled in null-magic! That would take ridiculous amounts of power.

The tunnel echoed with the pitter-patter of little hooves and a good deal of huffing and puffing. Persistent little critters. They were still within earshot when I heard Nightshade curse at them. *Why weren't they riding brooms already? How could pigs be so stupid?!* Bet they hated their boss.

I mounted Gladys to put more distance between us and picked a side tunnel that I hoped would be free of the grey goo. The thought of touching it was just too . . . icky. So, sue me! I'm female!

The luminescent glow continued as the tunnel made a sharp drop, but the goo dwindled the further I went. I stopped at a level spot, stepped away from Gladys, and extended a palm towards the rock. A null-magic field would give off an electrical sensation. Nothing. A bubble of hope fluttered near my heart. Could it be? I pushed against the warm stone. In fact, it was very warm come to think of it, and the air carried the distinct scent of sulfur. A trickle of sweat wandered down the side of my face. Guess I hadn't noticed what with running for my life and all that I was approaching the volcano. What now? How far could I stone-walk in the rising heat?

A scream of rage made me jump and look back. Nightshade was not looking good. Grey goo dripped from her clothing, makeup ran down her cheeks, and her mass of black hair looked like it'd been styled with a weed-eater. Pig men, now on brooms, were at her heels.

I transported Gladys to the surface before plunging into suffocating twilight. If I'd been on the surface, I could've cast a spell so I wouldn't feel the heat, but stone-walking has its limitations and, because of numerous null-magic fields, I couldn't move fast. The idea of spending eternity inside a volcanic mountain had little appeal though I suppose I'd be dead so would never know.

What next? Find Myrador? By now, he was aware his subterranean hidey hole had been breached. What would I do in his place? If I knew my enemies were all around an active volcano and I could do it, I'd . . . cause an eruption, catching them unawares.

Would he have that kind of power? I remembered watching Valgren shape an entire stream into a torus with no effort.

Magic was not billiard-ball physics, so equal and opposite reactions did not apply here. I suspected magic was from a deeper reality, one that pre-dated the world and what we thought of as physical laws. Perhaps it was more about feeling with the heart than thinking with the head. Though I felt I'd touched on a profound realization, there was no time to dwell on it. I needed to find Myrador.

Moving with care through hot stone, I realized it might be helpful to use the skills Dorian and I had developed while growing up – that of knowing when we were being watched. Would it work with Myrador? Or would it just tick him off when I invaded his thoughts, and he'd use the connection to find me?

First things first. I couldn't concentrate on locating Myrador while stone-walking. Too easy to lose focus. I needed a tunnel without a null-magic field – or to go topside. The stream of sweat that ran down my back and soaked my tunic made the decision for me. Tortured lungs were desperate for cool, fresh air. I lifted through running water and veins of pure gold while avoiding the tunnels, most of which hummed with traces of null-magic along their edges.

As the tips of tree roots appeared, I hovered, feeling for a trap. At least it was cooler here although there was still the peculiar metallic odour that accompanied stone-walking.

I decided to handle the situation like jumping into a cold lake in British Columbia. Hold your breath, steel yourself for the shock, jump far enough you don't mimic a cat making frantic efforts to latch onto anything in the vicinity . . . and try to muffle the scream when you hit the water. This was a lot like that, but the others were out there doing their parts. Mine was to lead Myrador into the trap. Hopefully I wouldn't materialize in front of him.

I popped into a cool breeze that felt like heaven. The sky was blue with a smattering of fluffy clouds, but the mountainside dotted with sparse pine trees didn't provide much cover. I glanced up, knowing that an invisible Bluescale was up there with Dorian who was probably still cursing and Scarlet still talking.

I peeked over a rocky outcropping to survey the valley. The silver thread of a sparkling stream twisted amongst rocks on its way to the sea, supremely disinterested in our self-absorption.

Valgren had once explained that Gaia was the consciousness of the planet while Nature consisted of the automated mechanisms that made things run. Gaia cared. Nature was indifferent. But since I'd never known Gaia to help with anything, I'd assume I was on my own. In fact, Gaia was still an abstract concept to me. The closest I'd seen of an intelligence was when Valgren had been encased and pulled into the ground by . . . something. I guess it'd been Gaia – and she'd brought him back to life. I'd keep an open mind.

Cool breeze through wet clothing soon had me shivering though I enjoyed the welcome change for a while. When it got uncomfortable, I dried my clothing with a flick of the wrist – a new skill I'd learned from Valgren.

The stream still flowed, the sun still shone – and I still had no plan.

"Bluescale, where are you?"

"The magic curtains are nearly in place!" he replied. "Any sign of Myrador?"

"He's around somewhere. Tell Dorian that Nightshade's in the tunnels. I barely escaped her and a herd of pig men."

"You didn't capture her?"

"Don't start, Bluescale! It's not like I had help. I wish Valgren was here."

"Don't we all?"

"What do you mean by that?"

"Uh . . . nothing. Every little bit helps."

"Right."

"No need for sarcasm."

"Myrador and Nightshade have been sealing tunnels, but I haven't seen him."

"Angus and Dorian just came to chat. I'll ask if they have any ideas."

"Don't tell Dorian you're talking to me. I'm sure he's still mad."

"If you'd been honest in the first place, he might not be." The connection broke.

Sometimes I hate brutal honesty, especially when it's directed at me. You see, if the other person is right, it might appear I could be wrong. And I hate being wrong. I fumed while waiting for Bluescale to re-establish communications. Whose dumb idea had this been anyway? Couldn't have been mine. Would I have been stupid enough to invite a maniac to chase me? I must've been out of my mind.

There was a soft mental click. "Angus says the curtains are in place."

"So, now I need to lure Myrador into the trap."

"I believe that was the plan."

How was I going to do that? I remembered my thought from earlier that, if I was Myrador, I'd destroy my enemies by causing the volcano to erupt, and we could bet he knew we were up there. I told Bluescale to let the others know I was about to make myself visible to Myrador and goad him into pursuing me.

"Angus says to be careful." There was a pause then, "Dorian says . . . never mind. I prefer not to use that kind of language."

Sigh.

I called Gladys, surrounded myself with a protection spell I hoped would be marginally effective, and began to skim the tree tops. I doubted Myrador could resist such a target. After all, I was one of his least favourite people. I don't imagine too many others had "spit in his eye" so-to-speak.

I found I was throttling Gladys every time a branch snapped or a bird flew up. I patted her. "Sorry about that." As the breeze stilled, fingers of fear marched up my back. I did a three-sixty and peered around. Nothing. Curious. It had felt a lot like something.

What was that noise? I halted Gladys and strained to hear. It could've been my imagination but . . . an almost inaudible rumble emanated from the ground. I settled to the grass and pushed my feet into the soil to the ankles. The low vibration I felt caused me to suck in a breath. That was definitely something!

"Bluescale! Watch out for the volcano!"

"We've got it covered, Raven. Any sign of our friend?"

"I'll fly towards the volcano. He can't be far, and I don't see how he could resist coming after me."

"Be careful. I don't have so many friends I can afford to lose one."

"I'm your friend?"

"Loosely speaking, of course." I heard the grin in his voice.

"Of course. I'm going to the edge of the crater, so I'll be in plain sight. By the way, hundreds of animals are stampeding down the mountain. Think they know something?"

"Animals always know."

"How did people get so stupid?"

"A question I've asked myself many times."

"The question was rhetorical, Bluescale." I heard a deep chuckle.

Rumblings from deep in the Earth increased and trees began to sway. I nudged Gladys forward until we hung suspended over a solidified lava bed that belched smoke in places. I felt like I was in a giant gun barrel with the hammer cocked – and Myrador's finger was on the trigger.

The opportunity wouldn't last long. Taking a deep breath, I dove straight into the gaping crater.

"Myrador, you coward!" I screamed. "Come out here and fight like a man! You send others to fight your battles while you hide like the cowardly rabbit you are! Are you that afraid of me?!"

I skimmed the circular walls, my voice reverberating throughout the giant bowl. "You'll never take Dorian's kingdom from him! We won't let you! You're just a sad little man who hides in a cave while delusions of grandeur dance through your crazy head!"

When in doubt, taunt. It had worked in grade school . . . on me. My mother would despair when I came home with a bloody nose and skinned knuckles. My explanation that I was restoring the balance of power was never adequate. I remember writing, "I will not fight", on the blackboard countless times. Not that I went looking for trouble, but kids are perceptive monsters and, if you're the least bit different, they sniff it out like the little bloodhounds they are. And then, of course, they pack like wolves.

My only defence was to make coming after me painful enough for the biggest bully that the others would scatter. A thin scar that slashed through my left eyebrow was evidence the strategy hadn't always worked as well as I'd hoped.

I pulled to a stop in the middle of the crater which was a half-mile across at that point. Fresh cracks showed in the crater floor through which red, glowing lava squeezed. Damn! Where was he?

I nearly jumped off Gladys at the sound of a gravelly voice. "I believe you're looking for me."

Chapter 30

Fear turned to anger as I spun to face Myrador. "So, you got brave enough to venture out of your hole! What's the plan? Think you can win against Altaria and Cumulos?"

A slight movement may have been a shrug. "I always win."

He approached until the nose of his broom was six inches from Gladys and stared into my soul. It was the first time I'd gotten a good look at his eyes – black and empty, slanted up on the outsides. Cheekbones were high, making a pale face thin and long which matched a thin, long mouth that slashed the lower part of his face. The man had never been pretty, but his looks hadn't been helped by a broken nose. Must've pissed off someone else at some point in his evil career.

"So, what's the deal, Myrador? Is there a point to all this 'taking-over-the-world' crap?"

Thin lips thinned further. "You wouldn't understand."

"You're right about that."

"You have a small mind occupied by small thoughts."

"Matter of opinion."

"It's a matter of *fact*." His lip curled in contempt.

"In your *opinion*."

He gave a condescending sigh. "Let's get this over with. Both you and your friend contaminate historical magic with your continental infection."

"Continental *infection*?" Brows met my hairline.

He made a dismissive motion. "You disturb good magic just by being here. I'm doing the magical realm a favour by getting rid of the pair of you."

Anger heated my stomach, and I growled, "That might be tougher than you think!"

"Probably not." As he made a circling motion, my head began to spin. Not literally, of course. To the best of my knowledge, I'm not possessed. It would be more accurate to say, it seemed the world began to spin which created the distressing sensation of not knowing which way was up. I clutched Gladys in a death grip and, before Myrador could complete the spell, shot towards the bubbling lava below.

My eyes burned from sulfur fumes and the blistering, belching heat. As I ducked around rock outcroppings, the dizzy feeling faded so I cast a protective spell to keep myself and Gladys from catching fire.

"Bluescale! You guys ready?" The dark blur that was Myrador was gaining. *"Bluescale! Answer me!"*

There was a mumble followed by, "Sorry. Had to turn off there for a bit. If I didn't tune out the pixie, I was going to throw her into the volcano."

"Bluescale, believe me, I understand but, in the next few seconds, the volcano will be swallowing me. Myrador's right on my ass! I know Nightshade's nearby, and there are pigs in the tunnels. I want to get them all!"

There was a pause. "Dorian says not to take chances. If Myrador's after you, pull straight up. The vortex has been activated. We'll watch for you. Make a ninety-degree turn in any direction on three."

"Three what?"

The question was followed by an insulting pause. "I'm going to count to three, Raven. When I say *three*, you change direction to horizontal – in any direction." I could sense his puzzlement at the appalling level of my ignorance. "I thought this would be easy for you. Don't human kids do this all the time?"

I ducked around a molten fountain that erupted in front of me. *"Kinda busy right now, Bluescale! Not a good time for a philosophy lesson! Keep it simple!"*

"Stupid."

"What?"

"Keep it simple, stupid. That's the saying."

"I know what the goddam saying is! Could we focus, please?!"

"You don't have to be so touchy. I'm just trying to help."

As blasts of power exploded all around, I couldn't spare the time to look back. Trees that had grown in the previously dormant crater tipped with a hiss into the rising bubbles of lava, and I was reminded once again of the indifference of nature.

Gladys bucked as a blast deflected from my shield. Time was short. Where the hell was Nightshade? She hadn't been that far behind. I'd make one more pass around the inside of the crater. If she didn't show, I'd settle for catching Myrador – if he didn't catch me first.

I tossed a stench bomb over my shoulder. I find it difficult to concentrate while vomiting so hoped it'd have the same effect on Myrador. At the speed we were moving, he'd be into the resultant cloud before he could react with a counter-spell.

Rock walls were a blur. I hadn't realized how big a volcanic crater could be. The Canadian Rocky Mountains didn't have active volcanoes – and I was grateful for that. In my experience, mountains were things of beauty, not imminent death.

Gladys ducked around a geyser of lava. The mountain was coming to life. If Nightshade didn't show in the next few seconds, I was out of there.

A flicker caught my attention – movement at a vertical slash in the wall. Could I be mistaken? Wind whipped my eyes so it was hard to tell. The spell I used to neutralize the heat did nothing to divert the wind. I'd have to work on that.

A swarm of giant bees poured from the opening. Now what? I was about to make a sharp direction change when I realized the bees were fat pig men wobbling on ratty old brooms led by an apparition from hell. Smug satisfaction enveloped me. I'm not sure what it is that makes women love to see other women in disarray, but I experienced a grand feeling of superiority as they neared. Of course, the sensation was short-lived as Nightshade's wand was pointed directly at me, and a ball of flame expanded behind her entourage.

"Now, Bluescale!" I screamed. *"I'm coming out now!"*

I shot straight up, coaxing every bit of speed Gladys could deliver, afraid to look back to see how close Myrador was. All I could do was fly an erratic course and hope to avoid the explosions for a few more seconds.

"I'm nearly over the crater rim! Watch for me!"

"Ten-four."

Great. Now Bluescale was talking like a trucker. Where'd he get this stuff? *"How far do I go?"*

"Until I count three. Remember?"

"Then for crissake, start counting!"

Silence.

"Bluescale! Now is not the time to get huffy! Have your snit later!"

"Are you sure you like her that much? Sounds high maintenance to me."

"Who the hell are you talking to?"

"Sorry. Forgot to close the conduit. Dorian had some input."

My body convulsed as a blast of power hit. A scream tore from my throat. I clutched Gladys' handle and hung on for dear life as the world tilted.

"Up, Gladys! Up!" I gasped. "Faster!"

I wished I could see the vortex. What if I went too far? I didn't want to spend eternity with Myrador, Nightshade, and a few dozen pig men. I sucked in a ragged breath. Just keep flying. It would be over soon.

"One! . . . Two!" Bluescale.

Excruciating pain shot through me on the word, "Three!" Acting on instinct, I jerked Gladys to the right and was astounded to feel upward pressure. Fighting to stay down, I caught a glimpse of a giant funnel spiraling to a point high above as the invisibility spell was neutralized by the others.

I could see Bluescale in the distance, Dorian beside him. A loud roar assaulted my senses as I was sucked skyward. A spiral of magic leaped from Dorian, and I was jerked clear of the funnel. A pig man slipped over the crater wall in an attempt to escape but disappeared in a puff of smoke as Bluescale spotted it. *Don't think about it, Raven. They'd do it to you in a heartbeat.*

There followed a deafening roar, and I realized the volcano had burst its seal. Myrador and Nightshade threw desperate looks below as a column of lava flashed upwards. Angus and the others reinforced the magic curtains to ensure there was no escape to the sides. Nightshade's long, dark hair was sucked straight up by the vortex, her efforts to remain stable twisting her face into an ugly grimace. The pig men floundered as they were caught in a crazy spiral that increased in speed the narrower it got. They looked like they'd been flushed down an inverted gigantic toilet.

Nightshade and Myrador struggled against the pressure until the lava had almost reached them. Then Nightshade, with an inaudible scream, was overpowered by the vortex and spun out of sight. Myrador, with deep hatred, showed his teeth in a snarl. Then he threw something towards me, relaxed, and let himself be taken. In seconds, he was a spinning, shrinking black speck – but I had a cold feeling in the pit of my stomach.

So engrossed was I in the spectacle, I barely noticed the tons of boiling lava that spewed towards me. When a glob the size of a car whizzed past, I jerked to attention but, before I could move, tendrils of something twisted around me, sucking tight.

Myrador! A final spell animated by his hatred. My panic-stricken struggles only caused the tendrils to tighten. Although my wand was in my hand, I couldn't come up with a single spell that would work. The crushing bands included a null-magic field that made the pig men's net seem like a toy.

I began to fall.

While I could still breathe, I screamed, "Bluescale! Help me!"

The mountain was covered in a glowing, oozing mass that crept towards the ocean where it would create a massive cloud of steam – but I wouldn't live to see it.

"Bluescale! . . . Dorian!"

The tendrils had reached my throat, tightening inexorably. I clawed at them, desperate to breathe.

"Valgren . . !"

I tumbled into darkness.

Chapter 31

What I saw didn't make sense. There was a woman on the bed below. She had pale white skin, and a fan of black and green hair spread over a snowy pillow. Her eyes were closed. Angus and Dorian's mages encircled the bed chanting spells as a healer placed crystals on the woman's body. Dorian was seated on the side of the bed holding her hand.

Seeing everything from a bird's eye view felt odd. How had I gotten up there? I felt as light as a bubble as I bobbed against the ceiling. And who was that woman? I thought about moving closer and was instantly at the bedside. A tremor ran through me as I recognized my face. Could I really be that pale?

As I scanned the others, I saw they were worried, but Dorian stared at the woman with a terror I'd never seen.

This was confusing. I was fine. In fact, I felt fantastic. The bit I couldn't reconcile was how I could be watching everything from a different perspective. If my eyes were closed, how could I see? My vision was perfect.

The body had dark bruising along the shoulders and around the neck, and there were scratch marks along the jaw and cheeks where I'd fought the spell. I remembered choking and falling through thick clouds of ash. It was all a bit hazy now.

I pushed Dorian's shoulder to let him know I was okay and was horrified when my hand passed straight through him. A second attempt was no different. It was like I was in a permanent state of stone-walking.

If he couldn't see me, maybe he could hear. "Dorian!" I felt like I was speaking from beneath a pillow, my voice muffled. If no one could see, hear, or touch me, how was I to communicate? In that instant, I got a whole new appreciation for the human body. It was a communications device for the third dimension – and I no longer had mine. How was I to get their attention?

Come to think of it, *was* I okay? I pushed at the mattress, not surprised when my hand went through it. A thought of floating at the ceiling instantly had me looking down at the others.

Finally, I faced that terrifying question. *Was I dead?*

My hands were faint blue outlines and my arms weightless. Icy fingers of panic clutched at me.

I growled that with all the magical people in the room, not one of them had sensed my presence. So much for magical infallibility. Then again, maybe this had nothing to do with magic.

I jumped as something skittered past. Cyril scrambled up the wooden bedframe to perch next to my body's head. Even in my present predicament, I thought his ropey tail was too close.

I was certainly in an odd situation. I'd never met anyone who'd been kicked out of their own body and lived to tell the tale. Then again – perhaps I wouldn't either.

Cyril stared down at my form. "I should've been there to protect her."

Dorian shot him a glance. "When I tried to stop her, it didn't do a damn bit of good. When Raven gets an idea in her head, it takes a block-and-tackle to jerk it loose."

"Will she recover?" Little round rat eyes looked almost as worried as Dorian's.

"It's too early to tell. Myrador's final spell was especially vicious, intended to extinguish both body and soul. She couldn't breathe for a long time – maybe too long."

"Raven told me she thought she was a Rider. If that's true, maybe Gaia will help."

Dorian made a grimace. "If Gaia was going to help, she'd have done it already. Raven doesn't have much faith in Gaia anyway."

"Mm. True. She's not exactly a trusting soul, is she?"

"She has reason, Cyril. The Americas aren't kind to a magical child."

Cyril eyed him. "I guess you'd know."

Dorian jumped to his feet and started pacing. "Where the hell is Valgren when we need him? Off on some oh-so-important mission for Gaia, I suppose, while Raven lays here maybe dying!"

Come to think of it, where *was* Valgren? He'd planned to be back for the attempt to remove Myrador, but he'd had no way of knowing I'd moved the timetable up by going after the dark mage alone.

I looked at the people in the room who worked so hard to save my life. They were my friends – real friends who accepted me for who I was (well, maybe not Talon). Scarlet fluttered into the room to alight on Dorian's shoulder and stare at the body on the bed. Expecting a tirade of criticism, I was stunned by her silence.

"Scarlet, please check on Frost and Talon," said Dorian. "They might've come up with something by now."

I was shocked when she buzzed out the door without argument.

Now I knew I could exist just fine outside my body, I was less worried. I didn't want to leave my friends in grief, but there was nothing I could do to get their attention.

"Ah . . . here you are."

My ghostly heart leaped at a voice near my elbow. I perceived a faint blue outline. "Valgren?"

"I thought you might've still been on the mountain," he said as if discussing the weather.

"How . . . *what?*"

"We're in an out-of-body state, Raven. Riders are adept at using this mode of travel to gather information and to check the far reaches of Gaia."

I made a tentative gesture and felt resistance when my hand touched his arm. "Why can I touch you and not the others?"

"I've adjusted to your frequency. It's similar to stone-walking. We shift our resonance to match where we want to travel."

"I've never heard of travelling without my body. I understand I can adjust my frequency to walk through the Earth, but I sure as hell never imagined this!"

"It wasn't on your itinerary for many months. Though most people have the ability to move without their body, the vast majority never figure it out."

It felt weird having a conversation with Valgren when we were both close to invisible. I could barely discern his face. "Can you let the others know we're here?"

"Not in this state. I left my body in stasis near the mountain so I could move faster. When Dorian had Bluescale call me, I flashed to where you were at the volcano. The instant I saw your body, I knew it was vacant, and you were close to death. The others transported you to Cumulos to a healer while I looked for your spirit."

"Is that what I am? A spirit?"

"Everyone is a spirit. The body is an indispensable tool for interacting with the third dimension as you've probably figured out, but you don't need it to live. We're all immortal."

He held out a ghostly hand for me to take. "Let's retrieve my body so I can let the others know you're okay."

I looked at the body on the bed. "But what if they can't fix it? And . . . and how do I get in? Is there some sort of ritual?"

I could see his faint smile. "No, Raven. You just lay on top of it, and let your spirit settle. In a few moments, you reintegrate."

"Does that mean someone else could move in while I'm out?

"No. You were paired at birth so only you can access your form unless you give someone permission."

"This sounds really weird, Valgren."

He chuckled. "We should get going."

I glanced again at my body. "What if it's not healed enough?"

"They found you in time, Raven. You'll be okay."

I took his hand and, with a blur of motion, we were above his body in a grassy glade in the forest. It turns out that when you don't have a clumsy body to haul around, travel is instantaneous. Angry clouds of ash boiled from the volcano in the distance, the odour bringing with it tremors of residual fear.

"After I return to my body, I'll still be able to see you," said Valgren. "I wanted you to watch the process so you'll have an idea of how it works. Return to Cumulos, and I'll help with your reintegration."

I watched as he lay face-up on his body. I could see two forms – the physical one and a ghost on top. In seconds, the ghostly form sank into the body.

Now, you see, this kind of stuff creeps me out. I could handle the idea of magic and evil mages, but ghosts creep the living hell out of me. And it was even worse to think I qualified as one.

Valgren's body drew a deep breath after which he opened his eyes. He smiled up at me and sprang to his feet. "Now, Raven, I want you to visualize your room at Cumulos. I'll be along shortly."

I felt a knot of fear. "You're letting me go alone?"

"Think about your destination. Focus and you'll be there. I wouldn't let you go if I thought you were in danger. You'll be fine."

His confident smile made me give a deep, ghostly sigh. I must be the worst student ever. I'd questioned every instruction Valgren had ever given me. How the guy didn't pull his hair out was beyond me.

"Okay. I'll see you there." I closed my eyes and envisioned my room. After a brief sensation of movement, I was again above the bed where nothing seemed to have changed. Dorian had returned to my side (the body's side). I could see how this could get confusing. Which one was I? I felt a profound sense of relief when, ten minutes later, the door opened and Valgren strode in.

On sighting the Rider, Dorian leaped to his feet. "Where the hell have you been?! Raven's dying!"

Valgren cast him a calm glance. "I was tracking her spirit."

"What are you talking about?" I could see Dorian had zero patience by that point.

Valgren turned to the healer who adjusted the crystals that dotted my body. "How much has her throat healed?"

The ancient woman lifted a wrinkled gnome face. "It was almost crushed, but we've directed Gaia's energy to repair the damage. Her injuries are painful, but the body could recover." She stood, which brought her head almost to his elbow. "Her spirit is gone. Without it, the body will not survive more than a few more hours."

Scarlet fluttered into the room to regain her position on Dorian's shoulder as he addressed Valgren. "You said you were looking for her spirit. What does that mean?"

"Your Highness." Valgren looked Dorian squarely in the eye. "Raven has capacities she's only beginning to discover, and Evil sees her as a light that can pierce its darkness."

Dorian frowned. "Won't that make her a target?"

"Constantly."

"She's that powerful?"

"Her potential exceeds that of most of the people in this room."

"That would explain a lot," said Dorian. "I've always said there was a giant target on her back, and bad things can see it. Now I know why. But how would such magic get concentrated in her? After all, she wasn't born in the magical world."

"Once in a while, a person of rare power emerges. No one knows why or how they get here. I suspect Raven might be one of those."

"Then why can't she wake up?"

"As I said, powerful light attracts great darkness. I think Myrador knew or suspected what she could be. His only chance to get rid of her was to do it fast, before she understood her power."

Dorian paled. "That's why he tried to destroy her soul with that vicious spell!"

"Exactly. If it had worked, she'd have ceased to exist on any level. It was the perfect solution because it would remove her as a threat forever."

"Isn't he gone now? He can't return, can he?"

"The dimensions are permeable at times and in places, and Myrador is intelligent. It's not impossible that he could find his way back."

"Then how can we protect Raven?"

Valgren sat on the side of the bed and took my (the body's) hand. "Raven is like a caterpillar. The butterfly she's destined to become will boggle your mind. She won't need protection for long."

As you can imagine, all the stuff he was saying freaked me out. I didn't want to be the biggest and best magic person. I just wanted to get along and enjoy my life and my friends. I floated closer to the body.

"Raven?"

"I'm here, Valgren."

He gave me instructions to copy what he'd done in the forest. I positioned myself above the body and shifted around until all my limbs matched.

Dorian stormed to the far side of the bed to stare at Valgren. "Are you saying Raven's here?"

"She is." Valgren continued to focus on me. "Shift your right foot a little." Dorian stopped talking and watched Valgren as I moved my ghost foot to the correct position. "Okay, let yourself drift lower. Take your time. It'll happen."

It felt like sinking into warm jelly – kind of creepy. All that blood and stuff . . . *yuck*. I'd be stuck in a body again. Funny, I'd never thought of it that way before.

"Almost there." Valgren was calm and confident as he always was around me. "A bit more."

My vision made a side-to-side shift, and suddenly I felt the warmth of his hand. I opened my eyes to scan the people gathered around and instantly regretted a deep inhalation as my throat screamed at me. I drew a more cautious breath and tested my limbs. Everything worked. The pain in my throat was excruciating, but I could swallow.

"Raven? Raven! You're back!" Dorian parked himself on the bed, grabbed my hand in a crushing grip, and brushed my hair back. "You scared the hell out of me!"

So, there I was, Valgren on one side and Dorian on the other, each holding a hand. In spite of my brush with death, it felt awkward. I rolled my eyes from one to the other then noticed Cyril next to my shoulder. To my horror, a thin snake was draped over my arm.

I blame my next action on stress. After all, it's not every day one returns from the dead – sort of. The screech that tore from my raw throat must've echoed throughout the castle as I lunged to the side and landed with a thump at Valgren's feet. A hail of crystals and healing stones scattered across the floor.

As Valgren helped me up, he had an inquisitive quirk to his eyebrow. I brushed my arm in reflexive horror and looked for the snake. "Where the hell is it?"

When I refused to sit on the bed, Valgren asked, "What did you see, Raven?" He scanned the sheets.

Cyril had scampered to the bedstead to watch the activity from a higher vantage point. I noticed his rat tail hanging down. Umm . . . It looked a lot like a snake. And he'd been awfully close to my shoulder. Might've been . . . To tell the truth, I didn't see much difference between Cyril's tail and a real snake. They're both creepy.

I put a hand to my forehead. "Uh . . . sorry. I'm a bit discombobulated."

A shrill voice came from the vicinity of Dorian's shoulder. "Are you sure she's the right person, Rider? Doesn't seem like a master mage to me."

"You know magic moves in silence, Pixie, and its currents are strong. Raven will learn to ride the waves – until she's one with the Riders." His green gaze locked with mine.

How could he be so confident in me? Something to consider another time. At that moment, my focus moved to gratitude that I was alive and could communicate again. I needed time to recover on many levels.

Chapter 32

The shrill whistle of a boiling kettle called me from a lounger on my sunny balcony. I poured water into a ceramic teapot and, as the tea steeped, slathered raisin toast with peanut butter. It was mid-fall and, though the sun was warm, the air was not, so I wore an Icelandic wool sweater. A pristine coating of new snow covered the mountains in the west – snow that would, in time, find its way onto the foothills before it turned Denver into a winter wonderland.

I reclined into the lounger, poured my tea, opened my e-reader, and gave a deep sigh of contentment.

It had been a month since my return from Cumulos and the realm of magic. Waking between Valgren and Dorian after my near-death experience had brought home to me just how confused I was. I needed a break from everything – and everyone.

After I'd recovered enough, I'd told Valgren I needed time to think. His revelations about my magical abilities had scared the bejeezus out of me, so I was going back to Denver – alone. He'd given me his enigmatic Gaia smile and said we'd see each other again. I swear, the more I got to know the man, the more mysterious he became. His encouragement of my exploration of a relationship with Dorian had me flummoxed. It was clear that, in order to retain my sanity, I'd have to make a choice before I returned to Cumulos.

I'd told Dorian I didn't know when I'd be back, but I needed time to sort things out. Although he didn't come right out and say it, I knew that if I continued my relationship with Valgren for much longer, he'd choose someone else as queen. The Kingdom of Altaria needed a monarch pair to ensure heirs and stability. I supposed I should've been grateful he'd been patient thus far.

Since the magical realm was relatively calm by then, I returned Bluescale to his stream and settled back into my apartment. At first it had felt awkward to reintegrate to human society, but I'd gotten to the point that I looked forward to pepperoni pizza and new books on my e-reader. And I'd stopped thinking about what might be happening on Cumulos or Altaria.

***

One afternoon, I met Reg in the hallway. He still skulked around my door, disappointed by the lack of magical activity.

He peered up at me through thick lenses. “Where did all your friends go?”

“Which ones, Reg?” I shifted my grocery bags to one hand and dug into my purse for keys.

As I continued towards my apartment, Reg trotted after. “Did your boyfriend dump you?”

“Why would you think that?”

“He’s not here anymore. Or did you cast a spell on him?”

“Yes, Reg. I turned him into a monster. He now has red hair, skinny legs, and a striped shirt.”

“What?”

“Never mind.” I slipped my key into the lock. “Nothing goes on in my place that doesn’t go on in yours.”

I was still facing him when I opened the door so was confused by his look of astonishment. I spun to look – and there was Talon seated at my counter drinking tea from a china cup.

Reg jumped up and down in an emotional frenzy, pudgy finger pointed at Talon. “It’s back! It’s back! The purple alien is back!”

Damn. Too late to deny so might as well go with it. “Here you were worried about witches, Reg, and it’s only an alien.” I gave him a humourless smile and slammed the door in his face.

I dropped my groceries on the counter. “What’s up, Talon? I doubt you’re here for the company. By the way,” I added with a burst of sarcasm, “help yourself to my tea.”

He rolled his eyes towards the door. “What if that juvenile tells its mother about me?”

“He already has. She thinks he needs a shrink.”

“He should’ve been culled.”

"Some days I'd almost agree with you, Talon. So, again. Why are you here?"

"Altaria is threatened by an old enemy."

"And that would be?"

"Did Angus tell you about the descendants of the Atlanteans?"

"It never came up." I began putting groceries away. "I'm not interested in returning to Altaria or Cumulos for a while, Talon. I need a clean break so I can sort some things out. The world of magic has existed a long time without me. It'll be fine. Besides, I can't imagine how my miniscule magic could help anyway, an opinion with which I'm sure you'd agree."

"True. You may have potential, but it's of no value if you don't learn to use it."

"What's the rush, Talon?" I snapped as I slammed a cupboard door.

"Dorian asked me to say he needs you."

My heart skipped a few beats. "What?" I could think of a few ways Dorian could have need of me, some of which brought a rush of warmth to my insides.

"He believes the Atlanteans are readying their warships to invade Altaria."

I dragged my wandering thoughts back to the issue. "Why would they do that?"

"Altaria is a wealthy country that's been targeted by greedy neighbours before."

"Dorian has an army and a navy, so what does he need with me?"

"I had the same question, but His Majesty felt Altaria would benefit by your spirit-travelling abilities."

"Dorian wants me back so he can use my out-of-body aptitude to spy on the invading armada."

"It would be helpful to know their plans in advance."

I scowled at Talon as I removed the lid from a pint of chocolate ice cream and dug in. "Why didn't he come himself?"

"When I asked him, he was evasive. Would you know why?"

Of course, I did. He knew what might happen if we were alone in my apartment. "No idea, Talon."

He finished his tea and floated in his cross-legged position. "What shall I tell him?"

I gazed out the window at snow-covered peaks for a long moment then looked straight at Talon. "Tell Dorian if he wants my help, he'll have to ask for it himself."

Talon narrowed his eyes, made a sharp gesture, and popped from view.

I swallowed more chocolate and pondered the wisdom of what I'd done. A month of solitude might've weakened me to the point I'd just made the blunder of the decade.

THE END

About the Author

One fine afternoon, D Kane got tired of a high-pressure day job and went home to write her books. Anything before that decision is now a distant memory. Fantasy, metaphysics, adventure, mystery and fun are arrows in her literary quiver. The Fifth Dragon series was written to give us all a chuckle and to remember that fantasy can be fun!

CPSIA information can be obtained
at www.ICGtesting.com
Printed in the USA
LVHW051658030220
645677LV00001B/153

9 781773 702858